Heritage of Threat

A Legion Archer
Book #3

J. Clifton Slater

I'd like to thank Hollis Jones for her help and diligence in keeping me on track while I wrote this story. Because of her prompts, eagle-eyed spotting of illegible prose, and pulling me back from my tendency to write esoteric phrases, she successfully supervised the creation of *Heritage of Threat*.

And, my sincerest 'thank you' to you. My readers are the reason I can spend my days doing research and writing stories. Rendering a hand salute to you for being there for me. Ready, two!

If you have comments, contact me:
GalacticCouncilRealm@gmail.com

To follow my progress on the next book, read blogs on ancient topics, or to sign up for my monthly Author Report, go to my website:
www.JCliftonSlater.com

Heritage of Threat

Act 1

Even before a group of Latin nobles took power from Tarquinius Superbus, the last King of Rome, and exiled him, Roman Legionaries were citizens. For almost three centuries, fathers and sons took their shields, helmets, armor, gladii, and spears when they left the farm and joined the Legion. They gelled into eighty-man units called Centuries for the fighting season, then disbanded and returned home for the harvest.

During the first war with Carthage, the Legion traveled overseas to fight for the first time. In order to occupy holdings, solidify sieges, and maintain blockades on the Island of Sicilia, the campaigns extended over several planting and harvesting seasons. And, although the harvest suffered from the absence of the farmers, the Consul Legions remained exclusively citizen's armies.

At the beginning of the second war with Carthage, the Goddess Nenia became very busy. The cost of citizens' lives at Lake Trasimene was estimated at 5,700 heavy infantrymen, 1,600 light, plus NCOs and officers. For the Battle of Cannae, the butcher's bill increased to 11,500 heavy infantry, 6,400 light, and their commanders. Then, the Battle of Silva Litana further reduced the number of military aged citizens by 5,700 heavy, 1,600 light, and their leaders.

Despite the efforts by the Legions to remove him, Carthaginian General Hannibal Barca continued to ravish the heart of the Republic. With the resulting loss of citizens, Rome was fast running out of eligible men between the ages of 17 and 46 to serve in the Legions. Something had to be done.

Welcome to 215 B.C.

Chapter 1 – A Profound Transformation

"One-fifth of our male population is gone," Consul Quintus Fabius exclaimed. "Those were our fighting citizens. Along with the infantry, death claimed three Consuls, two Proconsuls, and over a thousand staff officers. Including, if you'll look around the chamber at the empty seats, a third of our Senators."

"What are you proposing?" a man inquired from the back of the Chamber.

The voice neither challenged nor suggested support for Consul Fabius. The bland manner in which he asked the question made certain factions suspicious that his inquiry was planned beforehand.

Some groups of Senators had already figured out where the speech was heading. Of those, the traditionalists were not supporters. They stiffened their spines and prepared to reject the proposal. Other, more practical, Senators readied themselves for a hard debate on the floor of the Senate.

"Well, you've gotten a little ahead of me," Consul Fabius allowed. "But seeing as you asked. I put before you a proposal..."

Grumbling started to roll up and down the tiered levels of seating. A few Senators began growling 'no way' and the rest snarled back, requesting the naysayers to remain silent.

"Please, if you'll allow me?" Consul Fabius begged. After the initial outburst, the chamber settled. "We've lost too many citizens which diminishes our ability to fight and defend the Republic. Therefore, I put before you a scheme to fill the ranks of two Legions, as a test."

"And who do you think to fill the ranks with?" a Senator scoffed. "Debtors, thieves, and murderers?"

"Or train slaves to hold a shield wall?" another jeered.

Quintus Fabius scanned the chamber and swallowed to wet his throat before continuing.

"Yes," he stated.

"Yes, what?"

"We will draft slaves and criminals," Fabius told the Senators. "And train them to hold a shield wall, to advance, and to maneuver. In short gentlemen, we will train them to save Rome and our Republic."

Shouts of agreement, and curses against the idea, bounced off the roof of the chamber. Deflecting the strong emotions back onto the Senators, the echoes drove the noise levels to a deafening roar. Quintus Fabius let the outburst thunder while he waited patiently until the heat of the moment burned off.

"If you will settle down," Fabius advised, "we can open the floor for debate."

Groups of Senators bellowed for the opportunity to be the first, creating another wall of sound, this time with waving arms. One Senator pushed to his feet and raised two scarred arms over his equally scarred head. Then he stood, strong and silent, as if he, and not the columns, held up the ceiling.

"The chair recognizes Alerio Sisera," Quintus Fabius granted. "You have the floor Senator, state your opinion."

"It's not my opinion," Alerio responded. "It's the opinion of a seasoned officer and a Legion weapon's instructor, I once knew. He preached against teaching our enemies the skills needed to kill us. Thank you."

Alerio took his seat and the chamber erupted in renewed yelling and screaming.

"Not much of a speech," Hektor noted.

The assistant handed Senator Sisera a glass of watery wine.

"Truthfully, there's not much to debate," Alerio informed him. "Unfortunately, the Republic doesn't have a choice. Everyone knows that once the hot winds fade, the resolution will pass."

Despite the forgone conclusion, the debate and arguments continued late into the night.

***

Zip-Thwack

The arrow skimmed over the back of a large buck and split the bark of a tree on the far side of the clearing.

"It's a bowstring and an arrow," Jace scolded, "not a spear to be chucked."

"I got excited is all," Sidia explained while holding up the new hunting bow. "This is the best weapon I've ever owned."

"You mean a treasure for the mantle above your fireplace," Jace teased while stepping into the clearing. Sidia moved up beside him, crunched his forehead, and squinted at his cousin. Seeing the confusion, Jace told him. "A weapon is a dangerous tool. So far in your hands, the hunting bow is a work of art."

"It is pretty," Sidia agreed. Then Jace's meaning sank in and the Hirpini tribesman said. "Wait. Are you saying I'm not an excellent hunter?"

Jace pointed at the shaft jutting from the tree trunk.

"I'm saying you're not a good bowman, Cousin Sidia. As far as a hunter, you located and tracked the deer to this clearing. Your problem started when it was time to bring down the prey."

A trail of broken branches and deep hoofprints marked the path of the deer. The two wolf-men of the Hirpini Tribe crossed the clearing and followed the animal into the forest.

***

Miles later, the pair of hunters reached the top of a slope. Under the trees, the land turned rocky, making the animal tracks hard to follow. Jace dropped to a knee and studied the ground.

"Benevento is over there," Sidia mentioned. "We should turn away."

"And give up the hunt?" Jace questioned. He brushed dirt off a flat rock. The dusty granules floated into a depression, revealing a hoofprint and the direction of the deer. "He's slowing. Probably just ahead of us."

"That's not the only thing down there," Sidia cautioned. "The Latian overseer and his thugs are there."

"I thought this was Hirpini territory?" Jace asked.

"Well, it is," Sidia confirmed. "As a matter of fact, it's your mother's land. But the Roman's use it. And they aren't pleasant to trespassers."

"How can I trespass on my family's land?" Jace inquired. He stood and jerked his arm, indicating the far side of the slope. "Besides, we saw the buck first. By rights, the venison is ours."

Jace strutted over the crest and dropped down into the trees.

"Cousin Kasia, this could go wrong, really fast," Sidia remarked before he headed down the hill towards the land of the Otacilia Family. "Really bad, really fast."

"Venison, Sidia, think of all that tasty meat."

The wolf-men located a twisting and turning animal path descending the hill. Near the bottom, grass grew, the soil softened, and the deer's trail became clear.

"Venison," Jace said over his shoulder.

"Overseer," Sidia commented.

Near a creek, they observed trampled grass where the buck had stopped to drink. Only a few of the stalks had sprung back, most lay like tiny shafts of grain after a harvest.

"I bet we catch him just over the next rise," Jace remarked.

Sidia dropped to the creekbank and bent to sip the clear mountain water. Anticipation, and a wave of Sidia's hand, pushed Jace to continue the hunt.

The afternoon was pleasant with sunlight streaming between the leaves and branches. Underfoot, a summer's worth of greening had created a lush landscape. Jace walked with speed but didn't hurry. One thing about a productive stalk, it took energy and patience. Either the hunter would tire, lose interest, and turn back. Or, the animal would forget the touch of the shaft over its back and settle down to nibble on tender shoots. Because he was trained on Crete where hunts were successful or you starved, Jace already knew he would be ready when the buck stopped to eat.

A short distance later, a sense of calm washed over Jace. No birds sang. No bugs swarmed or butterflies fluttered. It was almost as if a large animal had invaded the realm of lesser species. Reaching down, Jace untied the cover of his quiver. Slowing to a walk no faster than the summer breeze through the trees, the archer eased forward. The arrow came out of the pouch before he saw the deer. The shaft gently touched the top of his thumb and the bowstring settled into the notch. Stooped forward, Jace Kasia parted some branches and peered across a clearing at the buck. As he drew the string, a smile touched his lips.

The fletching tickled his chin, then the spell broke.

"Thief. Stop right there, thief, or I'll cut you," a gruff voice bellowed from a distance.

The deer bolted at the uproar from the human voice. Jace relaxed the string on his bow and listened for Sidia's response.

"I'm no thief," his cousin pleaded. "I was hunting a deer. See my bow and my arrows."

"What I see is a tribesman looking to steal sacks of cucumbers and squash," the voice remarked. "You two, bring him to the field. We'll make an example of the thief for anyone else looking for a free meal."

Sidia grunted. Jace recognized the sound from their training sessions. A summer of building bows and wrestling let him know the grunt from his cousin had pain behind it and wasn't simply from rough treatment.

Jace didn't put away the arrow. He slipped through the empty clearing, and into the forest on the other side. Listening to the men holding Sidia, he moved parallel to the overseer and his thugs. When they reached the edge of the forest, Jace waited behind a bush.

In an overgrown field. Three farm workers, all of them from the Hirpini tribe, waited.

"See, we told you someone was lurking in the woods," one boasted to a thick set Latian.

Instead of thanking them, the overseer instructed, "Get back to work."

"What about him?" one of the overseer's thugs asked.

To emphasize his point, the man punched Sidia in the stomach. This time, not just air was expelled. The remnants

7

of his breakfast spewed out of the tribesman's mouth. It would have been a disgusting display by itself. But, Sidia jerked his head back just before puking. In a shower of thick liquid and chunks of food, the vomit sprayed the overseer from head to sandals.

Bent over and brushing at the mess, the Latian ordered, "Cut his throat."

The thug pulled a knife and brought it to Sidia's neck.

Zip-Thwack!

From supporting a blade level with Sidia's throat, the shoulder snapped as the arrowhead mangled bones, muscles, and tissues. The thug released Sidia and fell to the ground, while trying to extract the shaft of the arrow through his agony.

Zip-Thwack!

The other thug released Sidia when a second arrow impacted his hip. The man twisted away from Jace's cousin on his way down to the weeds.

"Run," Jace urged.

Before Sidia could gather himself and make for the woods, the overseer wrapped an arm around his neck. Choking and squeezing Sidia, the Latian used him as a shield.

"Drop the bow or he dies," the overseer threatened. "And don't you think I won't."

"I would never assume anything from a man who steals land," Jace remarked as he allowed the tension to lessen. The bow and string straightened and Jace lowered his arm. "This is my land. It belongs to my family and the people of the Hirpini tribe."

"This parcel has been worked by Republic landowners for decades," the overseer shot back. "Just because a raggedy dressed Latin says it's his, I should pull the workers back? No to that. And, understand this."

His elbow stretched as he tightened the tension across Sidia's neck. Adding to the young man's distress, the overseer lifted him off the ground. With feet kicking, Sidia visibly weakened.

"I was attempting to be nice," Jace advised.

He turned sideways and began walking to the overseer's left.

In response, the man rotated, keeping the semiconscious Sidia between him and Jace. Except, in order to see Jace, the overseer had to crane his neck forward so he could see around Sidia's head.

"You put arrows into my men. That's not what I'd call nice," the Latin challenged. "Just look at them."

"Can you hear that?" Jace asked.

He pointed farther to the left using his bow as an extension of his arm.

"All I can hear," the overseer said while leaning around Sidia, "are cries of pain."

"There you have it," Jace informed him. "Expressions of pain let you know you're alive. Their moans demonstrate that I was being nice."

"It's hard to kill with an arrow," the overseer offered. He jiggled Sidia as if trying to wake up the tribesman. After several shakes, he shrugged as if giving up on bringing him around. Then he told Jace. "What you did meant nothing."

The attention to the limp man in his arm, the conversation, and casual attitude while two of his men screamed in pain seemed wrong to Jace. When the overseer diverted his eyes to the cultivated field for a moment, Jace understood.

"With this," Jace exclaimed. He raised the bow over his head, "I have a choice. I can spare a life."

The overseer looked up and his eyes followed the beautiful war bow when Jace tossed it. In an arch, the bow floated up before flattening and falling back towards the earth.

The overseer stretched his neck, following the progress of the bow. He never saw it land. As soon as Jace knew the man was focused on the bow, he slapped the bottom on his war axe. The tap sent it sliding up the holding ring. Jace grabbed the wooden handle as soon as it cleared. In half a step, the Cretan Archer twisted to position the ax head. Then with a snap of his arm, he released the war axe.

Two and a half flips after leaving Jace's hand, the long blade of the war axe sailed by Sidia's ear and split the overseer's forehead.

"I can spare a life or take a life with an arrow," Jace explained as he yanked the axe from the brow of the dead overseer, "just as quickly as I can with an axe."

A check confirmed what Jace suspected. Legion riders were dashing in his direction. Although still on the other side of the cultivated fields, they would be on him and Sidia in moments.

"Come on cousin," he encouraged while pulling Sidia off the ground and hauling his limp form onto his shoulders. "The hunt is over. At least for us."

After collecting the war bow and the hunting bow, Jace Otacilia Kasia jogged into the woods, heading for the high ground.

Not long after, the cavalrymen penetrated the forest and raced along a trail to the top of the first rise. But their prey, being a trained archer, had changed direction mid slope.

Jace and Sidia were a mile away by the time the riders reached the crest of the hill.

Chapter 2 – Ransom for None

The Senate of Rome began their duties at dawn. People could argue with sunset, mid-morning, or midday. But no one could miss the rising sun at daybreak and plead ignorance as an excuse for being late to the chamber.

Cornelius Scipio tossed off his blanket, swung his legs off the side of the bed, and stretched. Pleased that it was still dark, he stood and walked across the tile floor to a washbasin.

"Master Scipio, do you require a carriage or a horse for the day's outing?" a servant asked from the doorway.

"Arrange for a carriage to drop me at the Senate," Cornelius answered. "I'll find my own way home."

"Yes, sir."

***

Before the bright orb appeared above the rooftops, Cornelius hopped down from the carriage and waved the driver onward.

"A good morning to you, Master Scipio," Hektor Nicanor greeted him.

The administrative assistant for Senator Alerio Sisera stood under a torch, just off the street.

"Hektor. Are you waiting for someone else, and I dropped in," Cornelius inquired, "or are you here for me?"

The Greek glanced from side-to-side. Once sure others arriving for the Senate were out of hearing range, he answered, "The Senator would like you to ride to the Carthaginian camp and ask about their intentions."

11

"It'll take me a day to ready a trip to Cannae."

"I apologize for the confusion," Hektor explained. "I was referring to the Punic camp outside the east gate of Rome."

Cornelius stiffened and his hands shot up, displaying his surprise.

"Why wasn't I mobilized with the city guard?"

"Because the Punics aren't here to attack Rome. At least not yet," Hektor said. "But their commander, an officer named Carthalo, has a message for the Senate from General Hannibal Barca. Senator Sisera wants to know what he has to say first."

"The Senate has much higher-ranking citizens than me to negotiate with Punic command," Cornelius pointed out.

"Indeed, they do," Hektor agreed. "And the Senate will appoint a delegation of worthy men this morning. But much later this morning. Before then, Senator Sisera wants to know the essence of Hannibal's message."

Cornelius tilted his head and searched the rooftops to the east. Full of stars, the sky held no sign of the coming dawn.

"I'll need to get to my father's villa and change into a toga," he began, but Hektor stopped him

"Are you familiar with the Maximus Villa?"

"It's a few blocks from here," Cornelius described. "I've never been there but I know the location."

Hektor waved his arm and from across the street, a driver snapped the reins on a team of horses. In a heartbeat, a Legion chariot came into the circle of light and stopped.

"There is a uniform and armor waiting for you at Villa Maximus," Hektor informed him. He glanced at the sky and added, "plus an escort of Legion cavalry. Get the information, Senior Tribune Scipio, and get it to me before the Senate sends the delegation."

"I have no Legion," Cornelius pointed out. "Therefore, I can't hold the position of a Senior Tribune."

"But you do owe Senator Sisera a favor for securing you a position in a marching Legion," Hektor reminded him. "Should I tell the Senator that you've refused the assignment?"

Cornelius Scipio didn't answer. He stepped into the chariot and instructed the Legion courier, "Take me to Villa Maximus."

***

After strapping on the senior staff officer armor and fastening the gladius over the armored skirt, Cornelius tucked the helmet under his arm and walked to where he left the courier. To his astonishment, ten mounted Legionaries, each holding a torch, waited in a protective formation around the chariot.

"Detail, attention," a Centurion of Cavalry ordered. Then he assured Cornelius. "Whenever you a ready, Senior Tribune."

"I'm ready…" Cornelius replied while placing one foot on the floor of the chariot. Then he stopped. A huge sculpture of the winged Goddess Bia reflected some of the torchlight. Cornelius removed his foot from the chariot. "Hold on, Centurion."

"Yes, sir."

Senior Tribune Scipio marched to the Goddess of Force and Compulsion. He reached down to his hip, but he had no wine or food for an offering.

The courier appeared by his side.

"Sir, you'll be needing this," the Legion messenger advised while handing Cornelius a wineskin.

"Goddess Bia, grant us the courage and strength of character to complete this mission," Cornelius prayed. Behind him, the cavalrymen added 'Goddess Bia'. Scipio poured a healthy portion of wine along the base of the statue while whispering. "Whatever this mission is."

He capped the wine and returned it to the messenger.

"Centurion," Cornelius said to the cavalry officer as he entered the chariot, "let's go show the contents of our hearts to the Punics."

"Yes, sir. Formation, forward."

They rode away from Villa Maximus in good order and made for the east gate. Over the rooftops, the first rays of the sun brushed the sky with soft colors.

***

If not for the steepled, multicolored tents of the Carthaginians in the distance, it would appear as if the Central Legion was on maneuvers. As prescribed for marching camps, ten-man Legionary tents bordered lanes and camp streets. But the lack of a stockade, and the placement of the infantrymen showed the Legion wasn't on maneuvers. This Legion stood before the walls of Rome, defending the Capital against an enemy.

Cornelius' procession left the city and approached the rear of the Legion.

"What Century?" a Legion sentry demanded.

"The Northern Legion," the cavalry officer from Scipio's detachment answered. "Stand aside, we're on temple business."

The announcement puzzled Cornelius. Why would a northern cavalry squadron be in the Capital and available for an escort assignment? And why was this mission temple business? Rather than ask, senior staff officer Scipio kept his chin elevated and remained aloof of the simple challenge by the sentry.

At the mention of a temple, the Legionary lifted his spear and stepped aside. The chariot and mounted Legionaries rode through the Legion lines, heading for the ornate tents of the Punic camp.

"I count twenty-five lances on the weapon's rack," the calvary Centurion mentioned. He concentrated for a moment then added. "And seventy or more horses in their corral."

"What does that tell us?" Cornelius inquired.

"They brought a lot of negotiators," the cavalry officer proposed. "Or the Punics are hiding their strength and doing it badly, sir."

"Why all the negotiators?" Cornelius wondered. "I'm sure the Republic isn't ready for the treaty tent, yet."

***

They crossed the empty zone between the Legion and the Carthaginians. Moments later, the chariot and honor guard approached the gaudy tents.

A Greek in a flowing robe rushed from the largest pavilion and scurried to the chariot.

"Greeting. Greetings," the Greek gushed. "May I assume you're here to accompany Commander Carthalo to your Senate?"

"No," Cornelius snapped as he stepped down from the chariot. Anger flushed his face as the memory of dead and wounded Legionaries flooded his thoughts. If he wanted to gather information and complete the mission, he had to remain civil. But holding back his resentment for the Carthaginians and their allies took all the blessings of the Goddess Bia.

15

The Greek paused and studied the youthful face under the Senior Tribune's helmet. Confused as to how much authority an officer just out of his teens could have, the man remained motionless.

Without thinking, Cornelius rested a hand on the pummel of the gladius. Then, to remove the temptation to kill the Greek, he removed the hand.

"Senior Tribune Scipio, should we head back, sir?" the cavalry Centurion inquired.

The mention of his rank reminded Cornelius of his responsibility and the reason he was in the Punic camp. His temper cooled enough for him to speak.

"Am I here only to enjoy the sunrise?" Cornelius questioned the Greek. "Or are you going to announce me?"

"I am Philo, a speaker of five languages, a scholar, and the main interpreter for Commander Carthalo."

"I'm not in the market," Cornelius told him. He brushed by the Greek and marched towards the tent.

Philo ran ahead and indicated the pavilion's entrance.

"This way, Senior Tribune Scipio," the Greek said, while holding the flap.

***

Cornelius strutted in and stopped. Not to allow his eyes to adjust, there were multitudes of candles casting light around the large tent. What caused him pause, were the Legion officers sitting on either side of a large chair. Their conversations faded at the sight of the Senior Tribune.

In a hoarse voice, the man sitting in the chair barked out a question.

Philo bowed and rattled off a couple of phrases in Phoenician.

"Commander Carthalo welcomes you to his tent, Senior Tribune Scipio," the Greek translated. "He wishes for you, health of the body and peace in your heart."

"I enjoy both. No thanks to his General and the Carthaginian invaders," Cornelius snapped.

Then he glanced up and down the rows of Legion officers. All ten were relaxed and held glasses of wine. But their bodies carried bruises and stitches and their armor was dented and held together by frayed leather straps. None wore a Legion dagger, or a gladius. In addition to being disarmed, there wasn't a helmet between them.

"If you aren't an escort, the Commander would like to know why you are here?" Philo inquired.

It tortured his soul, but Cornelius smiled in a friendly manner, then bowed respectfully.

"Think of me as a gate guard," he informed Philo in a soft voice. "Keeping beggars that crawl up from the sewer, and blackhearted thieves off the stoops of my master's villa."

The words contradicted the pleasantness related in his tone of voice.

"You dare insult me in my own tent?" Carthalo challenged.

"You dare to play a deaf mute to a representative of the Senate of Rome?" Cornelius questioned.

The two men stared daggers at each other for a moment. Then the Carthaginian commander shrugged and smiled.

"How did you know I spoke Latin?" Carthalo inquired.

"Philo asked a leading question, before you inquired about my purpose," Cornelius told him. "Plus, there's not an interpreter at your side. Yet, your prisoners were in mid conversation when I entered the tent."

"Very observant," Carthalo allowed. "Why are you here, Senior Tribune Scipio?"

"As I explained, I am a gate keeper. Tell me the message you wish to deliver in front of the Senate of Rome. I will deliver your words to the leadership, and they will decide your fate."

Carthalo brought a hand to his chin and began massaging his jaw. While the Punic Commander thought, Cornelius scanned the inside of the tent.

The headquarters for Carthalo's detachment had a wooden floor as befitted a commander. Other than the ten seats occupied by the Legion prisoners, small tables and chairs were scattered around a large campaign table. Out of necessity, lit candles and blazing braziers provided light. With the thick fabric of the pavilion, even at midday, little sunlight would penetrate the interior. As it stood, bundles of something rested in the dark at the back of the tent.

"I will tell you," Carthalo proclaimed.

Nine of the Legion officers nodded enthusiastically at the announcement. But the tenth prisoner refrained as if he didn't care what the Punic had to say.

Cornelius understood the sentiment. He too hated the Carthaginians. But the disparity of one in ten being a detractor struck him as odd. Plus, he was curious about what was hidden in the shadows.

"If you please, Commander," he requested, "I would like my Centurion of Cavalry to be a witness."

"Granted," Carthalo stated. "Philo, fetch the Legion officer. He will make an even twelve in my care."

"Except, sir," Cornelius informed the Punic Commander, "the Centurion and I have blades."

Carthalo indicated the spearmen stationed around the pavilion. Then he teased, "Aren't you the least bit nervous?"

"Commander. On a number of occasions in the last three years, I have been surrounded by your mercenaries," Cornelius assured him. "And while I lived, I can't say the same for your hired warriors."

The cavalry officer rushed into the tent with a hand on the hilt of his gladius. Taking advantage of the man's caution, Cornelius reached out to still the weapon.

"Hold your blade, we are safe for now," he told the Centurion. Then leaning forward, he whispered. "Work your way towards the back and find out what they have stacked there."

The cavalry officer looked left while moving his mouth as if counting the guards. Then he peered right and repeated the gesture. At no point did his eyes linger on the stacked material.

"What did the Senior Tribune mutter in your ear?" Carthalo asked.

"He said, sir, that you Punics are untrustworthy," the Centurion reported, "and I should be careful."

"You Latians are a war like people. Your reply is what I expected," Carthalo related. "I will now tell you the words of my General, the most excellent tactician Hannibal Barca."

Cornelius marched forward between the Legion prisoners. As he did, the spearmen shifted and Carthalo sat upright as if ready to leap out of his seat and defend himself. But Senior Tribune Scipio stopped before coming closer than two-blade lengths from him.

"I don't want to miss a word," he informed the Commander.

No one noticed the cavalry officer from the Northern Legion shuffle to the side and move towards the rear of the pavilion.

"Men of the Republic, hear his words," Carthalo proclaimed. "My intention is not to destroy Rome. Rather, my excursion onto your lands is a means to an end. That end being the easing of the Republic's aggressive stance towards my city. Allow Carthage to sail the seas unmolested and to trade where we will, and to reclaim our lost territory on Sicily and Sardinia. For this, I will cease war campaigns against the Latian people."

"Is that all?" Cornelius asked. "I thought it would be a longer speech."

"The General says much with less words," Carthalo boasted. "The ideas of a genius lay in his vision not in his rhetoric. There are of course minor demands, but they are moderate compared to the damage done to your Legions and relationships. You will carry this to your Senate?"

"Right away, Commander Carthalo," Cornelius said. "If you'll excuse me."

"Oh, one more thing, Senior Tribune Scipio," Carthalo advised. "Take the ten Legion officers. They have a speech of their own to deliver."

"Centurion. Did you get what I brought you in for?" Cornelius inquired.

"Yes, sir," the cavalry officer reported. "But we need to go over a part that I don't understand."

Chapter 3 – One of the Ten

Three of the captive Legion officers suffered from injuries to their lower extremities. Cornelius placed the

courier next to the team of horses so the driver could walk
the rig with the trio of wounded back to the city. A
cavalryman dismounted and took a position behind the
chariot to prevent the officers from falling out.

The other seven released officers marched ahead of the
chariot team and waited for the scattered escorts. Spread
apart, the cavalrymen lounged with their horses to either
side of the pavilion. Their casual attitude, and ongoing
conversations with Punic mercenaries, gave the impression
of men visiting the camp of a friendly Century.

"Centurion. What's your name?" Cornelius asked after
he mounted the surrendered horse.

"Caesar, Senior Tribune," the cavalry officer replied.

"Centurion Caesar, you should collect your men and
take us to the gate," Cornelius suggested with a hint of
irritation.

"Yes, sir. Detail, fall in," the cavalry officer bellowed.
Faster than Cornelius could have imagined, the Legion
riders said goodbye, mounted, and galloped to positions
behind the chariot and ahead of the released officers. After
they gathered, Caesar directed. "Detail, at a walk, forward."

"That went quickly," Cornelius remarked.

"Yes, sir. If you'll excuse me for a moment," Caesar
requested.

He kicked the mount and raced to the head of the
procession. After conversing with all of his cavalrymen, the
Centurion trotted to where Cornelius rode off to the side.

"The back of the tent is full of rolls of parchment,"
Caesar reported as he reined in. "And most of the Punic
soldiers have soft hands with ink stains on their fingers.
According to my riders, they couldn't fight off a flock of

sheep if the sheep were starved and exhausted. I don't know what any of this means, sir, but I hope it helps."

Between the speed of forming the procession and the intelligence gathered, Cornelius was curious.

"Who are you?" he asked.

"Last month, a war party of Gauls rode south with the intention of raiding Latin farms," Caesar explained. "We had the patrol area near the Sisera chariot racing facility. The Gauls came charging out of the trees, and my squadron punched them in the side. After a short fight, my cavalrymen are that good, the survivors fled. We met the manager of the facility, and he told us we were going to Rome. And here we are, the color guard representing Senator Sisera's chariot racing team on the next race day."

"And how did you get selected as my escort?"

"Hektor said you were brave enough to challenge the Punic Commander and smart enough to complete the mission, but maybe too emotionally involved for your own good. We're with the Northern Legion and aren't as deeply affected by the Punics," Caesar told him. "And forgive me, sir, but he said you are also foolhardy enough to start a fight in the middle of the Carthaginian camp. It's why my riders were spread out. If we had to pull you out, we would have collapsed around you, and fought our way back to the Legion line."

"Good to know I had reserve forces at hand," Cornelius admitted. "Here's what you're going to do this afternoon, Centurion Caesar."

"Yes, sir?"

"You're going to buy wineskins for your cavalrymen and hire a meat seller's cart to accompany you," Cornelius directed. "Send the bill to Villa Scipio. I'll pay it."

"Where are we going, sir?"

Cornelius indicated a hilltop outside the east gate.

"From there you can watch the show."

"What show, Senior Tribune?"

***

Cornelius left the Senior Tribune's helmet in the chariot but remained armed and dressed in the armor. With ten released prisoners in his charge, he wanted a proper Legion appearance to support the ruined armor of the released officers.

"Cornelius Scipio," Hektor greeted him at the bottom of the steps. "You return with company. I trust you also brought back information?"

"And a suggestion for Senator Sisera," Cornelius proposed while urging the former captives up the steps to the Senate building. "Order the Punic Commander and his scribes away from Rome. Don't negotiate, entertain an offer, or give him another day."

"He offended you that much?" Hektor inquired.

"Oh no, Master Nicanor. Commander Carthalo was gracious in his victory over the Republic," Cornelius stated. "And if his terms are not accepted, he is preparing an assault on Rome."

"He said that?"

"He didn't have to. General Hannibal's words told me the first part," Cornelius answered. "And Carthalo mapmakers, disguised as soldiers, showed me the Commander was ready to create maps of our defenses and the route through the city to the Senate."

"Tell me the General's words," Hektor encouraged.

"My intention is not to destroy Rome. Rather, my excursion onto your lands is a means to an end. That end being the easing of the Republic's aggressive stance towards my city. Allow Carthage to sail the seas unmolested and to trade where we will, and to reclaim our lost territory on Sicily and Sardinia. For this, I will cease war campaigns against the Latian people."

"Hannibal doesn't mention retreating back to Iberia," Hektor noted.

"He does not."

Both Hektor and Cornelius rushed up the steps. One to escort the Legion officers into the chamber. The other to advise Senator Sisera not to trust Commander Carthalo.

***

Quintus Fabius ran his eyes over the empty seats in the Senate. The vacancies had nothing to do with men avoiding their duty. If anything, because of their love of Rome, they had gone to war and not returned. Consul Fabius was of two minds. He wanted to take time and grieve the losses. Yet, to save the Republic, required him to stand strong and make hard decisions.

"I say we should meet with Commander Carthalo and hear him out," a Senator declared. "There may be a path to peace if we only listen."

"I second the motion," another said. "We've delayed long enough. Let us select delegates and meet with Hannibal's man."

"Do we send peacemakers or warriors?" Alerio Sisera injected into the conversation.

"You've been playing rhetorical games all morning," a Senator across the chamber complained. "First, should we send meals to the Carthaginian delegation. Then it's how big a response and next whether we should send an olive branch or cold steel. We've debated all of your quandaries and

24

settled each of your concerns. And now you propose another. It's almost as if you don't want us to meet with this Carthalo fellow."

"Can we just get on with it?" a fourth Senator shouted in frustration. "Consul Fabius, you need to select a committee."

Quintus Fabius had watched Sisera twist arguments and throw up roadblocks during the discussion about how to deal with the Punic emissary. Every question came with multiple choices, requiring deliberation. If Sisera's aim was truly to delay the meeting with Commander Carthalo, the tactic had worked, so far.

The Consul noted Hektor Nicanor when he raced into the chamber waving his arms. The antics continued as he dashed down the tiers to Sisera's seat. Assistants came and went from the chamber throughout the day. But they usually attempted to be unintrusive. Being an old campaigner, Quintus Fabius recognized misdirection when he saw it. Prying his eyes from Nicanor and Sisera, Fabius looked towards the door to the chamber.

Ten beaten and dirty Legion officers, a mixture of Tribunes and Centurions, marched or limped through the doorway. Bringing up the rear, and acting as their shepherd, came young Cornelius Scipio.

"Misdirection, no doubt."

"I have announcements," Sisera called out when Hektor stepped away from the Senator.

"I bet you do," Fabius thought. Then aloud, he stated, "the Senate recognizes Alerio Sisera. You have the floor, Senator."

"Senior Tribune Cornelius Scipio, please come down here," Alerio instructed.

"He's a youth without a Legion," a Senator on the far side of the chamber exclaimed. "You can't call him a Senior Tribune."

"Let me amend my statement," Alerio replied. "Senior Tribune Scipio of the Northern Legion, present yourself to the Senate of Rome."

No one could argue the assignment of the rank when it was attached to the Northern Legion. Alerio Sisera grew up at the border of the Republic in Tuscany. And the Senators influence in the Legion guarding the border was well known.

Cornelius marched down the tiers, and saluted Consul Fabius before turning about to face the Senate.

"As an assistant Aedile, you recently met with Commander Carthalo, did you not?" Alerio inquired.

On the other side of the chamber, a Senator shot to his feet.

"Since when did the Scipio boy become an Aedile?" he asked. "He's not twenty-five years old. How can he sign contracts for festivals to honor the gods? Or enforce building codes and oversee temples. Or manage the food supply for the city?"

"Was I not clear?" Alerio inquired. "It's within my power as the chairman for the committee to nominate Aediles. As such, I can assign a temporary assistant Aedile in times of crisis. And to me, having a Carthaginian attack dog tied up at the gates of my city is a crisis."

With the revelation of Alerio Sisera's true feelings, uproars exploded around the chamber. Mostly, the Senators expressed anger. But several voiced agreement with Sisera's motivation for dragging his feet all morning.

Cornelius now understood why Centurion Caesar told the Legion sentry that they were on temple business. Although a stretch, as an assistant Aedile, he did carry the authority of all the temples of Rome.

"Enough of the interruptions," Consul Fabius ordered. "Scipio, tell us what the Punic Commander had to say."

"Senators, the words come from General Hannibal Barca," Cornelius explained. "My intention is not to destroy Rome. Rather, my excursion onto your lands is a means to an end. That end being the easing of the Republic's aggressive stance towards my city. Allow Carthage to sail the seas unmolested and to trade where we will, and to reclaim our lost territory on Sicily and Sardinia. For this, I will cease war campaigns against the Latian people."

Alerio raised his arms to draw attention before speaking.

"Hold your tongue, Senior Sisera," Quintus Fabius directed. Then to the Senate of Rome, he stated. "Hannibal's words are clear. With those in mind, we will vote on one issue. Do we surrender the Republic and Rome to the Carthaginian? Yea or nay?"

Clerks recorded the votes and to Alerio Sisera's surprise, many voted to accept the conclusion that Rome was beaten. Enough however, voted nay, and the Republic survived.

"Senator Sisera, you have the floor," Fabius allowed after the vote.

"Thank you, Consul. I think we know what must be done with Commander Carthalo," Alerio replied. "And now, for those of you who missed the officers standing in the back, let me introduce you to the ten hostage negotiators. They represent eight thousand Legionaries who were taken captive at Cannae. And they, Senators, have information on the ransom demands for the return of our citizens."

"Did the eight thousand surrender during the battle?" someone inquired.

"No. They were guarding the Legion camp," Alerio told him. "These men did not run when confronted by a superior army. They stayed and fought until overwhelmed. But let's hear from the ten. Gentlemen, please come down."

The Legion officers moved slowly. Out of respect, the Senators remained silent as the ten filed down the tiers.

"How will you vote on the ransom, sir?" Hektor whispered. "Do I need to coordinate a voting block for you?"

"No. In this case, everyone needs to vote their conscience," Alerio answered. "As for me, I haven't decided yet. I need to hear the debate, first."

The ten lined up on the floor facing the rows of Senators.

One stepped forward, "I am Julius Hadrian, Senior Tribune of the Eastern Legion. We are your sons and fathers, and we beg for your charity and understanding. Yet, the ten of us have sworn to return to Carthaginian captivity if you deny the ransom..."

A man on the end of the line distanced himself from the other nine. Hadrian halted and peered down the line at the rebel.

"I'm a farmer and an experienced combat officer," the separatist boasted. "While the nobles here went along with the Carthaginian's plan, I left the enemy camp. But then, I went back for my bedroll. Ha, I've outsmarted the lot of you."

"Tell us who you are and explain the meaning of your speech," a Senator requested.

"My name's Zagonus, a Centurion with the Western Legion. And I also swore to return, if the Senate didn't pay the ransom. And I did return. I went back into the Punic camp after they released us. Therefore, my honor is intact. I'm going home."

Zagonus made it to the first tier when Quintus Fabius instructed, "Tribune Scipio return the Centurion to his place with the others."

Cornelius drew his gladius and motioned Zagonus back. But the Centurion sneered at the very young staff officer and took another step.

"I have no respect for the Punics," Cornelius informed him. Zagonus, wondering where the young officer was going with the dialogue, stopped. "But I love the Republic. And I will kill you as quickly as I have Carthaginian mercenaries to enforce Roman law. You would be well advised to get back in line."

The rogue Centurion glanced down at the steady blade then up at the steel in the young Tribune's eyes.

***

Once Zagonus resumed his position, Tribune Hadrian began where he left off.

"Although the ten of us have sworn to return if you deny the ransom, we want to remind you the wives and children of eight thousand brave men are depending on your generosity."

"Of course, we'll pay the ramson," a Senator announced. "How could we not free our citizens?"

"Earlier, you voted to surrender the Republic to Hannibal," another Senator barked. "So, in one day, you would hand over Rome to General Barca and send wagons full of silver to fill the Punic's war chest."

"This isn't about coins or property," the Senator said defending his position. "This is about families and the rights of citizenship."

"How about duty?" another countered. "A citizen who isn't ready to fight to the death to protect the Republic has no more worth than a dumb ox. Maybe less."

"You dare equate a man of Rome to a beast of burden?"

"If he lives in a corral and depends on another man to feed and water him, he is an animal," a Senator remarked. "And we need our Legionaries to know they must win the battle. Being taken alive cannot be seen as a way to return home. I will vote no to the ransom. And by extension, no to enriching Hannibal Barca and no to taking away our fighter's enthusiasm to win."

The Senate fell quiet as the legislatures contemplated the arguments. Then as six of Consul Fabius' Lictors arrived and signaled for Cornelius to leave the floor of the chamber, Senators began conversing with each other.

***

. Glad to be out of the heat of the debate, Cornelius strolled to the observation area and looked down. Senators were caucusing with each other and based on the number of angry hand waves, shoulder shrugs, and violent jerks of heads, the emotions were running high.

"I'm telling you we can sail to Egypt and a Ptolemy will hire us," a voice murmured.

"As Generals for a Prince, or even the Pharaoh, we could live like kings along the Nile River," another man offered.

Cornelius peeked to his rear to see who was talking about leaving the Republic. At the sight of four Legion staff officers huddled together, he bolted from his place at the rail. Barging into the Tribunes, he shoved them into a semicircle and drew his gladius.

"With all the passion in my heart, I swear, I would never desert our Republic, or permit any citizen of Rome to leave her during troubled times. If I ignore my oath, may Jupiter, the Great God, bring death to me and my family," Cornelius shouted. "This I swear. Now Tribunes, you will give your oaths. Or you can draw your gladius and, on this day, one of us will die."

The fiery declaration drew the attention of all the observers and the Senators on the upper tiers. Consul Fabius walked up the tiers until he could see the observation area.

"What's the meaning of this disruption?" he demanded.

Cornelius herded the four staff officers to the rail.

"Consul, these Tribunes are giving their oaths to the Republic," Cornelius stated. "They swear to either conquer for Rome or die on the field of battle. For them and me, there is no other hope for safety."

Quintus Fabius nodded and, forgetting his stately manner, almost danced down the tier.

"Senate of Rome. There is one question before you," he boomed from the floor of the chamber, "to pay the ransom, yea or not to pay, nay."

***

Late in the afternoon, after changing into a tunic, Cornelius rode through the east gate. Spying the cavalrymen, he galloped to the top of the hill.

"Greetings Senior Tribune Scipio," Caesar boomed while extending a wineskin. "Vino, sir?"

"What do you think of the show?" Cornelius asked.

Not far from the chaos of Commander Carthalo's camp, lines of Legionaries stood in combat formation. Behind them, mounted Tribunes watched the position of the sun.

"Carthalo has until sundown to leave," Cornelius explained between streams of wine. "If he's not packed and gone with the sun, the Central Legion will make sure he never leaves Rome."

"What about the guy the chariot delivered earlier, sir," Caesar inquired.

"The man in the chariot was Centurion Zagonus. After voting down the ransom, the Senate decided one of the ten should return to inform Hannibal of their decision."

Act 2

Chapter 4 – Become Romanized

Jace Kasia and Sidia Decimia jumped from rock to stone to rock as a mountain stream rushed under their feet.

"Fall off," Sidia cautioned, "and I'll be carrying you to Trevico."

"It's not me who should worry about spraining an ankle," Jace countered.

On the other side of the creek, they mounted another steep slope.

Sidia, being raised among the high mountains, moved with the grace of an experienced climber. And Jace, due to his archer training on Crete, rapidly scaled the hill beside his cousin.

In three miles the land rose almost two thousand feet. Long after they crossed the stream, the pair reached the stockade wall of Trevico.

"Front or back?" Jace asked.

"Chief Pacidia sent for us," Sidia answered. "If we're guests, I'd say we go through the front gate."

"The messenger only said we were summoned by the Chief of Chiefs," Jace warned. "It doesn't mean it's an invitation for a feast."

"It might be," Sidia suggested. "But just in case it's not, let's use the tradesmen entrance."

Around the corner, they noted a small gate and stalls for craftsmen. A forge burned hot with charcoal and, nearby, a cooper shaved barrel staves. Jace and Sidia glanced at the merchandise and the workers.

"I need a trade," Sidia complained as the pair strolled to the gate.

"Aren't you a farmer?" Jace asked.

"Yes, except I hate farming."

They reached the gate, and a soldier blocked their way.

"Business?" he inquired.

"We're hunters," Jace responded. He touched the bow case rising over his shoulder. "Come to get supplies before heading into the mountains."

It was either his Greek accent, or the idea of heading into the mountains that elicited a laugh from the guard. Because, they were already among the peaks.

"Alright, move along."

Several paces from the entrance, Jace wondered, "Is the town always so well guarded?"

"No. And it's busier than I've ever seen it," Sidia replied. "I wonder what's going on?"

Around a building, they arrived on the main street and spotted a reason for the activity. A Carthaginian nobleman and his bodyguards were gathered in front of a large building. Tied above the doorway, a flag clearly marked the structure as belonging to an important man.

"That's Chief Pacidia's banner," Sidia informed Jace. "It appears, he has visitors for the afternoon. Which is good for us."

"How so?" Jace asked.

"We have the afternoon for food and drinks. We'll see the Chief in the morning."

Away from the quarters of the Hirpini chief, they stopped in front of an inn.

"That's odd," Sidia remarked, "it's almost as if their looking for something."

Farther down the street, wagons were halted at the main gate and searched. While some guards examined the contents of the carts, others questioned the drivers and a few pedestrians.

"Or someone," Jace said. "Enough gawking, I thought you were hungry?"

"I am," Sidia confirmed. He held the door to the inn. "After you, cousin."

***

The waitress was fat, funny, and efficient. Sausage, goat cheese, flat bread from spelt grain, and mashed turnips with olive oil had filled the bowls. But now, empty dishes lay scattered on the tabletop. And except for a smear, a crumb, or a drop here and there, the food was gone entirely.

"The sustenance was hardy," Jace declared with a smile. He took a sip of beer and described. "Heavier than the cuisine on Crete and less spicy. Even so, the meal was satisfying."

"I envy you, Jace," Sidia said from the other side of the table. "You've seen so much of the world. And had adventures I can only dream about."

"Let me remind you, those adventures were deadly encounters," Jace cautioned. "Be careful what you wish for. They may come true."

Ignoring Jace's warning, Sidia lifted his mug in salute.

"To Hermes, may the God of Adventure bless me with a life less boring," Sidia prayed.

He spilled an offering on the tabletop before drinking to the God. Not to deny his cousin, Jace splashed out an offering from his mug then drank to the God.

"I hope you know what you're doing," Jace commented.

The door to the inn banged open drawing Jace and Sidia's attention. Peering over their mugs, they noted a big warrior duck under the doorframe. Once over the threshold, he drew back wide shoulders before expanding his chest.

"Dear God Hermes, is it too late to take back my request?" Sidia muttered. Holding the mug in front of his face, he shrunk down in the chair.

"I'm not a holy man," Jace teased, "but I sense an adventure has been granted."

"This isn't funny," Sidia barked while twisting in his seat to place his back to the room. "Pontia is Chief Pacidia's son and in line to become a war chief."

"If he hasn't been to Mefitis' ponds and added to her wall," Jace stated, "what's the problem?"

"Last year, he purchased four sheep from my father's farm," Sidia replied in a whisper. "But only three arrived at his flock."

"What happened to the fourth sheep?" Jace asked.

"It died on the trip."

"He can't blame you if his shepherd was careless," Jace offered.

"The sheep stumbled, fell, and died a mile from my farm," Sidia said.

"Was it unwell?" Jace questioned.

"Not according to the sales agreement."

Pontia shouted from the doorway, "Sidia Decimia. I've been looking for you."

The big warrior ambled to the table. With a smack, he pounded a big fist onto the wet tabletop. Beer, compressed between the wooden surface and the flesh of his knuckles, squirted into Sidia's eyes.

"Oh, oh," Sidia cried while rubbing at his eyes and blinking.

Ignoring the man's distress, Pontia snatched Sidia out of his chair.

"I've been looking for you."

"You've said that twice," Jace remarked while sliding his chair back. "Either, my cousin is deaf, or you're too simple to recall what you said."

"What did you say to me?" Pontia snarled.

"I said," Jace began in a normal tone before dropping to a whisper, "you might be both dumb and hard of hearing."

Pontia slammed Sidia into the chair, spun on Jace, and took a step forward.

"What did you say to me?"

"See. You've repeated yourself again."

Before Pontia could come up with a reply, Jace kicked his ankles. The big warrior's legs shot out from under him. As he toppled, Jace leaped up, wrapped his hands over Pontia's head, and smashed his face into the tabletop.

After snatching up his long pack and bow case from an adjacent chair, Jace suggested to Sidia, "We should go."

Sidia dropped coins on the table, grabbed his pack, and both men bolted for the exit. In mid stride, they waved at the waitress. In response, she clapped at their antics. And while laughing, she pointed at the front door.

"Yes ma'am," Sidia assured her, "we know the way out."

Still giggling, she indicated the doorway, several times. But, neither Sidia nor Jace understood.

"Pontia," two warriors carrying spears called out as they came through the doorway. "We could not locate..."

Sidia and Jace slid to a stop as spear tips poked at their faces.

"Thank you, Hermes," Jace said.

He dropped his pack to the floor and lifted his hands to show they were empty.

"Why thank, Hermes?" Sidia asked.

"Because, he is also the God who guides souls to the river Styx," Jace answered. "And we almost made the trip."

"I've been looking for you," Pontia said. His voice was muffled as if he spoke through a piece of cloth. And it came out breathy as if he had a stuffy nose.

"And you've found me," Sidia admitted.

He turned as the big warrior marched to stand beside him. A blood-soaked rag held against his nose accounted for the distortion in Pontia's voice.

"I wasn't speaking to you," the warrior corrected.

"You were looking for me?" Jace asked.

"You're Jace Otacilia Kasia, killer of overseers and a poor bowman," Pontia announced.

"Why do you say my cousin is a weak archer?" Sidia demanded.

"After murdering the overseer, he left two Latian foreman alive," Pontia replied. "They're the witnesses who will testify against him."

Jace hung his head. It wasn't in shame as the Hirpini tribesmen presumed. Rather, Jace Kasia sent a silent apology to his teacher for not shooting to kill.

"Erase your footprints, so your enemy doesn't know how many travel with you," Zarek Mikolas had taught. "And leave no one to point a finger at you for revenge."

He simply wanted to rescue Sidia and escape without taking a life. In hindsight, sympathy was going to get Jace crucified by the Romans.

"Take them to the empty shed," Pontia instructed. "We'll show them to my father in them morning. Then deliver the killers to the nearest Legion garrison."

"Killers?" Jace shouted which brought the tip of a spear to his neck. Calmer, he explained. "I killed the Roman. Sidia was being held by them. He did nothing."

"Not my problem," Pontia stated. "The Latians want two killers and that's what we'll deliver to them."

Jace and Sidia marched in front of the spears to a storage shed near a stockade wall. After shoving them in, the guards blocked the opening with a board.

"Congratulations," Jace said.

"For what?" Sidia inquired.

"For receiving the gift of an adventure from a God."

"I'm not sure if this is preferable to farming."

"Not sure?" Jace questioned. A few streams of light from the afternoon sun came through cracks in the walls. "When will you be. After we're tied to the wood and raised to rooftop level by the Romans?"

"This is not how I thought an adventure would go," Sidia admitted.

The two sat on the floorboards while resting their backs against the wall.

"What was in here?" Jace asked.

"I think this was the weapon's storage shed," Sidia answered.

"Where are the spears, swords, and shields?"

"I don't know," Sidia replied. They sat quietly for a spell before Sidia inhaled deeply and announced, "This is better than farming."

***

Sometime in the night, rain began falling on the roof of the shed.

"There is one advantage," Sidia commented.

"To being locked in a shed?" Jace inquired.

"The floor keeps us out of the mud," Sidia explained, "and the roof keeps us dry."

"But the disadvantage is we're locked in a shed. And with an overcast sky, we can't tell if it's daylight or still dark."

Moments later, the board moved and Pontia appeared in the frame.

"Get out here," he instructed.

While clouds filtered out a lot of the light, enough soaked through to let Jace know it was long past dawn.

Rain dripped down Pontia's face and he scowled, "I said get out here."

"Your nose is very red," Sidia remarked as he stepped out of the shed.

"That's because your cousin caught me off guard," Pontia stated, making an excuse for being bested.

Three spearmen behind the warrior nodded their agreement. Apparently, the fight as described by Pontia differed from reality. With their weapons leveled at the doorway, the trio made sure Pontia wasn't attacked a second time.

"Put down your spears and we can try it again," Jace offered as he emerged.

"I would gladly return the headache and broken nose," Pontia assured him, "but my father wants to see you two."

"You treat condemned prisoners very well," Jace remarked as they walked towards the headquarters of Chief Pacidia.

"Something's not right," Sidia noted. "Usually, murders are beaten as a sign to the Romans that the tribe takes the breaking of our treaty with Rome seriously."

"Then why are we unharmed?" Jace questioned. "Not that I'm complaining."

"Because my father wants to see you," Pontia answered.

***

They passed under the chief's banner, through the doorway, and entered a large room. Fur covered chairs for twenty advisers were arranged around a massive table. But only nine Hirpini elders were present. The Carthaginian, Jace and Sidia had seen the afternoon before, sat next to a man at the head of the table.

"Sidia Decimia. You own me a sheep," the man stated.

"Yes, Chief Pacidia," Sidia acknowledged. "I've been meaning to rectify that error."

"Some error," Pacidia remarked. He shifted his eyes. "And this must be Jace Otacilia Kasia. I knew your mother. A find lady and a good Queen of the Hirpini."

"I wish I had known her, sir," Jace admitted.

"Me too. She might have taught you not to go around murdering Romans," Chief Pacidia advised. Then he complained. "Half my nobles have become Romanized. They wear togas instead of our robes, sip vino rather than drink beer, and live in villas with flowering gardens, instead of houses with plots for vegetable. And they are demanding that I send you two to Benevento. It seems the garrison commander has your names etched on a pair of crosses just waiting for you and Sidia to be delivered to him."

"Yes, sir, I understand," Jace stated. "But Chief Pacidia, Sidia had nothing to do with the death of the overseer."

"That may be true, but the Hirpini treaty with Rome demands justice be delivered per the account of the eyewitness," Pacidia informed Jace. "And because of your weak archery, you left two. And usually, justice would be served."

"Sir, you said usually," Jace questioned. "Has something changed?"

"The gentleman to my left is Lieutenant General Hanno of the Carthaginian Expedition," Pacidia explained. "Last week, he sent me a nice gift from General Hannibal Barca. And yesterday, he brought an even better offer."

"We're not being sent to Benevento?" Sidia guessed.

"No. But you need to stay away from our eastern border. I'm sending you two troublemakers to our villages north of Venosa," the chief directed. "They have a rogue Marsican running the hills. Hopefully, despite your abysmal archery, you'll be able to kill the brown bear before it kills anymore sheep."

"And the treaty with Rome?" Jace remarked.

"The Hirpini Tribe has signed a new treaty with Carthage. We no longer recognize Roman authority in our lands. We've already sent warriors to join General Barca's army, which leave me short of hunters."

Servants brought out Sidia and Jace's long packs, quivers, and bow cases.

"Go kill the bear," Chief Pacidia ordered. Then he leaned forward and warned. "But don't murder any Carthaginian soldiers while you're hunting."

Chapter 5 – The Beast's Head

After five days of hiking mountain trails, generally in a southeast direction, Jace and Sidia stood outside the walls of Venosa.

"Aren't we supposed to be north of here?" Sidia asked.

"Yes, but I'm curious," Jace replied. "If the Carthaginians are so successful, why do the Roman's have a stronghold between the Punic army and the Hirpini tribe's border?"

"You don't think Chief Pacidia made a wise decision?"

"Who knows?" Jace admitted. "But I'll bet in Venosa, we can hire rooms with feather beds under a roof."

"And see if the Romans are packing to leave?"

"That as well."

The two strolled to the western gate. After a brief exchange with a guard, they entered the city.

"He didn't seem the least bit apprehensive about an attack from the Carthaginians," Sidia observed.

As they went farther into the city, they noted stacks of armor and spears in front of every building.

"Is this a Legion fort?" Jace inquired when they passed another stack of armor and weapons.

"Not that I'm aware," Sidia told him. "But years ago, the town was settled by retired Legionaries and their families. It appears more farmers have arrived this year."

"Those aren't the tools of farmers," Jace stated.

They entered a plaza and, seeing a crowd gathering, the two moved to stand behind the back row. Shortly after they arrived, a Legion Centurion hopped up on the low wall of a fountain. He unrolled a section of parchment and held it up as he read.

"Let it be known," he bellowed, "the Senate of Rome makes this offer. In order to raise two Legions to defend the Republic, we are taking recruits from slaves, criminals, and underaged youths."

"Not from here," a Latin man called out. "I need mine to work the fields. If they're going to do any defending, it'll be on the walls of Venosa. Not in a far-off district with a new Legion."

The Centurion ignored the man and continued, "Being a Legionary is not a job for everyone. To qualify, you need to be physically fit, have stamina, and be intelligent enough to learn."

"That leaves my brother-in-law out," another man shouted.

A burst of laughter erupted from the gathering.

"For those who qualify, you'll earn one hundred and twenty silver coins a year," the Centurion said, while ignoring the chuckles. "Plus, you'll be fed, have an opportunity to learn a trade, and get a chance to earn a pardon or your freedom."

"Twenty years ago, the recruiter spoke with more elegance," an older gentlemen told the crowd. "If he hadn't, I never would have signed up."

"Oh, yes you would have joined," another old man challenged. "Because you were sick of working on your father's farm."

"It was a good life in the Legions," the first one admitted.

Sidia nudged Jace in the ribs.

"Maybe I should join the Legion," he proposed. "It sounds like an adventure."

"There is one thing, the recruiter failed to mention," Jace advised. Sidia shrugged showing he had no idea what Jace meant. "You could get killed fighting the Carthaginians."

"That does lower the value of the benefits, ever so slightly."

"For the next five days, I'll be overseeing tryouts," the Centurion concluded. "Anyone who wants to test to become a Legionary, come to the plaza at midday."

Jace and Sidia wandered away with the crowd. While most of the citizens left, a few collected around the Centurion, asking him questions.

"Which inn looks the best, cousin?" Jace asked.

But Sidia didn't hear him. He was twisted around and looking at the recruiter.

***

Later in the morning than Jace or Sidia were accustomed to, they stopped by a butcher for fresh meat before leaving town. As the guard had done the day before, he easily passed them through the gate.

"Hannibal maybe boasting about how many battles he's won," Sidia commented. "But the men of Venosa don't seem worried about the Carthaginian or his army."

Several miles north of Venosa, Sidia announced, "That must be what it's like to be a God."

"What?" Jace asked, having no idea of the topic.

"The feathered bed, the high ceiling catching the evening breezes, and food served upon rising. A whole lot different than mornings at my father's farm."

"Your father was good to me when I got back from the north," Jace remarked. "He gave me a shed for sleeping and a place to build bows and arrows. And he fed me until I

45

could sell enough hunting bows to build a purse. Plus, it was peaceful on the farm."

"Says the man who lived through the attack of trees by the Boii tribe," Sidia stated. "You wouldn't understand. But there's nothing worse than sitting around watching crops grow."

"Sure, there is."

"What?" Sidia demanded.

"Starvation," Jace answered. Pointing to a hillside dotted with a flock of sheep, he instructed. "Let's go talk to the shepherd. He might know about the Marsican."

They left the road, entered a section of forest, and emerged on the other side. Where the trees ended, the land rose, becoming grass covered slopes.

***

While the shepherd didn't know anything about a rogue bear, he suggested the hunters continue over the crest. Two other flocks of sheep were known to graze in the adjacent foothills. After thanking him, Jace and Sidia hiked to the top and descended into a green valley.

"I wouldn't plant here," Sidia said judging the thin topsoil. "But the hunting would be good."

"I see birds," Jace offered, "and some old boar ruts, but not much else."

Sidia used a leg to brush aside the limb of a bush. Dropping to his knees, he sniffed at what appeared to be dark clumps of dirt.

"Those are bear droppings," he explained. "And from the aroma, it's been munching on something more substantial than nuts and berries."

"Lamb?" Jace questioned.

Sidia circled the droppings until he found the trail.

"Nothing stinks like meat merda," he stated. Facing towards the rising end of the valley, Sidia announced. "The bear went this way."

"Hold on a moment," Jace advised.

He pulled out his war bow and gently flexed the body and limbs over his knee. Once the wood and sinew were warm, he looped a bowstring around one end. Then he locked the end over the arch of his foot and bent the bow behind his other leg. Once the bowstring was attached, Jace stepped out from between the taut bow and the stretched string.

"Are you ready now?" Sidia asked.

Jace pulled a handful of arrows from his quiver. After sorting them, he selected five with matching shafts, and slid the rest back into the holder.

"Ready," he stated.

The two hunters marched up the valley.

***

Much later, the pawprints became more numerous. But it wasn't the tracks that bothered Sidia. Broken branches and uprooted plants identified the path of an angry animal.

"I've hunted bears," Sidia cautioned. "But I've never seen so much destruction."

Without talking it over, their footfalls softened and their breathing shallowed. Carefully, they slipped by branches to prevent the limbs from whipping back. Soundlessly, Jace and Sidia crept after the bear.

A healthy Marsican could maul and kill two men quickly. With the brown bear lost in madness and having developed a taste for blood, the stalk presented a higher level of danger than a typical hunt.

Two miles from where Sidia found the droppings, and higher in the valley, they heard heavy breathing and the sounds of an animal drinking. Sidia put out a hand, but Jace had already stopped.

"On the other side of those bushes," he murmured.

Jace scanned the surrounding trees before settling on a pine tree with thin branches.

"How fast can you climb that tree?"

"Not faster than a bear."

"You can get high enough, fast enough, to confuse the beast," Jace assured his cousin.

"You have a lot of confidence in my abilities," Sidia hissed.

Rolling his feet heel-to-toe to avoid footfalls and snapping twigs, Sidia Decimia crept to the designated pine. After shrugging off his pack, he gently lowered it to the ground. Then he reached in, pulled out a wrapped piece of raw meat and placed it on the ground.

To that point, the heavy breathing had been constant. But when the smell of beef drifted to the bear, it sniffed the air. Louder than a winded horse or the breeze of a summer storm, the massive Marsican gathered lungsful of air and meat scent.

Noting the difference in the breathing, Sidia reached up and grabbed a limb. Then he pulled his feet to a lower branch. From there, he climbed slowly, and as quietly as possible, to the top of the pine tree. Silently, he prayed to Hermes for the adventure to end. Then, realizing the request might be misunderstood, he settled for wishing the pine tree was taller.

Almost four hundred pounds of muscle and fur rose above the bushes. Towering to the height of two grown men, the bear turned its face searching for the source of the aroma.

Sidia clung to the trunk of the pine, attempting to keep his breathing shallow and the tremors in his arms from shaking the tree. The saving grace for Sidia was the poor eyesight of the brown bear. But what the Marsican lacked in vision, it made up for in its sense of smell.

From drinking at a stream behind the bushes, the Marsican pushed through the hedges and began sniffing and circling the pine tree. A great mound of brown fur on four massive paws, it tracked around the trunk, and stopped at the meat next to the pack. If the beast rose to full height, one swat could dislodge Sidia and drag him into the clutches of the bear.

Zip-Thwack!

The arrowhead penetrated the fur and skin a hand's width behind the bear's shoulder. After passing through the flesh, the shaft threaded between ribs, passed through both lungs, and exited out the other side.

In most successful hunts, the mortally wounded bear would gather the last of its strength and dash off into the woods. Even with ruined lungs, a bear could run a long distance before dying. But the Marsican was far from typical.

Enraged at the pain, the bear faced its attacker. Spotting Jace, the mad beast reared up, preparing to leap forward and rip the archer to sherds.

Zip-Thwack!

Zip-Thwack!

Madness and anger could temporarily overcome injuries to major organs. But no man or animal possessed the ability to resist two arrows through the heart. When the fates cut its strings, the fearsome beast dropped like a wet piece of woolen cloth.

Sidia scrambled down the pine and raced to the bear.

"Chief Pacidia will reward us for this," he gushed while placing a hand on the skull of the giant. His sprawled fingers fell short of spanning the distance between the Marsican's ears. "Maybe he'll forgive me for the sheep I owe him."

Jace circled the bear, examining the body. On the right hindquarter, he noted three lumps under the fur. With his skinning knife, he cut one of the bumps to find an old iron spearhead.

"What are you doing?" Sidia inquired.

"Trying to figure out why this Marsican was hunting during the day," Jace explained.

"It was mad," Sidia suggested.

"It was crippled," Jace corrected. "Look at its rear leg. This bear couldn't run far or fast."

"Then any hunter could have located it and made the kill," Sidia offered. "Why did Chief Pacidia need us?"

"Perhaps, he wanted us in this district," Jace proposed.

"What for?"

"I have no idea," Jace admitted. He lifted his war ax from the holding ring and took the first hack at the bear's neck. More fur flew than flesh or blood. "What I do know is this. Getting the beast's head separated so we can display it to the villagers is going to be a long process."

***

From over the rise, smoke drifted into the afternoon sky.

"I think I should carry the head this time," Sidia insisted.

He shifted the bear hide that draped over his shoulder. The thick fur, still heavy with fat and tissue, swung, forcing him to sidestep to keep his footing.

50

"But I like parading around holding the head up," Jace explained. To demonstrate, he raised the pole, lifting the skull and muzzle of the fierce Marsican high over their heads. "The children follow me around and I get to scare them with the head. Plus, the women. Ah, how they swoon in the presence of the hero who killed the rogue bear."

"You would deny your cousin his opportunity to bask in the glory," Sidia questioned. "All for the adoration of women?"

"Don't forget the laughter of small children," Jace replied. "It warms the heart."

"You aren't being serious, are you?"

"Not in the least," Jace assured him. "You can carry the head into the villages. For all I care, you can tote it back to Trevico and present it to the Chief of Chiefs yourself."

As if Jace would change his mind, Sidia seized the pole with the bear's head. After the raw hide had been transferred to Jace's shoulder, the two climbed the hill heading for the next hero's welcome and feast. It was what they expected after visiting two other villages.

However, as they neared the crest, the smoke, rather than dividing into individual cookfires, thickened into a single mass. At the top, Jace and Sidia peered down at burning huts, buildings, and dead bodies. Those alive rushed between structures trying to prevent the fires from spreading, while others treated the wounded.

Jace dropped the fur and sprinted downhill. Slower, because he would not relinquish the beast's head, Sidia jogged after his cousin.

***

"What happened?" Jace asked as he squatted next to an old man with a deep slash to his arm.

51

Applying pressure around the wound, Jace judged, by the slowing of the blood loss, that no major blood vessel had been severed.

"Carthaginian tax collectors," the man spit out. "Taxes my backside. They were scroungers come to raid our winter grain."

"How many?" Jace asked as he cut a slice from the man's shirt and began wrapping the arm.

"Five and a wagon driver. They didn't ask for a portion. They came in with bare blades and took all of our winter stores."

"But the Hirpini have allied with the Carthaginians," Jace informed him.

"Someone should tell that to their soldiers."

Sidia strolled up with an older woman collapsed against his hip.

"Is she hurt?" Jace asked while knotting the material over the man's arm.

"Not physically," Sidia answered. Then he placed a finger under the woman's chin, lifted her face, and urged. "Tell him what you told me."

"After beating down our men and taking our grain and dried vegetables," she whimpered, "they took my granddaughters."

Jace balled his fingers into fists, and asked, "How old are the girls?"

"Cassia is nine," the woman answered. "and Ophilia is eleven."

Jace came to his feet, reached over his shoulder, and extracted the war bow from its case.

While warming up the sinew and wood, he remarked, "This may be why Chief Pacidia sent us to the district."

"Pacidia," the woman said before spitting as if the name left a bad taste in her mouth. "He sent our men to the Carthaginians and left us undefended."

"We're going after them, right?" Sidia asked hopefully.

"Yes," Jace confirmed. Then he added, "And this time, we aren't leaving witnesses."

Chapter 6 – I See Witnesses

One stride per heartbeat allowed Cretan Archer Jace Kasia to cover miles without draining his energy. And while Jace closed the distance to the Carthaginian raiders, the cadence left his cousin behind. Although a man who could climb mountains like a goat, Sidia, on flat terrain, had to settle for watching Jace's head and shoulders pull ahead. But Sidia was game and continued at his own pace.

Miles later and gritting his teeth against the exhaustion, Sidia jogged across the plain until…Arms encircled his legs and he fell face first into the wild grass.

"What the…"

"Shut up," Jace cautioned. "You're as subtle as an Auroch during rutting season."

Sidia turned his head to face his cousin.

"You want to let me go? And maybe tell me what's going on," he inquired. "Or are you going to hold me down and give me a lecture on Auroch husbandry and herd migration?"

Jace slapped his shoulder and rolled away.

"Our tax collectors and the children are under a tree by a stream just ahead."

"Then let's go get them," Sidia encouraged.

"Six against two and the children need protecting during the fight," Jace told him. "It's a good thing you're on a quest for adventure."

"Why do you say that?"

With his back resting on the ground, Jace flexed the war bow while looking up at the streaks of sunlight in the sky.

"Because one of us gets to sneak into their camp, locate a shield, and then guard the children," Jace explained.

"This whole adventure thing isn't easy," Sidia commented.

"It never is," Jace confirmed. "You circle around and come in from the north. Once you have the shield in place, I'll move up the creek from the south."

Sidia inhaled then expelled the air between pursed lips. He pushed to his feet and moved towards the creek. Before Jace left the trampled grass, he strung the war bow, and selected five arrows.

***

Sidia crept along the bank of the creek. Where he encountered thick branches, he stepped into the water. In places where grass grew to the water's edge, he remained on dry ground. While moving, the tightness in his chest that he experienced in the pine tree returned. Then, as he caught sight of the raider's camp, he realized the fear wasn't paralyzing. In fact, it was invigorating.

High on the bank, the horses were hobbled next to the wagon. Deeper under the trees, a campfire pushed back the long shadows and reflected light off the shapes of three men. Closer to the creek, a second campfire revealed the presence of the last three soldiers. Sidia searched for the children but couldn't locate them. Fearing for their fate brought a lump to his throat.

After a raid, a soldier might get an impulse to take a villager or two. In the moment, owning a servant, seemed like a good idea. But on the trail away from the village, the ill-chosen captive might stumble and slow up the escape. At first the soldier would kick or strike his new possession to encourage them to keep up with the march. But eventually, angry at his own foolishness, the raider would murder the villager and leave the carcass beside the trail

Not having found the bodies of the girls along the route from the village, Sidia held out hope for their survival. Ignoring the dread, he shifted to scan the camp. A shield, propped up on a rock, rested close to the lower campfire. Sidia marked it in his mind and returned to searching for the girls.

At the upper campfire, a soldier dumped food into a couple of bowls and hiked to the wagon.

"Get up," he demanded while probing a blanket with his foot. The cloth beside the wagon wheel moved. In the deepening shadows, Sidia noted two heads appearing from under the fabric. "Here's food. Eat and understand, I won't tolerate you holding us up tomorrow."

"Trouble with your new pets," a raider from the campfire inquired.

"No. They just need to rest," the soldier replied. He placed the bowls next to the girls and strolled back to the fire.

Sidia had located the girls and he knew where to get a shield. All he needed now was the courage to take the shield, race to the wagon, and defend the girls. Dropping back into the grass, he tried to work up the nerve to act. But one thing held him back.

Jace Kasia had shown up at the Decimia farm last fall. According to the survivors of the battle at Cannae, he was an Otacilia and a second cousin to the Decimia clan. With that news, Sidia's family welcomed the long lost relative.

Over the winter and into the spring, Jace had crafted bows, made arrows, and taught Sidia how to fight with a blade and hunt with a bow. But as good as Jace was at hand-to-hand combat, and hunting with an arrow, Sidia had just one confrontation to judge the martial skills of his cousin. At the farm where they fought with the overseer, the two thugs had only been wounded by arrows. Those results didn't reflect well on the archery talent of his cousin when he was under stress.

Sidia desperately needed to trust that Jace could finish the rescue of the girls, successfully. He glanced at the camps and the wagon again then ducked back into the grass.

***

South of the raider camp, Jace squatted with one foot tucked under his haunch and the other extended downhill for stabilization. From the position, he tracked the man with the two bowls. Once he knew the location of the girls from the village, Jace refocused on Sidia.

From the tall grass, his cousin would raise up as if a rabbit watching for a predator. Four times Sidia peered over the stalks but didn't move.

"What are you waiting for?" Jace mouthed.

As if he heard, Sidia came out of the grass, sprinted to the camp, grabbed the shield, and raced uphill.

"Stop him," a soldier ordered from the lower camp.

At the upper camp, a soldier responded by lunging for Sidia.

Zip-Thwack!

In mid leap, the arrow pierced high on the man's neck. The force of the shaft rocked his head to the side. As Zarek Mikolas taught Jace, control the head and you control the body. The flying man rotated away from Sidia and fell to the ground limp and silent.

Sidia reached the girls. Then he squatted and used an arm to rake them in behind the shield. In response to the rough treatment, they screamed at the top of their lungs.

Having located the assailant, the last five raiders pulled their weapons and faced the wagon.

"They belong to me," the raider who took the girls shouted.

Quickly, he covered half the distance to Sidia.

Zip-Thwack!

In mid stride, the shaft snapped the thigh bone of the soldier's forward leg. The crippled limb twirled the raider off his feet. Screaming, he rolled down the hill. Because he fell away from Jace and made so much noise, the other soldiers paused to watch as their companion splashed into the creek.

To their detriment, they missed the Cretan Archer rising to his full height. With a better view of the battlefield, Jace sent his next arrow into the chest of a third soldier.

Zip-Thwack!

Pain followed the path of the shaft before the arrowhead stopped the soldier's heart, ending the agony and his life. As the body hit the ground, the archer shifted to select his next target.

Sidia was the only enemy in sight. The final three raiders sprinted towards the shield, the wagon wheel, and the threat. From off to the side, unnoticed by the soldiers, Jace Kasia sent another lethal shaft.

Zip-Thwack!

The Carthaginian soldier in the lead bent forward, folding his body around the shaft jutting from his stomach. Although painfully toppling onto his head, he ignored the sharp agony in his skull. For the aching in his gut, far exceeded the headache.

Zip-Thwack!

Hit in the shoulder, the next soldier lurched in a half circle. At the end of his stumble, he crashed into the sixth man. Both fell to the ground, but only one shook off the collision, picked up his spear, and pushed to his feet.

Jace took three short, quick steps. The shuffle allowed him to lean to the side and let the war bow slip from his hand and the quiver fall from his shoulder. While the weapon and pouch settled to earth, the archer came erect, lengthened his stride, and yanked the war hatchet from its holding ring.

***

All during the attack, the soldiers assumed the arrows were coming from the area of the wagon and the shield. After witnessing two of his men hit with arrows from the side, the sixth raider rotated to his left, dropped down, and lowered his profile.

An excellent tactic if more arrows were coming. But there were no more arrows from that direction. What came from the haze of twilight was a hatchet brandishing Cretan Archer.

The hatchet arched from high to low, hooking the shaft of the spear and driving the tip off to the left. Just before releasing the pressure, Jace stretched out and hit the soldier with an elbow.

Falling back from the blow, the man jerked the spear shaft, attempting to bring the spearhead to bear on his attacker. But the shorter weapon came around and chopped his forward arm. As he dropped the spear and grabbed at the deep wound, Jace ended his misery with a backhanded chop to the soldier's throat.

Six were down but three moaned and attempted to move.

"Don't let the girls see this," Jace shouted as he ran to the closest of the wounded raiders.

"No witnesses?" Sidia guessed.

"None," Jace confirmed.

***

The graves were as shallow as the prayers Jace offered for the souls of the soldiers. Although they could have traveled immediately, he delayed the trip back to the village until dawn. Once there was light, Jace examined the area. And while he erased footprints, Sidia buried the campfires. They left the area as natural as possible. From a distance, the six grass covered mounds appeared to be a part of the landscape and not the final resting places of a Carthaginian scavenging party.

***

When the wagon rolled into the village, the old woman sobbed. The two men who went to rescue the girls walked in front, guiding the horses. Cassia rode on the shoulders of the Hirpini tribesman. But there was no sign of Ophilia in the caravan.

"Grandmother. Are you missing an imp?" Sidia inquired. "Because I found this one on the road and I don't know what to do with her."

59

Nine-year-old Cassia used the flats of her hands to pat the sides of Sidia's face.

"My horse is in…," Cassia started to say but stumbled over the word. "He's inade…"

"Inadequate, is the word," Jace said helping her.

"Yes, my mount should be a horse, because he is inadequate as a shield bearer," Cassia exclaimed.

"Whatever are you talking about, child?" the grandmother pleaded while she searched the road behind the wagon.

"Jace said Sidia is inadequate because he couldn't keep two little girls safe behind a shield," Cassia announced.

"Not safe," her grandmother groaned. "What about Ophilia?"

"She cried so hard when the soldiers took us," Cassia replied, "and couldn't stop. She exhausted herself. Ophilia!"

A pile of blankets moved, and the slim eleven-year-old girl climbed off the back of the wagon.

"Jace and Sidia killed the raiders," Ophilia declared. She held up her arms and waved them in the air, while telling the villagers. "They were as brave as Spartan warriors and as quick as the arrows Jace used to slay all six of the evil ones."

Jace looked over with a scowl.

"Witnesses," he reminded his cousin.

"I was watching your archery," Sidia pleaded his case. "I didn't think the girls would have the courage to peer around the shield."

"We watched from the other side," Cassia told the visitors. "It was better than any old fable."

"You two killed six Carthaginian soldiers?" the old man with the bandage on his arm asked.

"They sure did," another villager informed him. "Shot six arrows and killed all six with one draw of the bowstring."

"Amazing," the old man shouted.

Jace locked eyes with Sidia, and repeated, "Witnesses."

***

Surrounded by the old folks and the youths of the village, they walked the horses to a storage building and began unloading the wagon. Just as the villagers finished, riders trotted into the center plaza. Jace and Sidia, were inside stacking bags. They missed the arrival.

"What happened here?" War Leader Pontia demanded.

The seven Hirpini soldiers with him looked around at the burnt huts, ruined public buildings, and fresh graves.

"Carthaginian raiders," the old man told the chief's son. Then his eyes flashed, and he demanded. "Where were our Hirpini warriors? Where was our protection?"

"General Hannibal Barca is going to beat the Republic," Pontia bragged, "and give our tribe back our independence."

"That's if we don't starve first," the village elder countered. 'You're here. Tardy, but here. So, you should join us for the feast. We're celebrating Jace Otacilia and Sidia Decimia. Two Hirpini who understand defending their people."

Pontia hopped off his horse as if preparing to attack the old man.

"We will stay for the celebration," Pontia stated. Then he suggested. "Perhaps you can tell me what Otacilia and Decimia did to deserve a feast in their honor."

***

Late in the afternoon, pots steamed, meat roasted over cookfires, and bread baked in ovens. A festive atmosphere permeated the town.

"More beer?" Sidia inquired.

"Not for me," Jace said. "Cretan Archers, like Spartans, are leery of anything that dulls our senses."

"That's fine, it leaves more for me," Sidia exclaimed. He took a sip and licked the foam off his lips. "You know, this adventure stuff is pretty good. The other day, I was fighting Pontia. Now I get to sit with him and share a meal."

"I believe it was me fighting and you...," Jace stopped in mid thought.

Heavy cavalry horses had a unique gait. The precise placement of hoofs evenly across a mounted patrol, identified a heritage of horsemanship. When ten riders cantered into the plaza, Jace drifted back under an awning.

"Please extend my apologizes to the village elders. But I'm feeling ill and will miss the feast," Jace told his cousin. He nodded in the direction of the riders. "However, I'm sure Captain Shama', of the Libyan Cavalry, will be happy to take my place."

Act 3

Chapter 7 - Sanctuary or Dismemberment

Jace may have relinquished his seat in the village circle, but he didn't miss out on the feast. Cassia, Ophilia, and their grandmother made sure their bowman received large portions of every dish.

"I simply can't eat anymore," he pleaded.

The dining room table was scattered with empty bowls. Through the window, the light of early evening faded. And Jace Kasia relaxed in the best hideout a man could ever want.

"We have baked sweet cake with honey and raisins," Cassia exclaimed as if the announcement would create room in his full stomach.

"It sounds delicious," Jace said trying to pacify her.

"Then, I'll fetch you a bowl," the little girl declared.

She ran out of the house before Jace could stop her.

"She's always been headstrong," her grandmother explained. "Please excuse her exuberance."

"I was raised as an orphan," Jace told the woman. "But I would hope if I had a little sister, she would be as full of life as Cassia."

The grandmother and Ophilia hugged Jace before heading for the exit. At the doorway, Ophilia stopped.

"No one has mentioned your deeds to the Libyan officer," she informed him. "Cassia will be back soon with the sweet cake. When her talking becomes too much, remind her she needs to get back to the feast."

"I will," Jace told her.

Alone, he paced the floor, wondering at the fates. Of all the towns on the border of Hirpini territory, what did they have in mind when they brought Captain Shama' to the village.

The last time he saw the Libyan officer of heavy cavalry, the Captain had threatened Jace with a beating if he skipped out on feeding a pair of captured Cretan Archers. After helping the two bowmen escape, Jace imagined the punishment had escalated, perhaps to dismemberment.

But other than cutting into his social life, the arrival of the Captain had not affected him. Perhaps the fates didn't have anything planned. Then hard, insistent kicks at the front door brought him to a stop.

With the hatchet raised to shoulder level, he went to the door and jerked it open.

"Sweet cake with honey and raisins," Cassia commented as she shouldered aside the door. Filling her arms was a large clay pot that threatened to topple her slight frame. "I thought we could eat together."

"I'm happy for the company," Jace lied while checking outside to be sure no one had followed the girl. He dropped the hatchet into the holding ring and took the pot from Cassia. "Come my fine lady, let us feast together."

Laughing, the girl strutted to the table and cleared off a spot.

"Tell me, Jace," she inquired, "what does super…superfluous mean?"

"Without a context, it's hard to say," Jace informed her while placing the large bowl on the table. "Where did you hear the word?"

Cassia grabbed two spoons and handed one to Jace. Then she carved out a chunk of sweet cake that hung over the sides of her spoon.

With the mouthful positioned in front of her lips, she answered, "Pontia told Captain Shama' that Sidia, and you were superfluous to the future of the Hirpini Tribe. Was that a compliment?"

She shoved the entire piece of sweet cake into her mouth and chewed contentedly. Jace stabbed the cake with the spoon, pulled out a taste, and licked it off.

"Cassia, can you do something for me?" he inquired.

"Yes," she agreed while scooping out another spoonful of cake. "What?"

"Something has come up and I need to leave," Jace told her. "But I don't want to interrupt the feast. Can you quietly tell Sidia to meet me where he found signs of the bear?"

"Sure," she stated. "Do I have to take the sweet cake back?"

"No, little lady," Jace informed her while collecting the gear for his long pack. "After you deliver the message, come back, and enjoy it."

She left and Jace finished packing. Then he gathered the items for Sidia's baggage. Moments after Cassia departed, Jace slipped out the backdoor, crossed the garden, and climbed over a side wall.

His caution proved correct. Two of the Libyan cavalrymen waited in the dark just outside the rear gate of the garden.

⁂

Sidia plopped an olive into his mouth and chewed while he talked.

"And I tell you, it was the meanest bear," he took a swig of beer to wash down the pieces of olive, "that you could ever imagine. But was I afraid? No sir, not Sidia Decimia. Nope, I took my bow and stalked the monster."

"How did you kill it?" a villager asked.

"I sent my cousin, Jace, up a tree to distract the Marsican," Sidia replied. He lifted his mug and sloshed beer when he saluted the head on the pole. "With the beast focused on the tree, I was able to get close while avoiding the massive claws."

The villagers leaned forward, their mouths opened, anticipating the conclusion to the story.

"Sidia," Cassia pleaded while tugging on his sleeve.

"Cassia, I'm in the middle of telling how I killed the bear."

"I know, but I have to tell you a secret."

She pulled on the material until he bent down to her level.

"Jace said he had to go," she whispered. "You can meet him where you saw the signs of the bear."

"Right now?" Sidia questioned. "Why?"

"I don't think he wants to be superfluous," she remarked. "You know, to the future of the Hirpini."

Sidia froze in place. Moving only his eyes, he shifted them up and down. With the movement, he swept the length of the table. On one end, Pontia sat with a tight, self-satisfied grin on his lips. On the other side, Captain Shama' looked ready to order an execution.

"Thank you, Cassia. Run along."

The little girl backed away before turning and sprinting towards the house and the large pot of sweet cake.

"Now, where was I?" Sidia announced as he sat upright.

"You were avoiding the claws," a villager reminded him.

"Of course. I edged to the side, notched my arrow, and drew the bowstring to my chin," he described. Pausing, Sidia took a drink of beer and made a show of swallowing. "Suddenly the bear turned to face me. Although it rose to its full height, as steady as a marble statue, I held my ground. Then I released the arrow, and the shaft went straight into its heart."

"But the bear pelt has three holes in it," someone pointed out.

"Well, I released two more arrows just to be sure," he explained. "You can't be too careful when dealing with snakes or diseased animals."

At the conclusion of the story, he stood and bowed to cheers and applause.

"Going somewhere?" Captain Shama' inquired.

"The beer, you know," Sidia replied.

He staggered out of the plaza, around a building, and stopped at the low perimeter wall. Pausing, Sidia glanced around to be sure he was alone, then he vaulted the barrier.

Several moments later, Captain Shama' shouted to several cavalrymen.

"Go get him. And send someone to the house and detain the other one. No one murders Carthaginian soldiers and gets away with it. Isn't that so, Chief Pontia?"

Everyone knew Pontia hadn't been to the pools of Mephitis, exposed himself to her vapors, and added to the Goddess's mud wall. The village elder started to correct the

Captain and school him on Hirpini customs. Before the elder spoke out, another man rested a hand on his arm.

"Don't say anything," he suggested. "Chief Pacidia's son has joined the Carthaginians against his own people."

Wisely, the elder held his tongue.

"That's right, Captain Shama'," Pontia proclaimed, confirming the idea. "Let all the villages know, Jace Otacilia and Sidia Decimia are outcasts and enemies of the Hirpini people."

After hearing the Chief of Chief's son make the decree, Sidia raced southward in the dark. Once he located Jace, they needed to talk.

***

The small fire in the dark was barely more than a candle flame. But in the night, it shined like a beacon. For all of Jace's skills in the woods, the location appeared to be a mistake, except, for two facts.

"That's not where I saw the bear dropping," Sidia muttered.

Angling westward, he walked the crest carefully placing his feet so as not to trip in the dark. Down in the valley, the flame fell behind. And that was the other fact. In order to see the flame, one needed to be on the slopes directly above the fire.

"Lo, cousin," a voice greeted him from the other side of the summit.

"I didn't think you'd be near the fire," Sidia commented. He stopped and complained to the gray image of Jace. "I was enjoying the feast until I got your message."

The cousins gripped wrists, then dropped to the ground below the crest.

"Was I wrong to pull you away?"

"No. Any longer and Captain Shama' would have taken me into custody," Sidia replied. "And adding to our problem, after I left, Pontia condemned us as enemies of the Hirpini people."

"That leaves us in a conundrum," Jace remarked. "To the east we have the entire Carthaginian army wanting to chop us into pieces. In the west, they have crucifixes with our names etched on the cross beams. And to the north, the Pentri Tribe has remained allies with Rome. And despite our actual standing, they would love to capture a couple of Hirpini spies."

Sidia gazed at the stars and exhaled audibly.

"Where can we go and not be immediately crucified?"

"I thought about Sicily," Jace suggested.

"From what I hear, except for Syracuse, the island is occupied by Legionaries," Sidia advised. "It seems the known world is full of soldiers from Rome."

"Not all, and certainly not in Crete. But I don't want to be there," Jace sighed. He paused for several moments before inquiring. "Have you ever heard of Alcibiades of Athens?"

"No, I haven't," Sidia admitted. "What does he have to do with our current situation?"

"Nothing and maybe everything," Jace replied. "After seven years of war between Sparta and Athens, neither side had made any progress. Generals Nicias and Laches negotiated a peace treaty. But a commander named Alcibiades, because he was young, was excluded."

"When was this?" Sidia inquired.

"Around a hundred and ninety years ago."

"Are you telling me a tale from a couple of hundred years ago will help us?"

Maybe," Jace stated. "Nicias and Laches' treaty had problems and Sparta sent a delegation to Athens to discuss the faults. After the first day of meetings, Alcibiades met with the delegation. Alcibiades told the Spartans that the Athenian assembly was arrogant and had secret ambitions to topple Sparta. But that he, Alcibiades, could use his connections to bring about resolutions that would be favorable to Sparta. But the Spartans needed to declare that they didn't have the full authority of Sparta."

"Wait, Alcibiades convinced a bunch of stoic Spartans to deny that they represented their country?" Sidia questioned.

"Historians say Alcibiades was a handsome man, a wealthy citizen, and a powerful speaker," Jace explained. "The next day in front of the assembly, when Alcibiades questioned the Spartan ambassadors, they followed his directions and admitted they did not have the authority to negotiate."

"They contradicted what they said the day before?" Sidia asked.

"They did," Jace agreed. "The direct contradiction gave Alcibiades an opportunity to denounce the quality of their character and cast suspicions on their intentions. In a rousing speech, he totally destroyed the credibility of the Spartan ambassadors. General Nicias, one of Athens original negotiators, tried to save the talks, but Alcibiades' ploy had ruined any chance of salvaging the meeting."

"But why?" Sidia inquired. "To what purpose?"

"Due to his uncovering the 'false' Spartan delegation, the assembly promoted young Alcibiades to a full generalship and granted him additional powers."

"What does a story of subterfuge have to do with our situation?" Sidia begged.

"Well, we are young, good looking, well spoken, and ambitious," Jace offered.

"The truth is hard to argue with," Sidia confirmed. "What are you getting at?"

"We're going to Venosa," Jace announced. "And we're going to join the Legion."

"We're what?" Sidia exclaimed.

"The Legion recruiter said he was looking for able criminals," Jace explained. "I believe we qualify."

"But that will deliver us to the Roman crosses," Sidia protested.

"We'll find our sanctuary," Jace assured him, "among the undesirables."

Chapter 8 – The Disagreeable Altar

"Wheat, peas, lintels, and barley," Leo Sandalius bellowed. He beat on the empty wagons as he walked around the idle transports. "Gentlemen. Where is my wheat, peas, lintels, and barley?"

"Aedile Sandalius, those products are bulky, and require the wagons to move slow," a teamster protested.

"Vino and olive oil are more compact," another explained. "Cushioned with straw, the amphorae can withstand faster travel."

"You assume master transporter that the God Mendacius has covered my eyes," Sandalius scolded. "But I am not blinded by his deception and treachery. Nor am I blind to yours. The citizens of Rome need vino and olive oil, I'll grant you that. But staples make the meal. I repeat. Where is my wheat, peas, lintels, and barley?"

"Well, we..."

Leo Sandalius jerked away from the teamsters and agents. The ends of his toga flew outward adding to the drama of his next order.

"*Assistant Aedile* Scipio, note the names of these transporters," Leo instructed. "If any return to Rome with any product other than wheat, peas, lintels, or barley, I want a duty tax. Let's base it on fifteen percent of the value of the goods."

"But Aedile, that will strip away our profit," a teamster pleaded.

"Then bring food into the city. That's your job," Sandalius proclaimed while twirling back to face the teamsters. "Seeing that Rome gets fed, gentlemen, is one of my jobs. Forgo your short fast trips, drive farther, and bring the citizens food."

After his speech, Aedile Sandalius stood stone faced. The drivers and shipping agents around him thought about arguing. But Aediles were authorized by the Senate to act in the public interest. Their word could not be challenged.

"Yes, Aedile," the drivers and agents said in turn.

"Very well," Sandalius concluded. "Come Cornelius, I have a complaint about a disagreeable altar."

"Yes, Aedile," assistant Aedile Scipio acknowledged.

He capped the ink bottle, rolled the parchment, and picked up the portable desk. After a servant packed the recording equipment into a small cart, Cornelius hurried to catchup with Leo Sandalius. The servant followed with the cart.

"Where they right about the speed of the wagons?" Cornelius asked.

"Goodness no," Sandalius replied. "Speed is only part of the trip because it's a shorter distance over good roads to haul vino and olive oil from the port at Ostia. Trekking into the country on dirt roads to collect farm goods takes longer."

They strolled through a commercial part of the city, examining store fronts and the exteriors of businesses. At one business, they stopped.

"Baker. The brickwork at your entrance is a disgrace," Sandalius shouted into the shop. "I expect to find them repaired by next week."

"Yes, Aedile," the baker called back.

They continued walking and inspecting while Sandalius talked.

"Most people understand the need for what we do," the Aedile explained. "Allow small things like the missing bricks at the bakers to go unrepaired, and soon, Rome's largest structures will be in ruin. It's especially true at temples and altars. Priests believe they are representatives of the Gods. And as such, they don't think the condition of their temples should be judged along with residential structures and commercial businesses."

The small procession turned down a tree lined street and passed along a row of tombs. Halfway down the block, two priests of the Goddess Miseria greeted them.

"Sandalius, we don't often get civil servants down this way," the older one said. "Would you care to leave a donation?"

Leo Sandalius bristled. It could have been the idea of contributing to the Goddess of misery, anxiety, grief, and misfortune that offended him. Or perhaps, the reference to him as being a civil servant disagreed with him. Although technically a civil service position, the Aediles had broader responsibilities and the power to enforce rules from both the Senate and the Temples of Rome.

73

"I have no plans to give you coins," Sandalius declared. He ran his eyes over the chipped brick exterior of the altar building, the weeds in the garden surrounding the structure, and the pieces of rags and packaging littering the grounds. "If this unsightly altar is as disagreeable inside as it is outside, I'm condemning it."

"But Aedile, the Goddess Miseria suffers because the Senate has banned public crying and other displays of sadness and loss. We can hardly be blamed for the lack of coins to support the altar."

"The Senate has also outlawed any mention of defeat or surrender to the Punic invaders," Sandalius shot back. "You don't see the priests of Pax, the Goddess of Peace, complaining and letting their temple fall into disarray."

"Their supporters are more numerous and more generous in normal times," the other priest offered.

"Is that a defeatist attitude?" Sandalius asked before turning to Cornelius. "Write down this warning to repair the altar structure and grounds, assistant Aedile Scipio. They have two days to bring the alter to a respectable condition. Or it will be torn down and the bricks sold to pay for the cost of demolition."

After the declaration, Leo Sandalius stepped through the entrance. A soft breeze blew into the roofless structure, gently ruffling the fabric of his toga. A whisper reached his ears. Looking up, he noted the sound came from the wind through the tree branches overhead. A small fire altar occupied one end of the structure. Facing the sacrificial flame, rows of benches, polished from generation of worshipers, radiated out from the altar. Despite being open to the elements, no dirt, leaves, or dust covered the floor nor any surface in the altar building.

When Aedile Sandalius went in, one of the priests raised his fingers to his lips and prayed. With the fate of the Goddess Miseria's altar in the balance, his action was expected. But something about the man's right hand caught Cornelius' attention.

"That scar on your hand," he inquired, "how did you come by it?"

The priest lifted the arm, which threw back the fabric of his robe, exposing the entire scar.

"I was with Longus Legions at Trebia," the priest responded. He extended his arm and an old wound, clearly from a long blade, ran from his hand down the side of his forearm. "A mercenary's sword sliced me open. At first, I was angry, but the wound saved my life. While I was in the rear being treated, my Century, all of my friends, were trampled by elephants or murdered by the Iberian heavy infantry. And because of this scar, I began studying about the Goddess."

"How so?" Cornelius asked.

"The loss of men I'd grown up with and others who I grew close to brought me to ruin," the priest explained. "When I got back from the north, I attempted to drink the capital dry of cheap vino. One day, I staggered by this altar after a funeral of a man I knew. Stopping in, I asked about the Goddess. And I discovered I had been celebrating in her blessings ever since the battle."

"Misery, anxiety, grief, depression, and misfortune," Leo Sandalius listed as he stepped out of the altar structure. "Cornelius, extend the deadline by two weeks for the exterior repairs. Inside is immaculate and truly a place worthy of a Goddess."

Cornelius started to write then stopped.

"Aedile, one of your jobs is managing festivals to honor the Gods," he stated. "With your permission, I'd like to organize a celebration for the Goddess Miseria."

"You want people to come to a festival and be miserable?" Sandalius questioned with a sour expression on his face. "Honoring the Gods isn't a lark, Scipio."

"When we honor Miseria, we will ask her to remove her blessings," Cornelius described. He looked at the priests. "I'm sure there's a way to demonstrate our need for relief from grief and misfortune."

Both priests nodded their confirmation.

"I do hate to see any religious structure destroyed," Sandalius remarked. "And it's important to learn what it takes to manage a festival for when you become an Aedile. You have my permission to put together a street festival honoring the Goddess Miseria."

"Thank you, sir," Cornelius said.

But in his mind, Tribune Scipio envisioned something more grand than a street celebration.

***

Later in the afternoon, after he finished his work for Aedile Sandalius, Cornelius rode to a villa near the Tiber river. From horseback, Cornelius could see the yellow of the river water.

"It's a miracle that your villa hasn't been washed away in a flood," Cornelius said while sliding off the horse.

"We're situated above the bend," Appius told him. "All the flooding happens downstream from here. But you didn't come to discuss engineering, did you?"

"No, Senior Tribune Pulcher, I did not."

"Oh no. When you start using Legion rank, I know something's up," Appius declared. "Are you planning an invasion of Carthage or maybe Egypt?"

"Not yet," Cornelius stated. "Although I do require military maneuvering."

"Come to the patio and we'll discuss your ridiculous requirements over a glass of vino."

"Why do you say ridiculous?"

"Because you're Cornelius Scipio and you don't do anything sane. Come on, I'll need a drink, I just know it."

They strolled around to the patio. Once seated, servants brought out vino.

"I'm charged with putting on a street festival," Cornelius explained. "What I need is the equivalent of a Legion baggage train to make it successful."

"You need a surveyor, a quarter master, a supply Sergeant, a transportation Centurion, Tribunes to officiate at the games, livestock handlers, and vendors for the crowd," Appius listed. "That's a lot of gear to crowd into a street festival. What area do you have in mind, the Forum?"

"No Appius," Cornelius told him. "I'm going to fill the festival grounds outside the east gate."

"Only major celebrations use that area. And they are planned a year or more in advance," Appius warned. "How long do you have?"

"Five weeks," Cornelius answered.

"You could train a Legion in those forty days," Appius ventured. "But there is no way to organize all the moving parts for a big celebration in that period."

"I will," Cornelius assured him. "But I need your help."

"You do realize that anything less than filling the festival grounds will be seen as a failure on your part."

"I do. But I have a plan."

***

Leo Sandalius had signed so many small contracts for the underaged Scipio youth, that he stopped reading them. When a piece of parchment landed on his desk, he glanced at the bottom searching for where to write his name. But there was no place to confirm the contract. Starting at the top, he read:

Leo Sandalius, Aedile of Rome, and citizen of the Republic
I trust this missive finds you in good health. Your presence is requested at a festival given in the name of the Goddess Miseria in two days hence. As a guest of honor, you will be seated on the grandstand with the other dignitaries.

Leo stopped reading and admired the moxie of Cornelius. Imagine calling a review stand a grandstand and having invited dignitaries for a street festival. The thought brought a smile to his face until he read farther.

A vehicle and a cavalry escort will pick you up at your villa shortly after dawn. If you are delayed, they will wait. However, the festival will start without you.
Hoping to see you at the eastern festival grounds,
Cornelius Scipio, assistant Aedile of Rome, Tribune of the Legion, and citizen of the Republic

Leo Sandalius came out of his chair, screaming, "Where is Cornelius?"

"Aedile, he sent word that he wouldn't be in for the next couple of days," a staff member informed him.

Gordian Urban, the other Aedile of Rome in the office, strolled through the doorway. In his hand he held an invitation.

"Your assistant Aedile has been busy," Urban remarked. "I had no idea you authorized such a big celebration."

78

"I didn't," Leo stated. Then he looked at the pen in his hand and realized that he had signed every contract. "I did. But just to show young Scipio how difficult it was to put on a festival."

"You're a brave man, Sandalius," Urban remarked. "If your boy doesn't fill the grounds, you'll both look like complete failures. And you'll never be elected to another public office ever again."

Leo Sandalius dropped the pen, then collapsed into his chair.

"I know," he admitted.

***

Unlike most days leading up to a major festival, there was little buzz or gossip in the villas of prominent citizens. Taking that as a bad sign, Leo Sandalius ordered servants to quietly remove small personal items from his office. It would save time and embarrassment when the Senate replaced him for dereliction of duty, squandering funds, and causing public embarrassment for the Republic.

Even though he didn't feel festive, at dawn of the day, Leo dressed in his Aedile toga, possibly for the last time, and waited for the fateful carriage ride.

Typically, the four wheels of a carriage and a team of horses made a distinctive crunching sound on the gravel of his drive. What came through the windows was closer to thunder than crunching. Rushing to the door, he peered out at five battle ready Legion cavalrymen and a chariot with an armored driver.

"Greetings, Aedile Sandalius," a calvary officer said. Then he removed his helmet and announced. "Sir, it is our pleasure to escort you to the Festival of Miseria."

"I don't understand," Leo admitted as he stepped onto the back of the chariot.

The driver placed a gladius in one of his hands and an olive branch in the other.

"You are a guest of honor," the driver told him. "Hold on with the gladius hand, sir. We'll have you there shortly."

"But the festival grounds are all the way across the city," Leo stated.

"Yes, sir," the driver acknowledged. "Centurion of horse. Aedile Sandalius is prepared."

"Forward, at a canter," the officer called. "Look sharp."

The escort, the chariot, the weapon, and the symbol of peace seemed too dramatic. Not until they turned onto the boulevard did Leo Sandalius understand why the elites of society had little knowledge of the festival.

Lining the boulevard were veteran Legionaries. Cheering and beating old gladii against ancient, cracked leather chest armor, they saluted him. He raised the gladius in response, returning the gesture and almost fell out of the chariot. It took some practice to figure out the balance.

The line of old men and crippled veterans extended to the east gate. Once through, Leo Sandalius smiled, and the worry fell away. Arranged by Centuries throughout the festival grounds were ranks upon ranks of infantrymen. Around the edges of the formations were the women and children of the Legionnaires.

As the chariot stopped beside the grandstand, units close by saluted him with a deep, "Rah!" The power of the expression sent a shiver up his spine.

***

"Welcome to the Festival of Miseria, sir," Cornelius greeted Leo at the top of the steps. "We have about fifteen thousand souls in attendance, so far."

"And you expect more?"

"Yes, sir. Once word spreads about sacrificial meat, games, entertainment, and wagons full of vino, more will come from the city as the day goes on," Cornelius assured him. "I'd say we have the start of a successful festival."

"Rah!" Announced the arrival of another guest of honor.

"Senator Sisera, thank you for coming," Cornelius greeted Alerio Sisera. "You know Leo Sandalius?"

"I should say I do," the Senator remarked. "It was my committee that recommended him for Aedile. Leo, you've done good work here. But really, a festival to honor misery? What were you thinking?"

"Cornelius put this together, Senator. He'll know more about the religious aspects than I do."

A series of 'Rah' proclaimed the arrival of several more dignitaries. As the important and wealthy mingled, Senator Sisera guided Cornelius to a corner of the grandstand.

"I made you an assistant Aedile to keep you out of combat," he scolded, "and away from political traps. But you've kicked over an anthill and went straight for a full-on battle. And not with a segment, but with the entire Senate of Rome."

"Me, sir, battling the Senate of Rome?" Cornelius asked in disbelief. "How could that be?"

Alerio Sisera lifted an arm and indicated the ranks of infantrymen.

"These Legions are here before the walls of Rome because you commanded them to be here," Alerio explained.

"Right now, you are the most powerful General in the Republic. And that is the biggest fear the Senate has."

"I assure you sir, I'm not their General."

"Oh really?" Senator Sisera questioned. "The Legionaries are standing in formation waiting for what?"

Cornelius slapped his forehead.

"They're waiting for me to speak to them."

"It's what a good General would do," Alerio offered. "I suggest, in the morning, you ride for Nola and attach yourself to the staff of Proconsul Claudius Marcellus. And stay as far away from Rome for as long as you can to avoid any charges of attempted Kingship."

"Yes, sir," Cornelius agreed. "Now if you'll excuse me, I need to get the festival underway."

"By all means, go," Alerio urged.

Cornelius crossed the stage to where a handful of priests stood in new brightly colored robes.

"Are you ready?" he asked.

"Thank you, Tribune Scipio for giving the Goddess this day."

"Just be sure to offer blessings and collect coins," Cornelius coached. "I'll get it started. The rest is up to you."

The five priests bowed as Cornelius strutted to the center of the grandstand and raised his arms.

"The guests of honor, and the dignitaries on the stage asked me why a festival to honor the Goddess of Misery," he bellowed. "Apparently, they have never been through Legion shield training. We honor her with every drill."

Laughter and cheers greeted the statement. All infantryman carried painful memories of bashing and getting beaten to the ground during recruit training. Cornelius waited for the ranks to quiet down.

"It toughens us up and makes us mean, like a pack of wolves," he ended the line by howling at the top of his lungs.

Fifteen thousand voices howled back.

"But we honor the Goddess Miseria today for a different reason," Cornelius shouted. "We ask that she, at least for the day, withhold her blessing. For we already carry the Goddess in the memories of fallen comrades. From the cries of wounded in battle, the burial details, and the funeral fires. We hold her misery, her anxiety, her grief, her depression, and her gift of misfortune in our souls."

He paused to allow the back rows to have his words repeated. When all heads return to face him, he continued.

"Today, we ask her to allow us to salute our fallen without guilt. To speak of them without feelings of depression. For today, we honor the Goddess Miseria as she allows us to recall our brethren with only good cheer."

Thousands of heads nodding told him that he had accomplished the task of explaining the religious meaning of the day. He had one more duty to perform.

"Goddess Miseria. Give me a sign to show that I honor you and your generosity."

The priest who was a Legion veteran marched to the center of the stage. When he approached, Cornelius held up a silver coin. After displaying it to the ranks, he handed the coin to the priest.

"For the men I've lost," Cornelius called out as if in pain.

The priest dipped a finger into a bowl of ashes. With two swipes, he placed a smudge on either side of Cornelius' nose. The smears resembled black tears.

"For today, the Goddess Miseria lifts her blessing for all men of faith," the priest announced as he deposited the coin in a purse.

"Officers of the Legions, dismiss your men," Cornelius shouted. "Let the festival begin."

When Cornelius turned, he noted Senator Sisera handing a silver coin to one of the other priests. And he understood that he had done a good thing by organizing a festival to honor the Goddess of misery.

Chapter 9 – Unassigned Staff Officer

Five days after the festival, Tribune Scipio rode through the fertile plains of Ager Falernus. Crops grew in fields that, two years prior, had been trampled by the Punic army. And while grain stalks covered farms and peas hung heavy from vines, the wrecked and burned estates remained in ruin. Few citizens of the Republic wanted to travel to their villas and chance another encounter with Hannibal Barca.

At a wooden bridge on the Volturno River, Cornelius reined in.

"Shouldn't the river crossings be guarded by militiamen from Capua," he questioned a Legion Centurion.

"That was before the city demanded one of the Consuls of Rome be from Capua," the combat officer answered. "We got word yesterday, the Senate told them to go sacrifice to Coalemus, the God of Stupid. In response, the city declared for Carthage. Since then, it's up to us and the garrison at Casilinum to keep Hannibal pinned to the south of the Volturno."

"Couldn't the Punic army just take the bridge at Casilinum and cross the river?" Cornelius asked.

"Why Tribune, that is a logical question in illogical times," the Centurion offered. "The truth is, sir, we're here to threaten the western flank of Capua. As long as we have enough strength, Hannibal will remain south of here to draw Proconsul Marcellus' Legions away from the city."

"I've faced General Barca on four occasions," Cornelius informed the Centurion while peering down the river. At locations, Legionaries patrolled both sides of the watercourse. "In none of the engagements, have I seen Hannibal afraid to engage just a pair of Legions."

"For the last few months, the Punics have been laying siege to Alfaterna. There's not much call for cavalry against the block walls of that old city. His cavalry, according to reports, is resting east of the Apennine Mountains. And he's using their presence as a show of force to recruit men for his infantry. So, his army isn't up to full strength."

"You're right," Cornelius commented. "These are illogical times. The siege has given both our army's space to recruit and train men."

"The siege might be good for the Republic and the Punics," the Centurion remarked. "But I can't imagine a siege is fun for the citizens of Alfaterna."

Cornelius nudged his horse forward while yanking on the mule's line. The beasts clomped across the bridge, heading south towards the Proconsul's Legions.

***

A week later and twenty miles south of Nola, a group of Romans watched the siege of the ancient city of Alfaterna.

Proconsul Claudius Marcellus sat comfortably on his horse. And while he and his staff leisurely surveyed the Punic positions, his thirty mounted bodyguards ranged in a wide half circle scanning for Punic riders.

"The city has resisted him for six months," Marcellus explained. He lifted an arm and indicated the massive block walls high on a hill. "And I'm sure they can hold out longer. Certainly, much longer than an army besieging a city while guarding hundreds of women and children."

"Why do you think General Barca collected them?" a visiting Senator inquired.

At every command post of the Punic forces, women, children, and old people were penned in corrals. The civilians were dirty from the living conditions. Yet, they seemed healthy and well fed.

"Maybe he's planning to send the prisoners to Carthage as slaves but hasn't had an opportunity to herd them to a harbor," another guest from Rome proposed. "Or perhaps, he plans to give them to his men as bounty."

"It's neither," a voice spoke from outside the Proconsul's circle of supporters. "General Barca has another use for them."

"Did you have something to offer, Tribune Scipio?" Marcellus inquired.

He turned to face in Cornelius' direction but didn't signal for the young staff officer to come forward.

"Hannibal does not burden himself with human baggage, Proconsul," Cornelius offered. "In every one of his conquests, he's sent prisoners off for ransom, or to slave traders, or he's executed them. But never has he caged and guarded prisoners. He has something in mind."

"You act like you know him," the Senator suggested.

"Not as well as I'd like," Cornelius responded without thinking. Then stammering, he attempted to correct the impression that he wanted to befriend Hannibal. "What I meant, sir. I need to know my enemy before I can defeat him."

"Are you my new Battle Commander?" Proconsul Marcellus asked. "Someone should tell Colonel Mettius that he's been replaced by an unassigned staff officer."

Cornelius remained silent while Marcellus' staff and visitors laughed. All were Plebeians, and each had a dislike for Patricians. Making a joke at the expense of a nobleman gave them pleasure beyond the humor of a jest.

"Gentlemen. Let's get back to camp," Marcellus instructed. "I can't see much change in the siege this late in the day."

Some reports from arriving couriers required the Proconsul's attention, and they delayed his departure. Finally, the General guided his horse around. But Cornelius' voice stopped him from trotting away.

"Proconsul Marcellus. You may have your answer," Cornelius alerted him.

"What is it now, Scipio?"

"They're opening the gates of the city, sir."

The entourage wheeled around to watch the massive iron bound gates swing open.

"After months of resisting the Punic army, the council of Alfaterna has surrendered," the Senator suggested.

"Not necessarily," Cornelius remarked. "I believe the Proconsul had it right in the first place."

From the opening, women and children, old folks, and cripples hobbled through the gates. Apparently, the city council was ejecting anyone unable to defend the walls.

"How so, Tribune Scipio?" Claudius Marcellus inquired.

"In so many words, sir, you said no side can sustain a siege with extra mouths to feed," Cornelius replied.

"That's nonsense," the Senator argued. "Marcellus was simply pointing out the strange case of thousands of women and children being held along the siege line."

"Are you putting words in my mouth?" Marcellus challenged the Senator. "Because when the Patricians got together and voted to revoke my Consulship because I was a Plebeian, you had very little to say."

"Well, there were extenuating circumstances," the Senator protested.

Ignoring his staff, Marcellus twisted to face Cornelius.

"What do you think Hannibal is up to?"

Before the tide of refugees reached the end of the gate road, Carthaginian mercenaries turned them around at spear point. And as the women, children, old, and crippled made their way back to the defensive wall, Hannibal fed his prisoners into the mass.

"General Marcellus, I believe he's adding mouths to the burden of supplies in the city," Cornelius said. "And if you are correct, sir, it is the beginning of the end."

"Hannibal Barca is a clever commander," Marcellus proclaimed. "He must have thought of that ploy months ago when he began collecting women and children."

"He always plans ahead, sir," Cornelius advised.

***

At dinner in the Tribune dinning tent, Cornelius sat alone. Paying more attention to a map spread on the table then to the bowl of stew next to it, he didn't look up.

"Something wrong with the food?" a man asked.

"The stew is fine," Cornelius replied while tracing a route between Capua and Nola.

"Capua and Nola," the man noted. "What about Naples?"

"It has a seaport for resupply, making a siege ineffective," Cornelius described. "That means it has to be taken by assault. And Hannibal is too smart to break his army on the walls of Naples."

"Where does he go next?"

"He's looking for allies," Cornelius said. "It's why he's south of the Volturno. He needs to control Capua's rear to show that he's capable of protecting his allies."

"I'll accept that. We need to know if Nola is solidly with the Republic," the man instructed. "If there's a possibility of the city joining Hannibal's camp, I need to know. Get to Nola and find out."

Cornelius snapped his head up then quickly followed by rising to his feet.

"Colonel Mettius. I didn't know it was you, sir," Cornelius apologized to the Battle Commander.

"We're two legions way south and out of reach from any reinforcements from Rome," Mettius said. "A turncoat Nola is the worst case for us and the best for Barca. I hear you're an assistant Aedile?"

"I am sir, for a few months now."

"Go to Nola and use some of that scrutiny the Aediles are famous for," Colonel Mettius directed. "And find out if I need to be in Nola to stop Hannibal."

"Yes, sir," Cornelius stated. "I'll leave in the morning."

"Eat your stew, Aedile Scipio," Mettius ordered before leaving. "Clandestine missions require that you keep up your strength."

***

Cornelius' baggage contained armor, weapons, maps, clothing for travel, social events, and lounging. But nowhere in his luggage did he have the wardrobe of a horse trader. It took long past sunup to buy the proper outfits and purchase four spare cavalry mounts.

With four horses on a line, he nudged his mount into motion.

"It's over," a Legionary shouted. "It's over."

"What's over?" Cornelius inquired.

"The population is abandoning Alfaterna," the infantryman told him. "And the Punic mercenaries are marching in."

Until then, the question of when Hannibal would move his army was uncertain. With the fall of the city, the Legion had only days to guess at the Punic General's next maneuver. Realizing Proconsul Marcellus and Colonel Mettius needed the information, Scipio kicked the flanks of his horse.

Moments later, Cornelius the Horse Trader rode out of the Legion marching camp. On the road, he turned north, heading for Nola.

***

It was possible to hide an entire army in the forest around Nola. And while units could get close to the city, command would have no communications with their soldiers because of the trees. This left three possible approaches for an attacking force.

Cultivated fields, especially the farms on the hills to the east, allowed for a view of Nola but wasn't threatening to the city. Another option, the attackers could emerge from the trees and enter cleared defensive zones. However, being near the walls, the soldiers were then in range of spears, javelins, bolts, arrows, and rocks sling by the defenders from the heights.

Cornelius rode through the forest on a wide trail. From far away, he caught glimpses of the guard towers through the trees. But the structures vanished behind spreading branches and thick leaves. Only when he left the trees did he see the towers and the circular defensive walls of Nola. But then he observed the third possibility for a hostile army to approach the city.

Three city gates led from Nola with roads running to the north-south highway. All three allowed access from the west side. The center one faced the coastline and Naples in the distance. On the northwest corner, the road from the gate stretched northward to Capua and the Volturno River. And giving access to farmers and transporters with business in the southern region was the southwestern gate.

With three major routes emerging from one side of Nola, and the need for a place to park wagons, bivouac large groups of visitors, and hold livestock, the land between the three roads was cleared outward from the walls for two miles. Should an enemy seek to assault Nola, this, the west side, provided best approach to the city for an army.

***

Cornelius walked his string of horses to the southwest gate. Above him, a spearman peered down from the watch tower.

"What's your business?" asked the guard at the gate.

"Buying and selling horses," Cornelius replied. Noting the two guards weren't Legionaries, he said. "I thought the Legion was here."

"You can find their headquarters off the plaza," the city militiaman told him. He pointed to the horses and added. "But it won't do you any good. Their cavalry is south of here watching General Barca lay siege to Alfaterna."

"That sounds boring," Cornelius remarked.

"Not if you're in Alfaterna," the guard offered.

"I can't argue with that," Cornelius agreed. Then he commented. "But for me, it's a relief."

"How so?" the militiaman inquired.

"I trade mostly in Republic towns," Cornelius complained. "The Legion always gets first pick and they pay poorly for good horses."

"They pay poorly for services and goods, everywhere. And they treat people bad while doing it," the guard stated. "Try the city stables. They're always looking for good horses."

The displeasure of one guard didn't prove the city was going over to Hannibal. But it gave a hint to the mindset of the population.

"Thank you," Corneous acknowledged.

He jerked the line and walked the horses into Nola.

***

As in most large cities, the main streets were wide enough for commercial wagons to pass each other. The side streets, however, inverted the width, allowing for barely a one-way flow of hand carts.

After a turn, Cornelius found himself facing the wrong way on one of the narrow lanes.

"Lo, can you point me to the stables?" he asked a man sitting in front of a store.

"Legion?" the man inquired. Then before Cornelius answered, he continued. "Don't know."

"Actually, I'm looking for the city stables."

"In that case, Latian, turn around and go to the end of the road," the man instructed. "Someone there can tell you."

"Are you new to Nola?" Cornelius inquired. "Because you don't seem to know much."

"I know this, I'm not the one who's lost," the man sneered. He stood and walked into the shop.

The naked hostility didn't tell Cornelius the city favored Hannibal. But it did hint at the preference of the citizens. After pushing the head of each horse until the beasts faced the other direction, he guided the string out of the tight space and onto a main road.

"Looking for the Legion stables?" a man in a robe of office called to Cornelius.

"The city stables, Magistrate," he responded.

"I'm a city councilman, not a judge," the man corrected. "Those are fine animals. I imagine the Legion cavalry would like them."

"Which is preferable, sir? The Legion or the city stables."

"Oh, the Legion, of course, but they aren't here," the official indicated a direction. "If you're in a rush, the Nola stables will pay a good price for your stock."

"Thank you, Councilman," Cornelius stated.

One city official favoring the Republic helped a little in balancing the other two opinions he encountered. Calling to the horses, Cornelius pulled the rope until the four riderless ones followed his mount.

***

The aroma from piles of horse manure near a stable was unmistakable. Once he detected the smell and the flies, Cornelius cut over from a main street and walked along a narrow lane until he found the corrals and pens of the city stables.

He approached a man with a shovel, loading manure into a cart.

93

"A councilman suggested I sell to the Legions," Cornelius said as he dismounted.

"Then wait for the cavalry to return," the stableman scoffed.

He never looked up from his chore.

"I had planned to sell to the Nola stables. Or anyone other than the Legion. But if you don't want my business, I'll go to another town."

Resting the shovel in the cart, the man stood and inquired, "You'd travel rather than deal with the Legion?"

"That's what I said," Cornelius told him before grabbing a saddle horn.

"Hold on, stranger. I'm Dallán. And I like your attitude."

"I'll admit Dallán, I'm not impressed with your Gaelic hospitality. Maybe it's best I leave."

"Let's put the horses in the corral and we'll go inside and talk," the stableman invited. "I think we share the same feelings about the Legion."

"We might at that," Cornelius admitted.

***

The pub was dark with only a few candles for light. Long beyond dinner service, the place held five patrons nursing mugs of wine. When the front door opened, only one customer looked up.

A man with wide shoulders stepped in and scanned the room. After noting each individual in the establishment, he marched to a table in the back and took a seat with a view of the front door.

"Good evening, Senior Tribune Aurelius," the serving girl greeted him. "Dinner?"

"Just a pitcher of vino," he told her, "and a mug. I've had enough company for one day."

Moments later, she filled the mug and placed the pitcher on the table. Then as she went to wait on other patrons, the senior staff officer took a long pull of the wine.

"Managing the emotions of others, makes for a long day," a young man offered.

He moved to the table beside the Senior Tribune. Taking the chair on the far side, the youth position himself in a nonthreatening location.

Senior Tribune Caius Aurelius ran his eyes over the rough work attire and sniffed the scent of horse that emitted from the man's clothing.

"Do I know you?" he asked.

"No. But I've been waiting for a veteran Legion officer to come in and take that seat," Cornelius informed him.

"And how would you know that?"

"After being in combat a few times, you don't trust your back to a room or a doorway," Cornelius replied. He bent across the table and dropped a rolled piece of parchment next to the pitcher of wine. "Get this message to Colonel Mettius and double your guard."

"Why would I do that?"

"Because Senior Tribune, there are Punic sympathizers in Nola," Cornelius informed him. "And they've sent letters to Hannibal Barca inviting him to free Nola from the Republic."

"There's always talk. Why should I believe you? And why should the Battle Commander?"

"Because General Barca replied to the letters," Cornelius answered. "He's sent for his cavalry to meet him at Nola. Senior Tribune, you have a battle coming, and you'd best be prepared."

"I repeat, do I know you?"

"I'm Tribune Scipio, an Assistant Aedile of Rome. And the staff officer assigned by Colonel Mettius to gather information," Cornelius reported. "Until I'm satisfied that we know enough, I can't declare myself. Don't let your Legion down, Senior Tribune. Or you'll find yourself a hostage of Hannibal Barca."

The senior Legion officer took a drink, then turned to face the other table. But the young man was gone.

"He must be a Tribune," Caius Aurelius admitted as he pushed the mug away and picked up the parchment. "Only a junior staff officer would pick a man's off-duty drinking time to drop a problem on his desk."

When Senior Tribune Caius Aurelius reached the street, he marched quickly away from the pub.

Cornelius watched from the entrance of an alleyway. After the Legion officer vanished from sight, Tribune Scipio stepped into the street. He walked in the opposite direction but at a slower pace. The planning session of Carthaginian supporters didn't meet until moonrise. Until then, Cornelius would patrol the city and get familiar with the features of Nola.

Act 4

Chapter 10 – Reject Legions and Freedom

A swift courier rode to the north and two days later, in a shower of dirt and stomping hoofs, he reined in at a Legion assembly and training area. The standard Legions of Consul Quintus Fabius occupied half the camp while the slave and criminal Legions of Proconsul Tiberius Gracchus filled the other quadrants.

In response to the news that Hannibal had ordered his cavalry and newly recruited spearmen to rendezvous with him at Nola, the routine of drills and exercises evaporated. At daybreak, the Legionaries disassembled the stockade walls. The lumber was stowed in wagons, and the transports rolled out to the cadence of four marching Legions.

Figuring Hannibal's Numidian Cavalry and his fresh foot soldiers would make haste to their General, Consul Fabius and Proconsul Gracchus agreed on Benevento as the best place to set up a blockade. Situated beside the Via Appia, the walls of the city created a solid barrier on one side of the roadway. On the other side, the Calore River would prevent the Punic forces from circling around the Legions.

Yet, even as the Legion commanders traveled, they sent scouts into the mountains. The fact was no one knew for certain the exact route the Carthaginian forces would take through the Apennines.

Three days later, the four Legions arrived at Benevento with no reports of the route taken by their enemy. However, waiting there was a message for Consul Fabius. He was informed that his presence was needed in Rome because of unrest by the citizens and possible treasonous activity. The Consul rode away with his entourage as the Legionaries began setting up their marching camp.

***

"Kasia, when the men finish with the defensive fortification," Centurion Thaddeus instructed, "set up a rotation for sentry duty."

"Yes, sir," Jace replied.

In the ditch, Sidia the Hirpini stopped to wipe sweat from his brow.

"The mountain is just over there," he said softly so his voice didn't carry. "Tonight, we could be out of camp, out of the valley and, halfway up the mountain, we're out of the Legion."

"Cousin Sidia," Jace stated. He dropped to a knee and leaned forward to keep the conversation confidential. "We can't go home. Bands of angry warriors sworn to the Chief of Chiefs are searching for us. I think the price for us from Carthaginian command is over three gold coins each. And the Centurion of the garrison at Benevento, just over the hill, has carved our names on two crosses. He's just waiting for us to call attention to ourselves to put us up on the wood."

"North then, we run north?" Sidia suggested.

"The Pentri Tribe has closed their borders. And farther north, the Boii tribe and I had a falling out over a few Samnite tribesmen," Jace said nixing the direction. "I think here in the middle of the Reject Legion, we're as safe as anywhere. Plus, the Republic feeds us, pays us, and provides the opportunity for lots of exercise."

"Reject Legion," Sidia scoffed. "Is that what you're calling us these days?"

"More correctly, Gracchus Reject Legion East," Jace corrected his cousin. He stood back from the ditch and sermonized. "You cannot leave out the name of our Proconsul."

The Legion's Senior Tribune strolled along the line of men shoveling dirt from the trench. He didn't trust the slaves and criminals in the Centuries he commanded, so as always, two Legion bodyguards walked slightly behind him.

"Kasia, is there a problem over there?" Seneca inquired.

Jace saluted the approaching senior staff officer.

"No, sir. We were discussing how to extract a big rock from the defensive ditch," Jace lied.

"Put more men on it," Seneca directed.

The Senior Tribune didn't wait to see if Jace followed his advice. In a few strides, he and his two bodyguards were beyond Jace without even looking into the trench.

"If he didn't have those thugs with him," a big Gaul boasted from the bottom of the ditch, "I'd take Seneca's head."

"And do what with it?" an Illyrian digger asked. "Dip it in silver and mount him on the mantle of your villa?"

"He doesn't have a villa," a Noricum spit out the insult directing it at the Gaul. He kept digging and added. "The stupid Gaul probably doesn't own a shed in the woods."

Catháir the Gaul tossed down his shovel and glared at the Noric.

"Anytime you feel the need for light duty," Fridolf the Noricum said responding to the act of aggression, "I'll gladly install the damages."

"Gentlemen," Jace pleaded, "can we finish this ditch without bloodshed?"

Sidia tossed a shovel full of dirt at Jace's hobnailed boots, and declared, "Gracchus Reject Legion. Now I get it."

***

High peeks to the west would soon block the light of the setting sun.

"Night's coming," squad leader Anker the Greek remarked.

"Is your guard rotation set for this evening?" Jace inquired.

The squad leader held up his hands and counted off on his fingers, "For the number three watch tower, I've got two at dusk. Then, two more during late evening. And another two, after a fight in the middle of the night. Two for the early watch, and the two at dawn will cover my squad's responsibility."

"Can't you separate the Gaul from the Noric?" Jace asked.

"I could, but then my Illyrian troublemaker gets to wake either Fridolf or Cathaír for the next watch," Anker explained. "And instead of a fist fight, it'll turn into a knife fight."

"I noticed Jerome keeps that sica sharp," Jace remarked. "Forget I said anything, Anker. Run your squad..."

A guard in the watch tower at the main gate shouted, "Open the gates. Scout patrol coming back."

Across the parade ground, Seneca questioned, "Didn't they just leave?"

100

The Senior Tribune and his bodyguards strutted to the gates. Shortly after the warning call, the gates swung open, and four riders galloped through the portal.

"Senior Tribune, we've located a detachment of the Punic army," one of the cavalrymen reported.

"Are they on the march?" Seneca questioned.

"No, sir. They appear to be setting up camp for the night."

"Then why did you cut your patrol short?"

"Sir, their camp is only two miles from here."

For an older man, Seneca moved fast as he headed for the Battle Commander's tent.

Not much later, a messenger ran from the Colonel's pavilion, jumped on a horse, and kicked it into motion. He raced out of the south gate and galloped a mile to the town of Benevento. Once inside the city walls, he rode to the villa where Proconsul Tiberius Gracchus and his staff were quartered.

As sun set, the courier rode back with orders that surprised a few people. The Legions would form attack lines at first light, per Proconsul Gracchus as delegated by the authority of Consul Quintus Fabius.

***

At dawn, the morning light revealed eleven thousand five hundred heavy infantrymen, thirty-two hundred skirmishers, and nine hundred Legion cavalrymen blocking the Via Appia.

"You can tell Consul Fabius is in Rome," Jace commented. Several heads turned, none of them understanding the remark. "When his father was Dictator, we waited for orders to attack the Carthaginians at Ager

Falernus. He never gave the order and General Hannibal and his army escaped."

A portion of the Legion cavalry stood beside their horses near the Calore River. Adjacent to the riders, the Maniples of Gracchus Legion West filled the area just off the riverbank to the edge of the roadside. The paved surface of the Via Appia ran between Fabius Legions North and South. They controlled the center of the Republic attack line. On the right, Gracchus Legion East completed the infantry ranks while the remainder of the Legion cavalry held the right flank.

Seeing the thin ranks of Legion horsemen, Jace recommended to the combat officer, "Centurion Thaddeus, we need to turn our ends and guard the flank."

From the Legions on the far-left side, cheering arose. Moments later, an even more robust roar of approval burst from Gracchus Legion West.

"Ever since I signed you up at Venosa, you've been a pain in my cūlus," the Centurion replied when the noise subsided. "Need I remind you. The cavalry is here to cover our flank."

Not being in a position to argue his point, Jace Kasia replied, "As you will, sir."

Horns sounded, announcing the arrival of the Proconsul. Battle Commander Ulysses Ovid instructed, "Gracchus Legion East, stand by."

"Standing by, Colonel," the Legion responded.

"Legion, turn about."

Three Maniples of heavy and ten Centuries of light infantry about-faced. With their backs to the enemy, the Legionaries shuffled their feet, many glancing nervously over their shoulders watching for signs of the Carthaginian army.

Battle Commander Ovid saluted Tiberius Gracchus as the General reined in and halted. After a few words with the Colonel, the Proconsul guided his horse around to face the Legion.

"Men of Gracchus Legion East, hear me and trust my words," Tiberius Gracchus encouraged. "I made this promise to your comrades in Legion West. For everyone who brings me the head of a Punic mercenary, I will free you. Or, if you're a convict, I will pardon you."

The Legion of slaves and criminals, like the ranks of Legion West, screamed out their excitement. When they settled, Gracchus continued. "Hannibal Barca is near Nola. Up the Via Appia is his Lieutenant General Hanno. And they want to meet and dine together. But to their great disappointment, my Legions stand in their way, my killers, the freemen of Gracchus Legion East. In the name of the Republic and your freedom, you will end Hanno's march right here at Benevento."

Wild cheering broke out when Tiberius Gracchus saluted the Legion.

"Freedom," Anker called over to Jace. "Isn't that good news?"

"Freedom," Jace repeated with a lot less enthusiasm.

"Come on cousin," Sidia teased. "Could you get any less excited about the concept?"

"I might," Jace whispered, "if we'd ever been caught and brought before a Magistrate. It's unclear if the Proconsul can commute a sentence of death for murder."

"What's wrong, Optio Kasia," Thaddeus asked from his position at the center of the Century. "Afraid of being free and having no jailer?"

103

"No, sir," Jace replied. "I'm worried about where we're going to put all the heads."

The slaves and criminals of the Twenty-fifth Century laughed at their NCO's remark.

Before anyone else could comment, Colonel Ovid commanded, "Legion East, turn around. Prepare to earn your freedom. Draw."

"Rah!"

Spread across the Via Appia were ranks of Punic mercenaries. Unsettling to the Legion cavalry, over eleven hundred Numidian horsemen flanked the Carthaginian spearmen. In moments, the foot soldiers rushed ahead to meet the Legion lines.

"Freedom," a Legionary shouted.

Only a few repeated the cry as the cost of that freedom plowed into the front ranks of Legion shields.

***

From his position as Optio for the Twenty-fifth Century, Jace dutifully split his attention. Ahead, he studied the men of the Thirteenth Century to be sure they held the end of the assault line. To the right, he attempted to judge the state of the cavalry battle. But on foot, he couldn't tell if the Legion horsemen were winning, just holding the flank, or losing.

Glancing back, he scanned the Thirty-seventh Century to see if they had reacted to anything he'd missed. So far, all three Centuries on the ends were focused on the enemy to the front.

"Our cavalry is holding them," Thaddeus shouted to Jace. "You were worried for nothing, Sergeant."

"Yes, sir, for nothing," Jace repeated.

In combat with tempers running hot, agreeing was preferable to debate. Especially if the statement expressed an outcome while events were still unfolding.

"Stand by to rotate the line," Centurion Hasti of the Thirteenth ordered.

Always being behind the Century in the combat formation, Jace and his men knew Hasti's voice. And the men of the Thirteenth understood Jace's and Centurion Thaddeus' tone. In shield-to-shield fighting, the only orders able to reach the men on the front line were audible instructions, making a familiar voice a requirement for a successful command.

"Standing by, Centurion," the Thirteenth responded.

"Advance, advance, step back, step back," Hasti ordered. "Third line, rotate forward."

The rotation maneuver provided the Republic's army with an advantage. While the front line of the enemy became exhausted, the Legions kept fresh arms and legs on the assault line. For months, the officers drilled them, transforming slaves and criminals into Legionaries. During that period, they practiced the rotation a thousand times.

Twenty-five shields smashed forward, and the Century's attack line stepped into the gap created by the shield thrusts. Then their gladii ripped in to fill the space when the shields withdrew. Before the Punic front rank could recover, the shields lunged again, and the blades stabbed. Anticipating the rotation, the third rank of the Century surged forward to replace those on the front line.

For a moment, Jace admired the smooth changeover. But then, the maneuver dissolved into chaos.

***

Breaking their training, the exhausted Legionaries on the assault line each grabbed an enemy by his shield and pulled him through the second rank as they retreated. Already tightly spaced, the lanes used by the third line to move up were clogged by the rotating Legionaries and their prisoners.

Plus, the extra bodies created openings and Carthaginian mercenaries flooded through. A heartbeat after the command to 'rotate forward', the infantrymen from the assault line attempted to cut the heads off their captures. Some had success while others failed to decapitate their prisoners. They discovered, the spearmen they pulled into the rear of their lines, were fighters.

"First and second squads," Jace bellowed as the battle developed behind the first maniple. "Move up and shut that down."

Twenty Legionaries from Jace's Century raced forward to join the fight and stem the breaches. With the First Maniple battling to its front and rear, Jace glanced over to Centurion Thaddeus for instructions. But the combat officer faced away while directing their third squad forward to patch another hole in the First Maniple line.

Then, a Numidian spear swept in from the side, taking Jerome the Illyrian from first squad and pinning him to the ground. A second spear stuck Centurion Hasti, sweeping him off his feet. An instant later, Jace realized the Legion cavalry had lost the war on the right flank.

"Still your breath so your hands are steady. Calm your heart so your eyes are clear. Focus your mind on the task."

The world slowed as Jace Kasia's archer training took over and his mind sorted through solutions.

***

"Pivot right," he shouted as he calmly walked to the rear of the Thirteenth Century, "Brace for a cavalry assault."

Pulling Legionaries back from individual fights, Jace shoved them into a line facing to the right. Lance Corporal Anker and the squad leader for the second squad noticed the start of a blocking formation. They began pulling their people out of the melees. Some fought the distraction because the Legionaries were busy chopping at the necks of mercenaries in order to take the head and claim their freedom. But soon, a rough broken defensive wall began to form along the Legion's right flank.

A young staff officer trotted from the center of the Legion and waved for Jace's attention.

"I'm a little busy, sir," Jace told him.

"Optio Kasia, Proconsul Gracchus has a change to make in the freedom agreement," the Junior Tribune reported. "He said to stop taking heads. If you want your freedom, win this fight."

"Timing is everything, sir," Jace told him. Turning from the young nobleman, Optio Kasia inhaled a deep breath, then ordered. "Thirteenth, Twenty-fifth, and Thirty-seventh Centuries, sweep right and form a shield wall, on my line."

Lifting his arms so he was visible, Jace moved deeper into the Legion and planted his feet. Even when a Numidian rider targeted him with a spear, Jace only moved enough to dodge the sharp point.

Two hundred Legionaries backed up and quickly formed two lines based on the rogue NCO's position.

"Cavalry shield wall," he bellowed.

The order was repeated until stacked shields blocked the spears thrown by the Punic cavalrymen. With the tall barrier acting as a hindrance to a cavalry charge, Jace glanced around for his combat officer.

"You've secured the Legion's right flank, Optio," Centurion Thaddeus noted as he marched to Jace. With eyebrows elevated in a questioning manner, the officer asked. "What are you going to do now?"

Chapter 11 – A Heroes Due

Headhunting for freedom and pardons had broken down discipline and erased the separation between the three Maniples. With the surviving Centurions sorting out the assault lines and attempting to get Legion East back into formation, no one remained to take command of the flank.

"I'm not sure what I'm supposed to do, sir," Jace admitted.

"You're going to control the flank and protect the main body of our infantry," Centurion Thaddeus informed Jace. "Don't let me down, Optio Kasia."

Thaddeus jogged away and was soon obscured by the dust, surging infantry shields, and flashing steel blades.

"Fridolf, collect five javelins," Jace ordered. "Catháir, you get five as well."

"What are we doing, Optio?" the Noricum inquired.

"You two are the biggest men in three centuries," Jace said as he shoved the pair shoulder to shoulder. "Sidia. Get in front of them and position your shield on top of the wall."

Once his cousin had shifted and his shield rested above another, Jace crossed his arms at the wrist.

"When Sidia drops his shield, I want ten javelins crossing at the shield wall and hitting the Numidian cavalrymen at an angle," he explained. "Make all ten count. I want them to know there's a price to pay for getting too close to our flank."

"Then what?" Cathaír the Gaul demanded.

"Collect five more javelins and throw again," Jace replied. "Throw until there's no one left to kill. Sidia, call the opening."

Instead of waiting for the results, Jace sprinted along his defensive line where he set up two more javelin traps. When he reached the Thirty-seventh Century, he grabbed their Sergeant.

"Give me pairs of your best javelin throwers," he instructed. "And men who know how to hold a top shield and give orders."

**

Brave and courageous, the Numidian Lieutenant led his horsemen into the fray. With heart and the soul of a warrior, the young officer routed the Republic horsemen. In a few years, he would grow to be as fine a commander as he was a war leader. Unfortunately for the Punic cavalry on that day, the Lieutenant had no concept of maneuvering after his initial success.

When the Legion cavalry raced away, he didn't give chase. Rather, he pulled back, gathered his men, and studied the broken rows of the Legion infantry.

Had Hannibal Barca been there, he would have sent the Lieutenant around behind the Legions as he had done at Cannae. Or, if Lieutenant General Hanno knew of the success, he might have pulled the Numidians back to save men and horses. But there were no senior officers close enough to advise the brash young cavalry Lieutenant.

In quick order, he spread his cavalrymen in a line, facing the exposed flank of Gracchus Legion East. When the horses stepped off, a few Roman shields linked together. Before the light cavalry reach full gallop, the spotty shield wall solidified. A few strides later, the height of the Legion shield wall doubled.

"Forward," he bellowed, waving his lance to encourage his Numidian riders. He personally wanted a hero's welcome when he returned home. It would help in the bridal discussions with Ozalces' father. Then, excited by a fantasy of life with the beautiful Ozalces, he shouted. "Knock down their barrier and kill the Legionaries."

Confidence flooded the Lieutenant's veins when the top shield in his path vanished. Clamping his knees tightly against the horse, he prepared to jump his mount through the opening.

To his left, the rider fell from his horse and the beast stopped. On the other side of the fallen cavalryman, the next, and then the next rider fell.

The shield wall proved too much for the riderless horses. They turned and collided with other Numidian cavalrymen. His charge at full gallop had dissolved into milling horses and riders with javelins in their sides. The Lieutenant twisted and looked to the right.

Just as on his left, the five riders near him were down. Their horses raced around in panic. Yet to his front, the hole in the wall remained open. Then a shield popped up and closed the opening.

Realizing he was alone, the young officer reined around, catching sight of gaps all along the line of his charging cavalrymen. Lifting his lance high in the air, the Numidian Lieutenant signaled for a retreat.

How the Legionaries managed to throw javelins and murder the riders to each side of him, he couldn't understand. But when the Legions surged ahead, he realized his cavalry was about to be cut off. Waving his lance, the Lieutenant led his remaining cavalrymen back to the Carthaginian lines.

***

"They're backing off," Sidia announced when he pulled his shield back. "Save your javelins."

"It's good they are leaving," Cathaír the Gaul boasted. "I killed so many, their mothers will cry for a year."

"Blah, I killed so many more than you," Fridolf the Noricum told him, "they'll say my name to scare children into behaving."

"Because you're ugly," the Gaul said.

Before the two began beating on each other, Jace strolled up.

"Is the fighting over? Are we now relaxing with wrestling matches?" he challenged. "Or would you two like to get in line and earn your freedom?"

The big men backed away from Jace's fury.

"I've had a change of heart," Sidia stated.

"Later cousin," Jace told him. "All right Legionaries, rejoin your maniples and extend our assault lines. There are mercenaries to fight, and we don't want to be left out when the Proconsul hands out pardons. To freedom!"

"To freedom," the Legionaries in the three Centuries shouted back.

In moments, the Thirteenth Century linked up with the First Maniple, the Twenty-fifth with the Second, and the Thirty-seventh with the Third. From the dust near the front, Centurion Thaddeus came at Jace in big quick strides.

"Are your people able to fight?" he asked.

"Yes, sir," Jace assured him. "All three Centuries are functional."

"I've assumed the position of line Tribune and I only care about Second Maniple."

"The Twenty-fifth Century is fit."

"You're now my Centurion for the Twenty-fifth. Standby to rotate forward."

"Yes, sir, standing by," Jace responded.

Without the confusion caused by the struggle to take heads, the three lines of the Second smoothly moved forward to replace the First Maniple at the front. Jace shifted the Tesserarius to his right, making him the Sergeant. And he pulled Sidia back, placing him in the Corporal's spot. Once his command staff was in place, Centurion Kasia studied the battle scene.

***

Physical combat between evenly matched opponents would evolve into a stalemate, unless influenced by another force. Confidence in victory qualified as a force and could be as effective as the arrival of fresh troops. Emboldened by the early confusion, the Punic forces crowded forward, bashing with long swords, and stabbing with short spears.

"Twenty-fifth Century stand by," Jace called. The warning order was repeated by his Sergeant, and his Corporal, and soon by the rest of the Century. "Second line and third line, two javelins. Assault line, advance, advance, step back, step back."

In two heartbeats, his words were repeated to him, "Second line and third line two javelins. Assault line, advance, advance, step back, step, back. Standing by Centurion Kasia."

Jace examined the Punic fighters that pushed and stabbed at the shields of his assault line. They were crowding forward, trying to break his ranks, and collapse the corner of the Legion formation. They needed a lesson in respect.

"Twenty-fifth Century, execute."

Two ranks of javelins arched from the Legion lines. Dropping into the third row, the iron tips on the weapons fell on unsuspecting spearmen. Thinking themselves safe, the Carthaginian soldiers panicked when thirty of them were struck down by javelins.

At the assault line, twenty-five Legion shields hammered forward like a possessed hardwood fence. Knocked back into the panic behind them, the soldiers weren't prepared for the gladii blades. Twenty-five spearmen died on Legion steel. Then the shield wall surged again.

The second flight of fifty javelins dropped into the backs of those bent to help the victims of the first javelin onslaught. Forty-five of the iron tips found flesh.

When the assault line stepped back after the second advance, the Punic spearmen did not follow. The Carthaginians were too busy carrying away their dead and wounded to tangle with Jace's Century. Plus, their confidence had been washed away by the blood of their mates.

With the pressure lifted for a moment, Jace ordered. "Third line, rotate forward. First ranks, step off the assault line. Good job."

***

The Second Maniple would rotate back and forward for the rest of the day. By late afternoon, the battle at Benevento rolled over enough bodies of Punic foot soldiers and

Numidian cavalrymen that the Legions approached the Carthaginian encampment.

"Centurion Kasia. Lead the Second Maniple around the Carthaginian camp," Thaddeus ordered with a wave of his hand. "Contain anyone trying to escape."

Jace and his Century faced right and fought as the vanguard for Second Maniple. The defenders attempted to stop the encirclement, but the Twenty-fifth knocked them down with their shields, stabbed with their gladii, and left the enemy spearmen bleeding or dead. As they neared the backside of the tents and supply wagons, a man in the bright armor of a Phoenician noble galloped away with two thousand survivors.

If he had his war bow and a few stiff shafts, Jace could have brought the Punic commander down. But like his infantrymen, he had only a gladius and a shield. He had no chance of stopping Lieutenant General Hanno.

Once the Legions surrounded Hannibal's reinforcements, the Legionaries turned inward. When the ring of shields tightened and infantrymen began to get in each other's way, Jace pulled his Century out of the fight.

From eighty men at the start, his Century was down to sixty-five. The missing men were laying in the path of the battle. At the end, if Proconsul Gracchus required heads to prove the bravery of his slaves and criminals, all he needed to do was glance down. The proof of their skills littered his path to victory.

***

Colonel Ulysses Ovid and Senior Tribune Seneca stood at the back of the platform. Proconsul Tiberius Gracchus prowled the forward edge of the stand.

"Legionaries of Gracchus Legion East, brace," he ordered.

"Rah, General," the Legionaries roared back.

"Stand easy. Yesterday, you defeated a Punic army and won your freedom," he informed them. "Not only did you earn your release, but you earned a rest."

Cheers broke out from the assembly of former criminals and slaves.

"Tomorrow, I'm taking a Legion and pursuing Hanno," Gracchus informed them. "But you still have a job to do. If Hannibal attempts to leave the west coast, I need my most ferocious infantrymen standing in his way. Do I have your oath that he will proceed no farther than Benevento?"

Almost thirty-five hundred voices shouted their acceptance.

"For the Legionaries and their squad leaders, Senior Tribune Seneca will issue papers of freedom," Gracchus explained. "For my NCOs, you'll meet with Battle Commander Ovid for your releases."

Praises for the Proconsul exploded from the Legion. When the men quieted down, Fridolf the Noricum lifted his face to the sky and shouted, "What about the hero, Centurion Kasia?"

Tiberius Gracchus placed a hand under his chin as if thinking.

"He is a rare breed isn't he. And I've given him a lot of consideration. As a Centurion promoted from the ranks, he earned his pardon. But he is to be given a medal and a cash reward. For those, he'll need to wait until a Magistrate arrives from Rome," Gracchus informed the gathering. Then he saluted and announced. "Gracchus Legion East, brace. Dismissed."

The Legionaries separated and broke into groups. Jace draped an arm over Sidia's shoulder.

"Yesterday, you said you had a change of heart," he reminded his cousin. "How so?"

"I've decided I hate being a farmer," Sidia replied. "I'm staying in the Legion. It feeds me, pays me, and provides me with adventure."

"I don't think this war was started just to amuse you."

"I could make an argument against that statement," Sidia offered. "But right now, I'm off to see Colonel Ovid and get my pardon."

"You better hurry," Jace advised. He stripped off his plumed officer's helmet, tucked it into his belly, and ducked behind the broad back of Cathaír the Gaul. "The Centurion coming this way is the commander of the garrison at Benevento."

"What does that mean?" the Gaul inquired.

"If the Centurion sees Jace, Centurion Kasia will never receive a hero's due," Sidia told him while turning his back to the approaching officer. "Because he'll be crucified before Magistrate arrives to sign his pardon."

"You there, Legionary," the garrison commander called to Fridolf. "I'm looking for Centurion Kasia. Do you know his whereabouts?"

Chapter 12 – A Tribune of Horse's Glory

For generations and across years of Legions, weapon's instructors advised, "You can hide behind your shield and live. But you won't accomplish your mission."

"Then we'll come out from behind the scutum," generations of enthusiastic Legion recruits had bellowed back.

"And you'll die," the instructors told them. After allowing the announcement to sink into the mushy brains of new infantrymen, the trainers clarified. "Unless you time your exposure to counter your enemy's blade and slip between his blocks."

"How do we do that?"

"Practice, drill, and rehearse," the weapon's instructors replied. "Standby. Advance, advance, advance. Those were pitiful thrusts. We'll run the drills again."

And somewhere in the choking dust, sweat dripping into their eyes, aching muscles, and blisters on hands holding the hilts of their gladii, Legionaries developed the skills to anticipate an enemy's next move.

***

"Colonel Flaccus," Claudius Marcellus questioned, "Do we stay here behind the walls of our marching camp? Or do we take the field?"

"It's the recruit's dilemma, sir," Valerius Flaccus suggested. "Come out at the wrong time, and Hannibal Barca will be all over us."

"Battle Commander, that's an interesting observation," Caius Aurelius allowed. "We don't know the Punic General's next move. But, Proconsul, thanks to Tribune Scipio, we know where he's going."

"Where's that, Senior Tribune?"

"He has to go to Nola to protect Capua's southern border," Colonel Flaccus spoke for the senior staff officer. "That's where he'll go next."

"Then gentlemen, no more guessing games," Claudius Marcellus declared. "In the morning, we march for Nola."

***

Cornelius the Horse Trader rested a foot on the upper course of stone.

"This should be telling," Capotosti the Cargo Broker offered.

A breeze from the west ruffled their clothing and hair, forcing them to squint into the distance. They weren't alone on the battlements of Nola. Beyond the militia in the guard towers, civilians stood along the top of the wall near Cornelius and Capotosti. On another section, the members of the town council also watched the developing clash.

To the west of the city, at the extent of the cleared land, two groups of cavalrymen faced off.

"I bet you'd like to get a herd of those horses?" Capotosti remarked.

"The Libyans cull their herds through hard riding. It tests the mounts, making them worth the price," Cornelius said. Then he added. "For those who survive, the trainers wash the animals in red vino."

"What? They wash their horses in perfectly good wine?" the Cargo Broker asked.

"I witnessed it myself," Cornelius lied.

It never hurt for a horse trader to have firsthand knowledge of equestrian practices. Silently, Cornelius sent a thank you to the memory of Jace Kasia for the story about washing the legs and backs of exhausted horses with wine.

"Then this shouldn't be a contest," the broker declared. "The Legion cavalry hasn't a chance."

The pleasure in Capotosti's voice at his assertion revealed his politics. Cornelius peered around to see if

118

anybody had noticed the pro Carthaginian comment. No one responded. If they heard, they either didn't care or they sympathized with the broker.

Capotosti's evaluation had some validity. The heavy cavalry from Libya could break a charge by the Legion riders. Usually, it opened the Republic squadrons to the hit and run tactics of the Numidian cavalry. But the light cavalry had yet to cross the Apennines and arrive with the rest of Hannibal's reinforcements.

"As you said," Cornelius told the broker, "this should be telling."

***

The Tribune of Horse yanked the reins, forcing his mount to stay and spin in one location.

"They are fat, slow," he told his squadrons, "ugly, and unhappy."

"They have helmets on, Tribune, and they're way over there," a Legion rider questioned. "How do you know they're ugly?"

"That's a fine horse your father brought you," the staff officer remarked. Then returning to his original speech, he said. "When they break our formation, don't panic. We'll wheel around, chase them down, and put them out of their misery."

"Why are they unhappy?" the same cavalryman inquired.

"I bet your father hired a real fine riding instructor for you," the Tribune offered. Then to the rest of his riders, he ordered. "Nola is ours and no force can deny us. Bring your horses online, gentlemen, and remember, we are Marcellus Legion. We may bend, but we never break."

"Rah!" came from the ten squadrons of Legion riders.

119

Across the field, an equal number of heavy cavalrymen milled around. Until the Legion gave them a target, the Libyans had no objective. But as soon as the horsemen from Marcellus Legion drew up and advanced their line, the Punic heavy cavalry solidified and pranced forward in formation.

***

"We might as well get to the gate house," Capotosti advised. "The first tradesmen to greet the Carthaginians will get the best contracts."

"I don't think a cavalry commander is going to be issuing business commissions," Cornelius noted. "Let's watch for the actual outcome."

Along the wall, men stepped back and made their way to the ladders. Just as Capotosti proposed, they anticipated a Punic victory and wanted to assure the city was opened for Hannibal's cavalry. Even as the civilians collected near the gates, signals from councilmen brought additional militiamen to the portal.

Recognizing the potential for violence, the cargo broker resumed his place beside Cornelius.

"Ugh, you're correct," Capotosti whined. "We'll wait up here. It's best to hide our allegiance, until the time is right."

"My thoughts exactly," Cornelius agreed.

The possible riot between those loyal to Rome and those seeking to hand the city to Carthage, unsettled Cornelius. If it came to open hostilities, he would have to side with the allies of the Republic. But it was too soon. He didn't have any idea who was leading the rebellion.

***

The two groups of horsemen were scouting parties with only a hundred cavalrymen on each side. The Republic cavalry represented the Legions of Proconsul Claudius Marcellus, and the Libyan cavalry carried the banner for General Hannibal Barca. Although just a skirmish, the survivors could claim the town as a prize for their General simply by riding into Nola and closing the gates.

Turf, kicked up by flying hoofs, soared into the air before falling far behind the speeding horses. Brutally putting heels to flanks, the Tribune of Horse forced his mount to thread between the riders at the center.

"Spread left," he shouted. Then to the other side, he screamed. "Spread right."

Peering over their mount's heads, the cavalrymen sorted out who they would engage with at the first clash. Hands gripped lances and knees locked down just behind the shoulders of their horses.

"Break right," the Tribune bellowed. "Break left."

Yanking savagely on the reins, the thirty Legion riders on each end cut a sharp ninety-degree angle and raced from the inevitable contact. In a heartbeat, the tips of the Legion wings rode away from the Punic heavy cavalry.

The forty in the center of the Legion line remained with the Tribune of Horse. And courageously, they charged into the mass of Libyan horsemen and horseflesh.

Lances, braced from the wide backs of sturdy Libyan mounts, ripped into Legion armor. Hosted on the tips by the momentum of the charge, Libyan's unhorsed Republic cavalrymen almost at will. Jerking their lances back, they deposited their victims on the ground.

Among the first casualties, the Tribune of Horse lay with the Legion dead.

Then the Libyans were through the Legion line, leaving only fifteen still mounted. All were bloodied, but still

121

defiant. The wounded Legionaries screamed at the backs of the retreating heavy cavalrymen.

In a glorious display of horsemanship, the Libyans divided into four segments. Two swept left while the other two swept right. Almost as perfect as four maidens tossing their long hair in the summer sun, the heavy cavalrymen curved around, planning to go back and finish…

The sixty Legion cavalrymen from the wings, having sped in from the sides, raced through their wounded comrades and plowed into the still turning Libyans. Caught in mid maneuver, the heavy cavalrymen fell victim to the Legion lances. Sixty well aimed tips in the sides reduced the Punic force to only forty fit riders.

Wisely, the Libyan commander waved for a retreat. As quick as the skirmish began, it ended with Legionaries dismounting to aid their wounded.

"Put the Tribune on a horse," a cavalry officer instructed, "and prop him upright."

"But Centurion, he's dead," a rider informed the officer.

"Not yet," the cavalry Centurion exclaimed. He indicated the city and the defensive wall. "Not until our Tribune of Horse rides triumphantly through the gates of Nola and claims the city for Proconsul Marcellus."

Understanding the symbolism, the cavalryman stated, "Sir, it'll be my honor to ride beside the Tribune."

***

The Legion victory brought little outward reactions from the witnesses along the wall. Down in the courtyard was a different story. Rough men lined up facing armored militia.

Most of the crowd on the ramparts switched from watching the winners of the cavalry skirmish to gawking at the new battle lines. Everyone expected a fight to break out at the gate. It seemed the entire town, except for possibly two people, couldn't take their eyes off the combatants.

The rioters facing the militiamen wore leather like teamsters, dressed as laborers in rough woolens, or had on the tunics of professionals. No single occupation dominated the malcontents. This lack of men from one industry made Cornelius' search more difficult. As one of the disinterested persons, Cornelius Scipio ignored the gate and searched for the only other person who wasn't fixated on the chaos of the courtyard.

The man would be the decision maker. His disinterest in the conflict at the gate had to do with his ability to initiate the fighting, or to dismiss the thugs. For either, the rebel leader didn't need to stare at the gate. But he had to collect clues for his next action from somewhere.

"What are you watching?" Cornelius whispered as he scanned the windows and doorways of the buildings near the defensive wall.

"What's that?" Capotosti questioned.

"Nothing, just looking for the nearest pub," Cornelius replied as he continued to shift from one dark opening to another. "I'm hungry."

"That's what I like about you, horse trader, you know exactly how to break the tension," Capotosti declared.

The two movements were connected and subtle. On the wall, a councilman's hand at waist level rocked back and forth in the recognizable signal for a wave off. It might have been any gesture for any number of actions. But a block from the courtyard and the gate, a man in the robe of a temple priest stepped into the street. He raised both hands in the air, then he spun on his heels, collapsed his arms into the folds of the robe, and quickly walked away.

Cornelius slowly dipped his chin and his eyes. At the gate, the insurgents backed away. Once a safe distance from the spears of the militia, they scattered in several directions.

"We should go eat now," Capotosti suggested.

"Hold on, I want to get a look at the Legion patrol," Cornelius told him. "They have several captured Libyan horses."

"Are you hungry or are you doing business?"

"Both," he informed the cargo agent.

The gate opened and the Tribune of Horse and two flanking riders came through the portal. At first Cornelius thought the staff officer was gravely injured. But as the trio rode into the courtyard, he recognized the limp and lifeless form of a corpse being held in the saddle by a pair of cavalrymen.

"Well, they killed a Legion officer," Capotosti laughed. "A Tribune and that's something."

Cornelius' hand closed over the hilt of his Legion dagger. The fingers squeezed hard on the silver wire wrapped handle of the gift Jace presented to him. In less than a heartbeat, the blade could be pulled and driven through the cargo agent's eye and into his brain.

"I'm looking for a horse trader," a Centurion of Cavalry shouted to the top of the wall. "These Libyan horses offend me. If nobody buys them, I'll sacrifice the lot to the Gods while cursing their riders."

"I'm Cornelius the Horse Trader," Cornelius called to him. "And I'll give you a fair price."

"That'll be the first time for a horse trader," the cavalry officer remarked. "Come on. Let's get on with the fleecing."

***

Cornelius followed the patrol to the Legion stables.

124

"What price for the Libyan animals?" the cavalry officer asked as he dismounted.

"I'll need to examine their hoofs," Cornelius replied.

"I'm not in the mood for trader's games," the Centurion growled. "Will you give me a fair price or not? I've dead men to bury and priests to pay for prayers."

"I understand, Centurion," Cornelius assured him. He knelt beside a horse and lifted the left front leg of the beast. "But come down here and have a look."

"Not long ago that horse was well enough to carry the man who killed my Tribune," the officer told Cornelius. "I don't know what flaw you're finding to lower the price. But I don't like it."

"Just a moment of your time," Cornelius pleaded.

After a huff, the cavalry officer squatted and leaned forward to better see the hoof.

While maintaining his grip on the foreleg with one hand, Cornelius used the other hand to clamp onto the officer's wrist. Pulling down, he almost unbalanced the man.

"Stop acting like a raw recruit," he demanded between clenched teeth, "and pay attention."

"Say your name again, horse trader," the Centurion demanded. He attempted to jerk his arm away. "When I put my blade between your ribs, I want to curse you."

"Cornelius Scipio, assistant Aedile of Rome, and a Tribune of the Legions," Cornelius informed him. The titles didn't register through the Centurion's anger. Cornelius tried a different approach. "You can keep worshiping the God Coalemus and let your men die in back alleys. Or you can listen to me."

"I don't worship the God of Stupid," the Centurion protested. "And my men have just beaten a contingent of heavy cavalry. Why should…?"

"Because naked blades wait in the dark recesses of Nola," Cornelius warned. "And while I don't want to reveal my true identity, yet, I will in order to save the brave cavalrymen who captured this city. Despite a Centurion with the common sense of an infantry recruit."

"You're really an assistant Aedile of Rome?"

"And a Tribune of the Legions," Cornelius told him. "There are dangerous Punic sympathizers in Nola. Until the Legions arrive, keep your men close and post guards on your equipment and mounts. Do you understand?"

"Yes, sir," the Centurion acknowledged.

"Good. Now jump up and curse me," Cornelius instructed. "Deny my first two offers. But take the third. And I'll leave with the horses."

"Where will you go Tribune?"

"Back into the alleyways until I can identify the leaders of the resistance," Cornelius replied. Then in a loud voice, he stated. "The hoofs are ruined. I'll give you a silver for each. But you have to include the saddle."

"A silver?" the Centurion bellowed as he stood up. "I can get better than that for the horsemeat. Do better, you thief, or get out of my sight."

Act 5

Chapter 13 – Marcellus Arrives

From the mist that came with dawn, men swaddled in wolfskins burst through the tree line. Soon the cleared area to the west of Nola filled with racing Velites. The leading edge of the Legion skirmishers stopped before the defensive wall of the city while those behind bloomed outward to create a human fence. Shortly after the light infantry appeared, ranks of heavy infantrymen stomped down the road.

Behind the first few Centuries, Proconsul Marcellus and his large staff rode into view. Flags, banners, and silver armor caught the light of the morning sun, causing the General's entourage to glow as if they were an assembly of Gods.

In Nola, the city council members climbed to the ramparts. But after spotting the approaching commander, they reversed course and scurried back down.

"Open the gates," the Cavalry Centurion ordered.

Behind him, fifty mounted Legionaries waited to ride out as escorts for General Claudius Marcellus. The rest of the cavalrymen stood with militiamen at spots around the gate. Their placement assured the gates would open and remain open until ordered closed by Proconsul Marcellus.

"We should have reduced their number last night," Capotosti complained.

"What happened?" Cornelius inquired.

"The cavalry officer was smarter than we thought," Capotosti replied. "He posted guards and didn't allow his cavalryman to wander around the city alone."

"Come my friend," Cornelius implored, "let me buy you breakfast."

"Don't you want to see the arrival of our conqueror?"

"I've seen Legions enter cities," Cornelius told him. "They keep coming until even little boys with dreams of glory get bored of the spectacle. Besides, I'm hungry."

"If your purse is over filled from buying and selling horses and saddles," Capotosti exclaimed, "I guess the least I can do is help you spend some of it."

"An excellent idea," Cornelius allowed. "I saw a nice pub near the Temple of Ceres. Being adjacent to the home of the Goddess of Agriculture, Grain, and Fertility, the place must have good food."

"Need I remind you that butcher shops are located near smelly stockyards," Capotosti cautioned.

"If we get there and the pub stinks, we'll leave coins at the temple and have the priests pray for the owner of the restaurant."

"I had no idea, horse trader, that you were religious."

"No more than any tradesman," Cornelius replied. "But you know, we all need blessings sometimes."

General Claudius Marcellus rode through the gates. And thanks to a handful of men rushing around encouraging the crowd, the Proconsul was greeted upon entering Nola by a rousing cheer. As ranks of marching Legionaries entered the city, Capotosti and Cornelius strolled away from the courtyard. Behind them, the vocal public greetings continued for the infantrymen of the Republic.

***

The table and chairs on the patio afforded Cornelius a view of the temple. Across the street, four polished, wooded steps led from the stone walkway to the sanctuary of Ceres.

"You were right," Capotosti granted as he spooned in a mouthful of thick stew, "the food is excellent."

"It's a pretty temple," Cornelius noted. "Newer than I'd expect."

"Nola is almost six hundred years old," the cargo broker informed him. "But no buildings have survived the years. And while some of the stones in the walls came from ancient stoneworkers, they've been used in different places since first being laid."

"Fire does promote new buildings and jobs for craftsmen," Cornelius offered.

Across the street, a vagabond shuffled to the pretty steps of the temple and promptly sprawled across the polished wood. Appearing as comfortable as if he rested in a fine feather bed, the unfortunate closed his eyes in slumber.

Cornelius dipped a piece of flat bread into the barley stew and lifted out the dripping morsel. Bending his head to get an angle on the food, Cornelius hunched over the bowl. Then he stopped.

Rushing from the temple, a priest hurried to the vagabond. On his knees, the cleric of Ceres used both hands to urge the man to a sitting position.

The bread remained suspended between Cornelius' fingers. Moisture dripped back into the bowl of stew as the bread hovered only a few fingers' width from his mouth.

Yesterday, the same priest had passed on the signal for the malcontents at the gate to abandon the uprising. Today, Cornelius had a better view of the man's Punic features.

129

When the cleric waved to Cornelius, it struck him as odd.

"Me?" he asked, the bread still hanging in front of his face.

"Not you, Master," the proprietor corrected. "Cleric Eshmoun requires a bowl of stew for the unfortunate."

"Oh," Cornelius said as he wolfed down the piece of bread.

"You look perplexed," Capotosti remarked. "Is everything alright?"

"Everything is perfect, broker. Even better than I could have hoped for," Cornelius responded.

"Would you like to meet the priest?" Capotosti inquired. "His family is very important. With him being the priest of a temple and his brother a city councilman, they are good people to know."

"I would like to meet the cleric," Cornelius assured him.

***

Cleric Eshmoun was as tall as Cornelius but lacked the broad shoulders and prominent nose of the Roman.

"Cornelius the Horse Trader is one of us," Capotosti told the priest. "He's already taken the captured Carthaginian horses from the Legion."

"Buy and selling livestock proves nothing," Eshmoun declared.

With a rag in both hands, he moved fluidly around the temple, dusting around artifacts and polishing wooden shelves.

"You fed the poor man sleeping on the temple steps," Cornelius said. "At most temples, guards would have driven him off with their clubs."

130

"My generosity proves nothing," Eshmoun told him. "Perhaps I don't like people starving to death under the eyes of the Goddess of Grain."

Cornelius opened his coin purse and pulled out a generous amount of silver.

"This, as you say, proves nothing," Cornelius stated while dropping the gift into a collection plate. "Let's just say, I also don't like the idea of people starving in front of the Temple of Ceres."

"But that does prove something," Eshmoun corrected. "You were on the wall with Capotosti and saw me pass on the signal. Why didn't you report me to the Legion cavalry officer?"

"Because I'm a horse trader, not a slave of Rome," Cornelius explained. "Your business is yours to mind and mine is to buy horses as cheaply as possible."

"I can respect a man with a clear motive," Eshmoun said. "You can earn a lot of coins if you're favored."

"By the Goddess Ceres?"

"No, horse trader, by the Carthaginians when they take over the city."

"We'll get the best contracts," Capotosti proposed.

"I'm a man of business," Cornelius advised the rebel priest. "You'll find me unwilling to fight armored militia at the city gate."

"But you know livestock and I'll need someone to manage the Legion baggage trains," Eshmoun stated. He went to the collection plate and emptied the coins into his purse. "We'll talk after General Hannibal Barca arrives."

***

The next morning, the blare of trumpets reverberated off the defensive stones of Nola. General Claudius Marcellus and his two Battle Commanders climbed to a guard tower.

"They were only a half a day behind us," Colonel Flaccus noted.

"If you hesitated, Proconsul, our Legions would have been caught in the open," Mettius added.

"Our journey aside gentlemen," Marcellus submitted, "what do we do now?"

"We can't sit behind the walls," Mettius stated. "It's bad for the morale of our Legionaries. And the illusion of us hiding gives the Punic mercenaries heart."

"I relish the idea of catching Hannibal fresh off the march," Marcellus chuckled. "Let's go offer battle to the Punic General before he sets up his camp. We'll see how the strategist handles a spontaneous invitation."

**

While the heavy infantry and elephants of the Carthaginian army were still in the woods, Legion skirmishers dashed from Nola. They charged almost a mile ahead of the Legions before stopping to jeer at the Punic light infantrymen.

"Perhaps you would like to rest before we kill you," an Optio of Velites challenged. "Never mind, you can rest in Hades."

Across from the Legion NCO, the Punic light infantrymen jumped up and down while waving their spears in the air.

"I don't need a nap before or after murdering Latian farmers," an Iberian light infantry officer shouted back.

As in all battles between Hannibal's forces and the Legions, the Latin men stood about the same height and had nearly identical equipment. Only a few variances of style and color from regional craftsmen marked the difference in shields, chest armor, and helmets.

For the Punic light infantrymen, their gear matched their country of origin. Iberians, Celts, and men from the Punic coast dressed in the style of their heritage. But the outfits and weapons weren't the only difference.

No matter which area of the Republic they came from, Legion skirmishers trained in Legion tactics and had a single language. Both gave them an advantage.

"Forward, throw, three rotations," a Centurion of Velites ordered.

"Forward, throw, and three rotations," the Legion light infantrymen shouted back.

Across the skirmish line, the Iberians, Celts, and Punic men didn't catch the meaning of the words or the ramifications.

"Velites, execute!"

Five hundred and thirty-three Legion light infantrymen ran forward and launched javelins into the air. While they ran back, a second rank raced forward and threw. Before the third rank moved, the first flight of javelins came down among the lightly armored Carthaginian skirmishers.

Shields, arms, shoulders, and necks fell victim to the long-tipped weapons. Those not dead, limped away while trying to dislodge the javelins. Then, to the horror of the Carthaginian skirmishers, the third flight of Legion javelins dropped into the panicked light infantrymen.

A few spears attempted to answer the Legion assault. But the response was disjointed and halfhearted.

"Velites, standby," a Legion officer alerted his light infantrymen

"Velites standing by Centurion."

Again, the single language and training paid a dividend. The limited cavalry Hannibal had at his disposal emerged from the tree line.

"Retreat to the Centuries," the Legion officer ordered. "Run!"

All sixteen hundred Legion light infantrymen raced around and sprinted for the ranks of Legionaries. Behind them, Thessalian cavalrymen dug in their heels and urged their mounts forward.

But the order to withdraw immediately filtered through the Velites, allowing them to respond quickly. Before the cavalrymen reached them, the skirmishers dashed between the ranks of big infantry shields.

"Welcome to the First Maniple," a Centurion of the heavy infantry boomed when the cavalrymen approached the Legion shield wall. "Will you be staying to die? Or do you have to rush off?"

"Rah," came from the Legionaries on the front lines.

Trumpets blared from Punic command and Hannibal's army stepped back. As they began sorting out their baggage train, Flaccus rode to the Proconsul.

"General Marcellus. Unless we're going to march over there," the Colonel offered, "I believe the Punics have had enough for one day."

"I believe you're correct," Marcellus agreed. "Let's go back to Nola and celebrate our moral victory."

***

Although a large city, the injection of eight thousand Legionaries, two hundred mules, two wagon trains of gear, teamsters, and animal handlers created permanent congestion in the streets.

"I can attest to you, Proconsul, the city of Nola is loyal to the Republic," a councilman declared.

"I'll have to take your word for it," Claudius Marcellus replied. "But you'll have to forgive me. The introduction of two Legions into a situation can create allegiances despite prevailing public opinion."

"We have a few Carthaginian sympathizers," another councilman admitted. "But the council and our militia favor Rome as our protector."

A commotion at the doorway to the council chamber drew their attention.

Battle Commander Mettius marched to the Proconsul and saluted.

"You were correct, General Marcellus," he exclaimed. "Hannibal is done for the day. In fact, sir, his army is settled around cookfires. Orders, sir?"

"Orders, yes," Claudius stated in a flat tone. "Instruct the supply men to distribute extra rations."

"We're not mobilizing, sir?"

"No, Colonel Mettius, we're not going to challenge Hannibal again," Claudius informed the Battle Commander. "For months, we've danced around the movements of General Barca. But now we've gotten ahead of him for the first time. And we have the advantage. I'll not give him the satisfaction of engaging. Tonight, let the city and our Legionaries celebrate my arrival."

"Yes, sir, tonight we celebrate the coming victory of General Claudius Marcellus."

The councilmen stood and raised glasses of wine in salute.

"To the victory of General Claudius Marcellus," the rulers of Nola cheered.

Of the eight councilmen, three went with the flow, two were guarded in their adoration, two were genuine in their praise, and one had to grit his teeth as he toasted the Roman General.

Chapter 14 – Heads on Walls

Every establishment in Nola was packed from wall to wall. And every doorway had people lined up, trying to push their way inside. After experiencing some of the shoving, Cornelius Scipio decided to remain in his rented room for the night. Unfortunately, on the street side, drunken conversations penetrated the wall, and the back of the room was only slightly less noisy.

A banging on the door brought Cornelius to his feet.

"Go away," he shouted.

"You're wanted at the temple, horse trader," a man said.

In two strides, Cornelius crossed the floor, unlatched the door, and flung it open. No one waited outside with more information. Not wanting to waste the chance to get in on the rebel's plans, Cornelius grabbed a leather cloak, left his room, and ducked into the crowds.

Blocks and sore elbows later, he arrived at the restaurant across the street from the temple. Unlike the day before, the patio overflowed with customers. Turning to the temple, proved a pleasant surprise.

Torches blazed along the front of the sanctuary and the polished steps reflected the flickering light. The illumination caused the entrance to shimmer as if the Goddess herself had just walked up the steps to her temple.

"The Goddess Ceres welcomes you," a young cleric greeted Cornelius. "In this mayhem, she offers sanctuary from the mobs and solstice for the soul."

Cornelius dropped a coin into the young man's hand and took the steps to the temple. Inside people stood silently while an older priest spoke. Before Cornelius could catch the drift of his words, a hand grabbed his elbow, and guided him to the rear of the temple.

"I'm so glad you came," Eshmoun said as they entered a back room.

"What's going on? I was relaxing in my room, and someone knocked on my door and told me…"

"You're wanted at the temple," Eshmoun said finishing the sentence. "The messenger only knew that phrase and had no idea what it meant. I'm glad you understood."

"Understood might be giving me more credit than I deserve," Cornelius admitted. "Why am I here?"

"General Hannibal Barca has arrived," Eshmoun informed him as if the information wasn't known to everyone in Nola. "Tomorrow, my associates will seize the gates and open them for the General. What I need is a captain to control my men when they take the Legion baggage train."

"You expect one man to manage a hundred wagons and keep your street thugs from stealing everything?"

"Please, horse trader, they are patriots not thugs," the priest scolded. He picked a large knife from a table, held it up, and twisted it, causing candlelight to reflect off the wide blade. "This is for my thug. The men taking control of the wagon train will use clubs and overwhelming force to secure the supply wagons. Once they have possession, you'll keep the wagons in place."

"You're going to present the supplies to Hannibal?" Cornelius guessed.

"Yes, as a welcoming gesture. And you, as one of my captains, will be rewarded handsomely," Eshmoun answered. He cut the air with the blade. "Shrewd, don't you think?"

"Smart. But what's up with the knife?"

"I need a way to turn the population against the Legions," Eshmoun explained. "One of my thugs, as you call them, will murder a Legion officer. In revenge for the street crime, Legionnaires will slaughter civilians. After the carnage, General Marcellus will declare martial law and isolate everyone in their homes. When the Legions march out to face Hannibal, the citizens will revolt, and we'll close the gates."

"Trapping the Legions between the outer walls of Nola and the Carthaginian army," Cornelius concluded. "It sounds as if you have it all figured out."

"This has been in the planning stages since Capua declared for Hannibal," Eshmoun said. "We've had to pull a lot together quickly."

"My compliments," Cornelius offered. "As I said before, I'm not a fighter. Let me know where the knifeman is going, and I'll avoid the area. If you're correct, the infantrymen will make a bloodbath of the city streets."

"It's perfect, isn't it," Eshmoun suggested. A thick set man came in from a backdoor and stopped at the edge of the candlelight. The priest spun, held out the knife and gushed. "And here he is, the key to the entire plan."

"Who is he?" the thug demanded.

"I'm no one, friend," Cornelius stated.

He lowered his head and walked slowly towards the rear door. Growing impatient at the deliberate pace, the killer moved into the candlelight just before Cornelius passed into the dark.

A moment later, Cornelius Scipio was out of the temple and in a dark alleyway.

***

In the thongs packing the streets, Legionaries mixed with the citizens of Nola. Wine and beer flowed, and the city, flushed with Roman coins, was in a festive mood.

Sandor the Carpenter slipped through the crowd. Under orders from Cleric Eshmoun, he looked for a Legion officer. Hidden beneath his tunic, the carpenter clutched the hilt of a large knife. For blocks, he searched for the right victim. Many streets from the Temple of Ceres, Sandor noted a young man in the armor of a Centurion in the distance. The stalking began in earnest.

One street away, then a half a block, and finally, the officer stopped to speak with several Legionaries. Sandor slipped ahead, located a store front, and anchored himself in the path of the young combat officer.

When he finished conversing with the men from his Century, Centurion Horace resumed strolling through the streets. He reached a storefront and got jostled by a pair of drunks which he easily shook off. Then with the speed of surprise, a fat blade slashed across his face.

Horace fell back as his assailant dropped the knife and fought an arm that cranked down on his windpipe. Quickly, Sandor, the failed assassin collapsed under the weight of a tall, Latin civilian who seemed intent on breaking the carpenter's neck.

"Knife," someone shouted when the weapon clattered to the street.

The rebels wanted to cause mischief, of that there was little doubt. Except, the streets were full of drunken infantrymen. And there was nothing drunken infantrymen liked better than fighting with blades. At the announcement of a knife, every Legionary on the street drew his personal blade, dropped into a fighting stance, and scanned for an enemy.

"Stand them down," the Latin holding the carpenter instructed Horace. "We don't want a massacre on the streets of Nola. At least not yet."

Visualizing the sharp steel passing in front of his eyes again and again, the young combat officer didn't process the orders.

"Centurion. I am Tribune Scipio," Cornelius stated. "And I need to speak with Colonel Mettius."

"The Battle Commander?" Horace asked.

Realizing the young man wasn't over the shock of nearly having his face separated from his skull, Cornelius peered at the circle of Legionaries surrounding them.

"Would someone please, for all that's good, give the Centurion a drink of vino?" he asked.

Two wineskins hit Horace's chest and the officer managed to catch one and take a long pull.

"You're a Tribune?" he asked with red wine dripping from the corners of his mouth.

"Very good. And you are a Centurion. And this waste of flesh attempted to murder you," Cornelius explained. "And we need to see Colonel Mettius, tonight. Understand?"

A change came over the young combat officer. His back stiffened, his eyes cleared, and he bellowed into the night.

"Seventh Century, stand by."

From blocks around, the call came back to him, "Centurion Horace, standing by."

On a Legion assault line, during a battle, no infantrymen could stop to decipher a flag, understand the blasts of a horn, beats of a drum, or guess if an errant command was meant for them. In the chaos of a shield and gladius fight, there was one thing Legionaries understood and trusted. And a moment later, their combat officer exercised his control.

"Seventh Century, on me," Horace ordered.

From blocks away, eighty highly trained Legionaries bellowed, Rah! And heartbeats later, they crashed their way through the crowds and the mass of people to create a barrier around their Centurion.

"Sir, Seventh Century is formed and accounted for," an older man announced.

"Thank you, Optio," Horace said. "The Tribune and I need to patrol to Legion headquarters. Kindly assign two men to guard the prisoner and lead us out."

"Are you in a rush, sir?" the NCO inquired.

"Yes."

Horace spoke just that one word. But the result far exceeded the simple affirmation.

"Give me a protective wedge," the Optio instructed. "Nothing stands in our way. Nothing delays our passage. Seventy Century forward."

There were few thing to match the sheer determination of a terrorized team of oxen, a panicked buck, or a stampede of horses. Counted among those unstoppable forces was a trained Century on a mission. The masses parted either on their own accord or they were roughly shoved aside by the wedge. In any case, the walk to the headquarters of Marcellus Legion North went smoothly for Cornelius and Centurion Horace.

***

Not long after the Seventh Century delivered the officers, Colonel Mettius marched into a room and halted at the head of a feasting table. For several long moments, Mettius stood waiting by the elbow of the Proconsul.

"We will venture out tomorrow and see if Hannibal really wants a stand-up fight with two Legions," Claudius Marcellus stated to the table of Tribunes. After he finished speaking, Claudius glanced up at the Colonel. "Are we under attack, Battle Commander?"

"No, sir," Mettius explained. "But I wanted you to know what Legion North was doing tonight."

"It's your Legion and I trust you," Marcellus informed him. "Unless you're marching out to get into a drunken brawl with the Punics, I'll assume you know what you're doing."

Through the windows of the villa, the sounds of drunken carousing drifted into the banquet room.

"That sounds closer than I heard earlier," Marcellus remarked.

"Yes sir, it should be louder," Mettius told the Proconsul. "Because it's coming from the ramparts and the guard towers."

"Our sentries are drinking and participating in the celebration while on duty?"

"That, sir, is what we want General Hannibal Barca to believe."

"And whose idea is that?"

"Tribune Cornelius Scipio, sir. He has a plan."

142

"To get our guards drunk?"

"Yes, sir. And to sleep late in the morning."

"As I expressed earlier Colonel Mettius, it's your Legion. I just hope you know what you're doing."

***

Punic scouts sat in bunches below the walls of Nola. On a typical night, they would stay back to avoid the occasional arrow, javelin, or lead pellet. But on the night of the celebration, they rested near the stones, knowing the guards were too drunk to look down.

As the sun came up, they noticed two things. The front gate sat ajar as if carelessly slung open and forgotten. And there were no shoulders or heads of sentries visible on the ramparts or in the guard towers. Messengers ran to alert General Hannibal Barca that the militia guarding Nola was asleep.

No trumpets blared. No NCOs bellowed out loud orders. In what felt like a mime show, the Punic heavy infantry slipped on their armor as they strolled to within a half mile of Nola.

"There's the gate," a young Carthaginian officer pointed out to another Lieutenant. "Let's go. Let's take the city."

"General Barca has won every battle against the Latians," the other officer advised. "I'll trust his intuition over the invitation of an open gate."

As they talked, rows of infantrymen gathered. And even as the core of Hannibal's army staged in the open, no one on the walls of Nola sounded the alarm.

"Attack the gate," a Captain shouted.

"About time," the Lieutenants remarked. Then to his NCOs, he called. "Forward to the gate."

There was a moment while the NCOs translated the orders to the local languages before the ranks surged. But once the instructions were clear, the Punic army stepped off.

In the noise of armor clanging, leather creaking, and men breathing hard, no one in the Carthaginian army heard Battle Commander Mettius.

"Marcellus Legion North, standby."

"Standing by, Colonel," the Legionaries roared back.

Chapter 15 – The Third Legion

Eight hundred strong, the skirmishers from Legion North squeezed through the portal. As they emerged in the open, the Velites ran in a suicidal attack at the shields of the Punic heavy infantry.

Half sized shields, gladii, and short lances had little chance against the full shields and infantry spears of the Iberians. Stabbed, cut, and brought up short, they bounced off the infantry shields and sprawled in the dirt dead or wounded. The mismatch of Legion skirmishers attempting to move a barrier of steel, leather, flesh, and muscles had the expected result. The Legion light failed to penetrate the Carthaginian ranks and died trying.

The rows of mercenaries cheered the massacre. But under the shouting, the voices of Optios and Centurions ordered, "First Maniple Legion North, standby."

Because under cover of the dust, while the Punic heavy infantry gloated at the mismatch, the Legion heavy infantrymen came through the portal, unmolested. Formed up in ranks, they responded, "First Maniple, standing by."

"Advance, advance, advance."

"Advance, advance, advance."

And from having their way with the Legion's light infantrymen, the Punic army came shield to shield with the Velites' big brothers. And the Legionaries of the heavy infantry would not die as easily, nor would they give ground, nor grant mercy.

***

Three fingers height was the space between the short brim of the Legion helmet and the top of the Legion scutum. Limited to a narrow view of the assault line, Legionaries could only concentrate on four things during a battle. Hearing orders from their NCOs and officers, the feel of the infantryman to the left, and the sense of their companion to the right. The fourth, and most important, according to the Legion trainers, consisted of seeing the enemy to their front.

"Three fingers of view are all you'll get and all you'll need. A blade three fingers wide, and a stab, three fingers deep into the guts of the man in front of you. Three-fingers is all an infantryman requires for victory."

All the joy of the Carthaginian front rank vanished when a solid line of shields smashed into them. For a moment, they saw the faces of Legionaries before the shields withdrew, leaving only the three fingers gap. But the Iberians didn't have time to contemplate the eyes of the Latians across from them.

Three hundred gladii stabbed three inches into guts. Over the shields, the Maniple's second rank stabbed anyone untouched with their spears. Every Punic infantryman who murdered a Velites, died in the first vicious advance. By the third advance, the Punics solidified their lines, and the battle became a shield wall pushing match.

Seeing the concentration of Republic forces in front of the western gate, a Carthaginian Captain ordered the ranks in the rear to circle around and attack the Legionaries from the side.

***

"Colonel Flaccus, the field is yours," Claudius Marcellus announced as he settled his helmet on his head. "I trust, we will meet later to celebrate our victory."

"Yes, sir. It's an appointment," the Battle Commander responded. "Marcellus Legion South, draw and stand by."

"Draw, Colonel Flaccus," his Legion said in a cacophony of gladii being pulled from sheaths and slammed into shields. "Standing by."

"Senior Tribune Aurelius, proceed," Flaccus instructed.

Caius Aurelius signaled half the Legion and they marched for the southwestern gate. As they moved, Colonel Flaccus led the other half to the northwest gate. By the time the two senior officers reached their gates, Proconsul Marcellus and his entourage had ridden through the west gate to join Colonel Mettius in the ongoing battle.

***

Cornelius stood on the rampart and watched as elements from Legion South jogged from the gates as if arms intent on hugging the Punic army. Where wings of mercenaries had maneuvered, attempting to flank Legion North, they now faced outward, fighting a withdrawal from the shields and blades of Legion South.

"Tribune Scipio, orders?" the Centurion assigned to the west gate inquired.

"We've rounded up Priest Eshmoun and his Councilman brother and as many rebels as we could locate," Cornelius replied. "Other than a horse and a command so I can go down there and help, I have nothing."

146

"It's going to be a long day at the grind," the combat officer remarked. "We're evenly matched. But if we had another Legion, we could end the Punic invasion right here at Nola."

"But we don't have a third Legion," Cornelius reminded him.

Below them, the two sides were kicking up a fog of dust. So much in fact, the lower half of the combatants on the assault line were lost in a blanket of silt and powder.

"There is one benefit to fighting with your back to a wall," the Centurion offered. "Our infantrymen don't have to worry about cavalry."

Cornelius peered at the rear of the Punic army. He easily located General Hannibal Barca and his command staff. At other battles where Cornelius saw Hannibal, the Punic General had claimed high ground. But at Nola, the land to the west was flat fields or forest. Still, Hannibal's head rotated as he searched for a weakness in the Legion lines.

"We caught you unprepared," Cornelius declared. "If we had enough cavalry, we could ride behind the Punics like they did to us at Cannae."

"But Tribune, as you pointed out," the Centurion said, "we don't have a cavalry detachment or a third Legion."

Shifting his eyes to the three-sided assault line, Cornelius studied the dust cloud that threated to obscure his view from on top of the wall. In his mind, he visualized the wall of powder and wondered how much of the fighting Hannibal and his commanders could see through the boiling wall of dirt.

"Centurion. Hold the gate," Cornelius told the officer.

"Sir. Where are you going?"

"To find a third Legion," Cornelius informed him.

Then in a rush, he leaped on the ladder and slid down to the courtyard. Once on firm ground, Tribune Scipio sprinted towards the headquarters of the Legions.

***

The grind reduced the enthusiasm of the Legionaries. Rotating to the front and sucking on dust while they fought, then choking on more powder while in the rear, beat on the infantrymen as much as the enemy.

"Is there any way to break out of this?" Claudius Marcellus asked.

He used a hand to cup his eyes, trying to see the Battle Commander more clearly. It did little good in the haze.

"No sir. It's dry, all the way to the trees," Mettius informed the Proconsul. "The best we can hope for is rain."

A glance at the clear blue sky, informed the Proconsul that rain wasn't likely.

"This isn't a battle," Marcellus suggested. "This is the death of passion. And perhaps the ruin of two good Legions."

"How do you figure, sir?" Mettius questioned.

"After this mess, it'll take a year of training to regain the confidence of our men," Marcellus explained. "That's for the Legionaries who stay. There's no chance to reach the ones who will pack up their gear and go home."

"Disengaging our assault line from the Punic line will be hard," Mettius offered. "If we're going to withdraw, General, we need to start soon."

"I don't see another option," Claudius Marcellus admitted. "Let's get word to Colonel Flaccus and Senior Tribune Aurelius."

But the blare of four trumpets echoing from the western gate stopped the orders.

148

A solo trumpet might have signaled a maneuver. But long notes from four of the instruments carried a vague announcement of the start of a ceremony. Whether it was a ritual for the religious, the political, or a civil affair, didn't matter. The quartet had no importance or meaning on a battlefield. Yet, they sounded again, the sharp tones sailing over the shield walls.

On the far side, Iberian infantrymen in the fourth rank and beyond stretched tall, trying to see what the trumpets proceeded. They weren't the only ones questioning the meaning of four instruments.

"What is that?" Proconsul Marcellus demanded.

"I have no idea, sir," Mettius admitted.

Where the dust had been bad, the swirling from a thousand footsteps billowed into the air. Arched high, the silt created a long tunnel of dust starting at the western gate and angling off to the left.

A few moments after appearing, the ghostly channel turned as if to flank the Punic army. Seeing the danger, Captains raced back to Hannibal to warn him.

"General Barca," one gushed. "They have engaged a third Legion. And from the length of the procession and the dust, we believe they're bringing their cavalry out."

"It could be a maneuver to envelop us, sir," another Captain offered.

Hannibal scanned the battle one more time. Then he turned and searched to his rear.

"Were standing in the middle of cavalry territory," the Carthaginian General remarked. "Order a withdrawal. We can't afford to lose men to the Legion cavalry."

"It wouldn't be an issue if your Numidian cavalry was here," another commander said.

"But they're not, are they?" Hannibal commented as he reined his horse around. "Get our people out of the fight and out of the dust. I want ambushes in the woods to cover our retreat."

"Yes, General," the Captains replied.

***

The battle ended before anyone, except the infantrymen on the assault line, realized it.

"Congratulations, General Marcellus," Mettius boomed.

"What are you talking about?" the Proconsul inquired.

Claudius Marcellus wasn't paying attention. He had his eyes fixed on the dust screen that obscured the third Legion.

"General Marcellus, you are the first Roman commander to go shield-to-shield against Hannibal Barca and beat him. Congratulations on the victory."

The words sank in, and Claudius slowly turned. The Punic army scurried away as fast they could while carrying their wounded.

"Do we go after them, sir?" Colonel Flaccus asked.

With the cessation of hostilities, the dust fell to earth and the ranks of Legionaries emerged from the haze.

"No. We know Hannibal likes traps," Marcellus informed his Battle Commanders. "I'll not hand back a moral victory just to take a few heads. Let the Punic army chew on their defeat and the failure of their General."

"As you will, sir," Mettius acknowledged.

"And Battle Commander, wipe that stupid grin off your face," Marcellus scolded Flaccus. "The Legionaries will think you've lost your mind."

"I am trying, Proconsul, I really am," the Colonel begged. "But you beat Hannibal. And I am so proud to have been a party to it."

In the settling dust, the tunnel over the third Legion collapsed. First to appear were flags of plain cloth and banners of rough-cut material. Even the poles holding the flags were simple trimmed logs.

Then the heads of mounted men materialized. A few had on helmets but almost none were Legion. And rather than lances, they held javelins. A weapon totally inappropriate for use by cavalrymen.

When the swirling dropped to knee high, the rest of the third Legion emerged. And Proconsul Marcellus began laughing and wiping tears from the corners of his eyes.

The third Legion was mostly mules, horses, donkeys, oxen, and teamsters holding tree branches. At the head of the procession of draft animals, sat four mounted trumpeters. In front of the musicians, a Tribune in ceremonial armor sat proudly on a stallion.

"Battle Commander of Marcellus Legion the Third," Marcellus called to him. "Won't you join us?"

Cornelius lifted his helmet and saluted.

"I wasn't sure if I would be up on charges or acknowledged for daring a ploy, Proconsul," Cornelius admitted. Nudging his horse to the General's command staff, he added. "I've witnessed General Barca in four different battles, sir. And Proconsul Marcellus, you are the first to beat the crafty Carthaginian. Sir, it would be my honor to read the report of your victory to the Senate of Rome."

"He is an assistant Aedile," Flaccus advised, "and a decorated Tribune of Rome,"

"And better still, sir," Mettius added. "Tribune Scipio is from a noble family and is well respected. His voice carrying your name will reverberate throughout Rome."

"Scipio, you are aware the Patricians in the Senate stripped me of my Consulship after a day," Marcellus warned Cornelius. "Are you as confident in your offer as you were before?"

"General Claudius Marcellus, commander of Marcellus Legions North and South, Citizen of the Republic, and champion of Nola," Cornelius exclaimed. "I, sir, am humbled by the honor to be your voice in the Senate of Rome."

Looking around at the Legionaries who turned at the loud announcement, Cornelius barked, "Rah!"

Over seven thousand voices replied in a single roar, "Rah!"

Not surprising, other than a few whinnies and bleats, the third Legion was silent.

Chapter 16 – Through Enemy Territory

Two days after Hannibal withdrew from the battlefield and marched his army away from Nola, two hundred and seventy-two Numidian and Iberian horsemen appeared at the west gate.

"State your business," the Centurion called down from the ramparts.

"We've come to join Legion General Marcellus," an Iberian Captain replied.

The Centurion vanished from view. Once in the courtyard, he sent a runner for his Senior Tribune and called out his Century. When Senior Tribune Caius Aurelius climbed to the top of the wall, eighty heavy infantrymen stood ready inside the gate.

"Hannibal is renowned for his tricks," Caius challenged the horsemen. "How do I know you aren't here to rescue the rebels?"

"We know nothing of rebels," the cavalry Captain replied. "But we do recognize the power of the Republic. We offer your General years of combat experience."

"And in return for your lances?" Caius inquired.

"We want farms when the fighting is over," the Iberian officer told him. "Places where we can raise children and crops."

"Dismount and walk your horses in single file," Caius Aurelius ordered. Then we moved to the back of the wall and called down to the Centurion. "If any of them make a move to rescue the prisoners, kill them."

"Yes, sir," the Centurion acknowledged. "Century standby."

"Standing by, Centurion."

"Open the gate."

***

At the town square, four blocks from the west gate, Cornelius saluted General Marcellus. He was the only officer on the platform in woolen traveling attire.

"Sir, I'm leaving for Rome," he announced.

"Don't you want to stay for the executions?" Marcellus asked. "It's your investigations, after all, that convicted them."

"No, sir, I need to get to the capital."

"And my request about Casilinum?"

"Yes, sir, I'll get word back to you on the state of the garrison."

A courier jogged into the square. Moving quickly, he barely acknowledged the seventy men on their knees in front of the reviewing stand.

"Sir, we have cavalrymen from the Punic army," the messenger stated, "looking to join your Legion."

"And the morale lift continues to give benefits," Marcellus remarked. "Our Legionaries are proud of the victory and now, it seems, Hannibal's army is shamed."

"What do you want to do with the horsemen, sir?"

"Bring them here so they can witness what happens to traitors," Marcellus instructed. He turned back to Cornelius. "Are you sure you want to leave? Things are just getting interesting."

"General, I've a long way to go before I can deliver your words to the Senate," Cornelius told him. "And the first part of the journey is through enemy territory."

"In that case, Tribune Scipio, you are dismissed."

Cornelius saluted, about-faced, and marched off the reviewing stand. As he headed for the stables, the voice of Proconsul Claudius Marcellus reached him.

"You have been convicted of rebellion against Nola and Rome."

The seventy rebels whined at his declaration.

Once on his stallion, Cornelius took the reins for a string of three horses and a pack mule. He nudged the horse into motion and his small caravan left the corral. A block over, he crossed paths with a long line of Iberian and Numidian cavalrymen leading their mounts towards the town square.

"For your crimes, I sentence you to death," Marcellus instructed. "Centurions, cut off their heads."

The seventy prisoners screamed and pleaded as Legion officers marched down the rows. One by one, the officers chopped and hacked at the necks of the rebels until the heads fell from the bodies.

Cornelius reached the northwest gate. For a moment, he thought he heard the voices of Cleric Eshmoun and Capotosti the Cargo Broker begging for their lives. Then he was into the portal. When he emerged on the other side of the defensive wall, the sounds of the condemned faded away.

***

He had twenty miles of wagon trail to cover before reaching the solid pavers of the Via Appia. And while he felt the urgency of a Legion courier on official business,

Cornelius understood that a horse trader would move at a relaxed pace.

The easy trot carried him to the top of a gentle rise, where he caught sight of marching men. Reining in, Cornelius walked the horses while he counted. Even though hanging back looked suspicious, he remained patient. Once he had a count of five hundred African heavy infantrymen, Cornelius pushed the horses back to the trot. The last thing he needed was to be questioned by a Punic infantry Captain.

Moments later, he rode up beside the formation.

"Capua is nice this time of year," Cornelius suggested.

"We're not going to Capua," an NCO told him. "We've been assigned to clear North Casilinum."

"Is there trouble in the river city?" Cornelius gasped. "Should I go around?"

"No need. It'll only take us a day to clear away the garrison."

"Thank you for your help," Cornelius lied before nudging the horses into a cantor.

Moments later, he waved at the Punic Captain as he rode by the front of the formation.

General Marcellus wanted to know if the garrison still held the north end of Casilinum. Apparently, they did for now. But the Carthaginians had plans to remove the Legion garrison from the town. And they were sending the African Corps to do the job.

As if the clear blue sky had darkened, announcing an approaching storm, Cornelius yanked on the line to the string to get them in motion then he dug in his heels. At Cannae, he witnessed the infantrymen from the Punic coast. The African Corps was brutally efficient, disciplined, and ferocious. The garrison holding North Casilinum needed to be warned about what was heading their way. Throwing off the veneer of being a horse trader, he rode hard, covering the rest of the miles quickly.

***

Off to his right, smoke from tradesmen's fires in Capua drifted into the sky. The defensive walls appeared on the plain, and just as quickly, the city fell behind him. Fields of spelt grew on cultivated land for the next three miles. Then, rows of trees in snakelike patterns came into view. From outside the town of Casilinum, Cornelius couldn't see the Volturno River, but he knew the tall trunks marked the southern riverbank.

As with any shipping and transport town, Casilinum had more warehouses and commercial businesses than grand villas. But what it lacked in country estates, the river town made up for in services for visitors. The southern portion of the town followed a sharp U-turn in the river. Guiding his horses, Cornelius took the road into the crook and located a stable.

"I'm traveling north in the morning," he told the animal handler. "If I can get across the bridge."

"That's the question of the year," the stableman replied. He opened a corral and waved the string through the gate. "If it's not the militiamen from Capua with their hands out, it's the Republic garrison across the bridge."

"Sounds like a couple of bribes will clear the way," Cornelius guessed.

"For a lucky few. Most travelers get hung up on one side or the other waiting for a guard officer to get sick of looking at them. Or, until they don't have enough for the bribe on the other side."

"And they turn them back?"

"That's right. Once Hannibal gets here and clears them out, business can get back to normal."

There was no doubt the stable manager referred to the trouble with both the militia from Capua and the Legion garrison.

"Most commerce travels during the day, right?" Cornelius questioned.

"That's correct."

"Meaning the overnight NCO doesn't collect many tolls."

"Very few on both sides," the stableman summed up. "You're going to cross the bridge tonight?"

Cornelius tipped the stableman and asked him specifically to guard his bags. Especially the valuable Legion armor that he hoped to sell farther north. It was better to let the man know about the weapons and gear, than to have the man discover the Tribune armor and report him to the militia.

"I am going to cross tonight, even if it costs me more. Now, where can I get a good meal to tide me over?"

***

Although not a cold night, the rain sent chills up the spine with each dribble of water that slipped down a man's back. To ward off the damp, a fire roared beside the militia barricade. Some of the light cast illumination on the bridge surface. It only extended for about ten feet, leaving the remainder of the two-hundred-and-forty-foot span in darkness. At the far end, another big fire glimmered through the rain from the Legion side.

"Lieutenant, I'm Cornelius the Horse Trader. What's it going to cost me to cross in this foul weather and not wait."

"I'm a Sergeant," the militia NCO corrected him.

"Does that mean you don't want the fee?" Cornelius asked. He held a silver coin between his thumb and forefinger and rocked it. The metal caught the firelight and reflected it into the NCO's eyes. Noting the man's greed, Cornelius inquired. "I guess, I could stay here with you by the fire until daybreak. But will you be accepting tolls then or will it go to someone else?"

The man chewed on the inside of his cheek while glancing around searching for something. Perhaps a sign that he should wait or not.

"Open the barricade," the Sergeant told his militiamen as he snatched the coin from Cornelius' hand. "Move fast horse trader."

"Much appreciated."

Remembering the games the stablemen warned about, Cornelius, whistled and slapped the rump of each horse. Then with his pack mule in hand, he followed the horses onto the bridge.

"Hold on a moment," the Sergeant called to him.

"Horses," Cornelius responded as he jogged with the mule onto the surface. "They might get scared and jump."

Halfway across the Via Ponte Vecchio Romano, he located the four horses. They stood quietly in the rain. And just as the sun attempted to break through the rain clouds, Cornelius walked the string to the north end of the bridge

"What are you doing there?" a guard asked.

"You know I was out for an evening stroll and found myself in the pouring rain, on a bridge over a deep river, speaking to a goat-headed kid," Cornelius responded. "Where is your Officer of the Day?"

"We don't have an Officer of the Day," the sentry told him. Then he shook water off an oiled skin and demanded. "Did you call me goat-headed or a kid?"

"Yes. Where is your Sergeant of the Guard?"

"Optio Sertor is around here somewhere," the sentry remarked.

"What would you do if the militia attacked? How would you get hold of Sertor?"

"Oh, they haven't tried us since the raid where we lost our Centurions."

A bad feeling came over Cornelius and it wasn't all from the downpour at dawn.

"Tell you what," he said to the dense sentry, "pretend this is a raid and call the Optio. Or open the barrier and let me get off this bridge."

"Captain Sibidiena won't like it. He gets upset when we collect tolls."

"Who said I was paying a toll?"

"Everyone who wants to cross the bridge pays a toll."

Cornelius kicked the barrier. The pole jumped off the supports and rolled into the Legionary. Both the top of the barricade and the infantrymen fell to the ground. As he stepped over the youth, Cornelius snatched up the spear, and walked his horses off the bridge.

"Casilinum garrison, I am Tribune Scipio, standby," Cornelius bellowed.

Discipline might have been lax, the chain of command unlinked, but the training of Legionaries never faded.

"Standing by, Tribune."

"Get on the street, now."

"Getting on the street, now, Tribune."

In the heavy rain, with a hint of dawn in patches, two Centuries of Legion infantrymen responded to the orders. They raced from a pair of houses.

"Sir, I didn't know you were an officer," the sentry pleaded as he pushed off the ground.

"I can tell. Give me your gladius and take the spear," Cornelius instructed. "Guard my back but keep your mouth closed."

"Yes, sir," the hardheaded Legionary acknowledged.

They exchanged weapons, and Cornelius marched down the street between the gathering Legionaries.

"What's the meaning of this," a man with a bushy beard and broad shoulders roared. He burst from a third house and headed straight for Cornelius. "Who do you think you are too..."

A gladius can be used to stab, chop, hammer, or in the case of the bearded man, trip.

Cornelius dropped to his knees, slipped the blade between the man's legs, and shoved sideways as he stood up. The bearded man hopped away as the sharp blade neared his manhood.

Cornelius slammed a shoulder into him. Off balance, the man fell to the wet street. The gladius blade traced along his belly and his chest before stopping at his throat.

"I am Cornelius Scipio, a Tribune of the Legion and an assistant Aedile of Rome," he shouted. "Who is this barbarian to question me?"

"That sir, is Captain Sibidiena of the Praeneste heavy infantry," an Optio said as he ran up, "an ally of the Republic and a commander of five hundred."

"So far Optio, I haven't heard anything that's preventing me from slicing his throat for insubordination," Cornelius remarked. "Speak now, or he will forever hold his tongue."

"Now look here, Tribune," Sibidiena blustered.

But the gladius lifted from his neck and the flat of the steel slapped his beard, before returning to threaten his windpipe.

"When I want to hear from you, I'll let you know. Optio, I'm waiting."

"Tribune, we only have two Centuries to hold the north end of Casilinum," the Legion NCO explained. "Without the Praeneste heavy infantry, we couldn't fulfill our duty."

Cornelius pivoted slowly around Sibidiena's neck. As he moved, his head rotated searching the gray of morning. On the other side, he spit on the wet road.

"I don't see an Officer of the Day or any infantrymen on the street except Legionaries," Cornelius observed. "If this is a Captain, he is a poor leader of men. It's better if I replace him."

"Please understand, Tribune," Sertor begged. "He and the Praeneste Company were supposed to go to Cannae. But they received news of the defeat when he reached Casilinum."

"So, he stayed here and set himself up as a warlord," Cornelius declared. As the day lightened, he looked through the rain at the faces of the Legionaries. They were paying attention but didn't look convinced. "As an assistant Aedile of Rome, I sentence Captain Praeneste to death for disobeying an officer of the Senate of Rome."

"He can't do that, can he?" Sibidiena shouted.

"I'm afraid Captain Sibidiena, he can," the Optio assured him.

"Wait, wait, Tribune," Sibidiena requested. "I can follow orders. Just tell me what you need."

"Can a man who swears an oath at sword point be trusted?"

"On the life of my mother," Sibidiena blurted out, "I will obey your orders."

Cornelius raised his chin and locked eyes with the Legion NCO.

"Tribune Scipio, the Praenestes are devoted to their mothers, sir," Sertor informed him. "If he makes a pledge in her name, it's as good as a blood oath from anyone else."

Cornelius stepped away from the Captain and handed the gladius to the sentry. Then he looked up at the rain falling in the light of dawn.

"Our first order of business, Captain Sibidiena, Optio Sertor, is to build a stockade wall with oak gates," he told them. "Because, Hannibal Barca is sending five hundred African heavy infantrymen to remove us. And gentlemen, we will not surrender a foot of our bridge. Rah?"

While he was addressing the Captain and the Optio, Cornelius knew the Legion infantrymen heard every word. And he didn't need to see their faces to know the Legionaries were convinced of his prowess.

"Rah!" exploded from the men.

Chapter 17 – More Than Defensive

Every evening after hiking all day, Legionaries in marching Legions constructed defensive camps. As a result, infantryman knew the procedure and the techniques of building enormous stockades. The camps, in addition to the tall walls of planks and guard towers, had a defensive trench around the perimeter. The Legionaries at North Casilinum, however, instead of duplicating the elements in a standard camp, needed only build and brace a single barrier wall.

By midday, a trench cut across the road at the start of the bridge. On either side, the ditch sloped down to the edge of the river.

"That was fast," Cornelius remarked as he inspected stacks of beams and boards. "Where did you get the lumber?"

"I had the men disassemble a house, sir," Sertor answered. "I chose it because it had a barn on the property. We'll reinforce the doors and use the old hinges to hang the gates at the bridge."

The Tribune and NCO walked the construction site inspecting the work of the Legionary carpenters, foundation men, and engineers. When not fighting, all Legionaries were craftsmen of one kind or another. As the staff officer and the NCO neared the start of the bridge, Captain Sibidiena strolled from around the corner of a building.

"Tribune Scipio," he called out, "here are the tolls we collected."

He held up a sack bulging with coins then shoved it at Cornelius.

Cornelius indicated the NCO and directed, "Optio Sertor, give me a count of the coins and an accounting for the distribution of the funds."

After the directive, he turned and hopped into the trench.

"And how much is your share, Tribune?" Sibidiena questioned.

Cornelius stomped back and forth in the trench to be sure the Legionaries had tamped down the bottom. Once assured the section he was in passed inspection, Cornelius looked at the bearded Captain.

"My share is nothing."

"Compared to what?" Sibidiena challenged. "Nothing as in you'll give us a little and take the rest. Or…"

Interrupting the Captain, Cornelius asked, "Optio, how are the treasuries for our Centuries' burial funds?"

"Sir, after the funerals for our Centurions, there's almost nothing left."

"That is unacceptable," Cornelius stated. "But the men will be pleased to hear that Captain Sibidiena has donated half his personal share to the Legion burial funds."

"That's very generous," the Optio offered.

"I'll go along with your stupid game, Scipio. But I still want to know your share."

"Sergeant Sertor, I changed my mind. Put the Captain down for the same share as me in the fund," Cornelius told the NCO. Then he saluted Sibidiena and confessed. "Neither of us will take a coin from the tolls, Captain. You, because you aren't trusting. Generally, a man who sees cheating in others has a problem with honesty. Therefore, we'll be magnanimous and direct all our coins to our infantrymen."

"I like wealth," Sibidiena admitted. "And I have a problem trusting a man with a mysterious motivation. Like I said, I want the things coins can buy. What do you want, Tribune Scipio?"

Cornelius vaulted out of the ditch, landing in front of the Captain. Leaning over, he put his face three fingers from the Praeneste officer's beard.

"What I want is peace in the Republic," he growled. "But I can't have that because a barbarian has invaded my country. So, while I have wants, my life is dedicated to the defeat of Hannibal Barca. Until the Senate gives me Legions to command, I'll settle for small battles. We beat him for the first time at Nola. And believe me, I will do whatever I must to defeat him here at this bridge. What do I want you ask? It's simple, Captain. I want victory."

He didn't ask for the response. But of their own accord, the Legionaries and irregular infantrymen working on the wall and bridge gate shouted, "Rah!"

***

Once confident that the work was progressing, Cornelius said, "Show me to the garrison's offices.

Sertor indicated the direction. But halfway to the headquarters, Cornelius stopped. He spun and pointed back towards the gates.

"The garrison offices are useless that far from the bridge. This situation is a funnel," he described. "All the action will take place at the narrow end as if we're filling a barrel. And we need to be there with our men when the Africans come. Not blocks away, hunkered down in a fine estate. Locate a headquarters within a javelin's throw of the bridge and move us there."

Shortly after, the first house on the bridge approach was cleared and desks installed for the commanders of the garrison. Cornelius sat at one desk writing dispatches. Across the room, Captain Sibidiena's desk occupied the far corner. On Cornelius' side two camp tables for his NCOs filled the adjacent corner, and the far corner had an empty deck.

"When is Captain Ceionia due back?" Cornelius inquired.

He didn't look up but continued to work on the dispatches.

"I imagine the rain held him up, sir," Optio Pollio, the NCO of the second Century, reported. "He's touring the positions of his light infantrymen."

"Have militia crossed the river to get behind us?" Cornelius asked.

"Not since the Perugians arrived and began patrolling the riverbank."

As he finished the messages, Cornelius marveled at the fates. Originally, the garrison consisted of two Centuries. Plenty of shields to assist the Capua militia in guarding the Via Appia and the bridge. But things changed when Capua and South Casilinum declared for Hannibal Barca.

The defeat of the Legion garrison should have been short and swift. As it was, they lost both Centurions in the initial clash on the bridge. But the fates directed Captain Sibidiena and his Praeneste heavy infantrymen to North Casilinum. Shored up by the big shields of the irregulars, the garrison fought the militia to a standoff at the bridge.

Two days later, another Company bound for Cannae but too late to participate in the battle, joined the garrison. Captain Ceionia and four hundred and sixty Perugian light infantrymen took command of the north riverbank. With them in place, no militia dared cross the river to attack the garrison from the rear.

And most spectacular of all, the fates delivered Cornelius to a garrison under siege and in need of leadership.

***

"Tribune Scipio. These are the men I've assigned as messengers," Optio Sertor announced as he entered the offices.

Behind him, four Legionaries marched to the center of the room.

Cornelius stood and selected two pieces of rolled parchment from the desk.

"This message is for Proconsul Marcellus," Cornelius told them. "It informs the General that we are holding the bridge but need reinforcements. Two of you will carry the same message to assure the Proconsul receives the report."

"Which ones of you are familiar with the land south of here?" Sertor asked.

Two of the Legionaries raised their hands. Cornelius handed them the messages for Marcellus.

After taking two more pieces of parchment from his desk, Cornelius rolled them and tied each with a length of string.

"These dispatches are for Proconsul Gracchus or the Legion commander at Benevento. I'm asking for reinforcements. No offense to our friends from Praeneste, but I'd like six Centuries of Legionaries on the bridge when the Africans arrive."

Optios Pollio and Sertor laughed. Not because the comment was humorous. Their responses identified the truth of the remark. Auxiliary forces were fine for filling out Legion commands. But in the opinion of the Optios, there was no equal to having trained Legionaries in an assault line.

Once the couriers left, Sertor addressed Cornelius.

"Sir, Benevento is forty miles from here," the NCO advised. "Nola is half the distance. Why even send a message to Proconsul Gracchus? We have little chance of support from him."

"The distance is greater, but the resistance is almost nothing," Cornelius responded. "Between here and Nola could be the entire Punic army if they're marching for

Capua. Going east, the Legion controls the roads. I don't know who will or can respond. I'll take help from either."

"Agreed, Tribune," Pollio said.

Outside, cheering interrupted the conference.

***

Cornelius and the two NCOs dashed from the headquarters building. They rushed into the street and slid to a stop. The view of the bridge ended at a monster wall of wood with a double gate suspended in the middle. But that wasn't the action eliciting the cheers.

On either side of the wall, guard towers rose above the stockade. And crossing high above the gates was a walkway. Legionaries standing on the walk bowed and saluted the workers who participated in the construction.

"Congratulations Optios," Cornelius exclaimed. "You've given us a chance to defeat the Punic infantry."

"Yes, sir," Pollio said. "That wall will stop them."

"The gates in that wall," Cornelius pointed out, "are there not to stop the Africans. The gates are hinged, meaning the wall is more than defensive. We will open those gates and take the fight to the Punic infantry."

"And we'll defeat them before our gates," Optio Pollio declared.

***

Since early morning, Tribune Scipio marched back and forth on the walkway over the gates. When the sun came over the horizon, it painted the rooftops of Casilinum, the top of the stockade wall, and the form of Tribune Scipio. In the morning light, his red cloak and the horsehair comb of his Tribune's helmet identified Cornelius as the new garrison commander. Across the bridge, men of the militia pointed at the wall and the pacing Roman officer.

169

After initial greetings, the staff officer ignored the sentries in the guard towers. He didn't want company or conversation.

A ladder leading to the left guard tower creaked as someone climbed. Moments later, an auxiliary officer appeared on the walkway.

"Tribune Scipio?" the lean, clean-shaven officer inquired.

"You must be Captain Ceionia."

"Yes, sir, and we need to talk."

"About the tolls?" Cornelius questioned.

An odd expression passed over the officer's face as if he had an upset stomach. Then the Captain pointed upriver.

"Don't know about tolls, sir," he admitted. "What we need to discuss are the number of boats being staged on the south bank at the curve in the river."

"Fishing boats?" Cornelius inquired.

"Some are and others are flat bottomed barges," Ceionia described. "And a few are river transports. But they all have one thing in common. They float."

Cornelius took a couple of steps away before walking back.

"As in, they are capable of floating infantrymen across the river," Cornelius offered.

"That's my guess," Ceionia answered. "But Capua militia ate steel the last time they tried a crossing. What's changed, Tribune? This wall or something else?"

"Five hundred infantrymen from Hannibal's African Corps," Cornelius stated. "I passed them a couple of days ago coming from the south."

"Let me suggest that the main body might not be in South Casilinum, yet," Ceionia advised. "But their planning staff certainly has arrived, and they've gone to work."

170

"Where do you expect them to land?"

Ceionia turned and faced downriver.

"The banks before the bridge are too steep and the current too swift," the Captain from Perugia replied. "But two thousand feet from here, the riverbank flattens just before the water drops to another level. Only river transports can make the trip. Small boats overloaded with men in armor can't make the passage. So, it has to be the two-thousand-foot mark. That's where they'll come ashore."

"Then that's where we'll meet them," Cornelius declared. Then he closed his eyes and mumbled something unintelligible. Moments later, Cornelius lifted his eyebrows and asked. "Don't you wonder why the boats are in plain sight? I do. Tell me Captain, have you ever seen a bull with one horn?"

"No, Tribune," Ceionia replied.

"The Carthaginian God El, the Father of Gods and Men, is represented by the bull," Cornelius explained. He held up both arms and cocked his wrists, so his fists pointed at each other. "As a follower of El, General Barca pays homage to the God in his attack formations. A solid center like the head of a bull accompanied by infantry and cavalry on each side, like horns."

"You don't think the shallow riverbank and the bridge are the only points of attack?"

Cornelius brought his fists together in a pincher action.

"I realize you just returned from inspecting your positions," Cornelius admitted. "But Captain, I need to know where the other attack is coming from. Find me the second horn."

"It'll be east of here," Ceionia suggested. "If there are signs of a staging area, I'll find it. If there's nothing else, sir?"

"You're dismissed. Oh, and thank you."

"My men and I came to fight but we were too late for Cannae," Ceionia said. "But we're not to late for Casilinum. You can count on us."

The Perugian Captain quick stepped to the ladder, gripped the sides, and slung his body outward. He vanished below the walkway and Cornelius faced the bridge and ran his eyes along the length of the elevated roadway.

"I know your tricks Hannibal," he whispered. "And I know how to counter them."

For all his bravado, Tribune Scipio did not have the infantry to engage the African Corps on three fronts. Even though he suspected one place of attack, his area of operations needed to be centered around the bridge over the Volturno River. It locked him into a defensive position where attrition spelled defeat. Plus, he had no indication where the Corps would launch the third attack. Despite the warmth of the morning sun, Cornelius Scipio shivered.

Chapter 18 – The Bull's Head

Senators and leaders in the Republic held the belief that one must remain above the mundane. With minor tasks delegated to underlings, great men freed their minds for thinking about important matters. As a nobleman and a citizen of Rome, Cornelius Scipio agreed with the philosophy. Thusly, he regretted wallowing in mud for the final twenty feet. It went against every ideal of the principle.

"If we hadn't been looking, we would have missed them," Ceionia said.

The Captain released the weeds that screened him from the Tribune and crawled from the muddy trail. Easing into a swollen stream, he and Cornelius grabbed a rope that prevented them from washing down the channel. In a few feet, the bed tilted, and the water began to rush faster.

"Here they are," Ceionia announced.

The Captain hooked Cornelius' arm and pulled him out of the wash and onto a flat piece of stone. Downstream, the rainwater shot into the air creating a small waterfall.

"The steps are ancient," Ceionia explained. He patted the granite, his hand splashing water off the hard surface. "My scouts think they were here before the bridge and the Via Appia. Built over a hundred years ago for carrying grain sacks down to the river."

"And you believe this is the second bull's horn?"

"Behind the warehouse on the southern bank are ropes and boats," Ceionia described. "They weren't there last week. I still don't understand why you wouldn't let me post guards on the steps."

"If the African Corps doesn't use these stairs, they'll cross somewhere else."

"And you want to catch them unaware," Ceionia suggested. "But when, sir?"

"That, Captain, is the question," Cornelius admitted. "I would guess shortly before or after they attack us on the bridge."

"If you look over the weeds, you can see breaks in the foliage where the granite pieces step down to the river."

"Can your infantry pin them to the water's edge until I get some heavy infantrymen over here?" Cornelius inquired. He peaked over the weeds, scanned the flat spots, and dropped down. "The steps are wide."

"They would have allowed pairs of porters to carry heavy loads up and down from the river," the Captain ventured. "Or permit six shields abreast to climb off a barge."

Cornelius grabbed the rope and rolled off the slab. Once in the stream, he climbed hand over hand back to the muddy trail.

***

Optio Pollio extended his arms at shoulder height.

"If they came across five shields wide and stacked fifteen deep, it'll require an equal pressure from our defenders just to stop their forward progress," the NCO described as if attempting to extend his hands the width of the bridge. "It'll take more than eighty Legionaries to defend against the initial push."

"We only have one hundred and sixty in total," Sertor summed up. "As much as I hate to admit it, we'll need to mix Praeneste infantry with our Legionaries. It's the only way to check the African assault."

Near the end of his talk, the door blew open and Tribune Scipio came in from the rain. His hobnailed boots trailed mud across the office floor.

"What do you hate?" Cornelius inquired while shaking water off an oiled wrap.

"We're analyzing the bridge defense," Pollio answered. "It'll take more than a Century to throw back the initial assault."

"It gets worse than that," Cornelius said as he hung the wrap on a hook. "We need to cover three simultaneous attacks. Captain Ceionia located the third staging area."

"Aren't we assuming too little of the Praeneste infantry?" Sertor remarked. "They may be good fighters."

174

"The Legionaries practice with gladii and shields every day," Cornelius challenged. "Since they've been here, how many days has Captain Sibidiena drilled his infantrymen?"

The two NCOs exchanged glances before Pollio commented, "Then we are defeated before the battle begins."

"Not necessarily," Cornelius proposed. "If we were attacking a pair of gates, what would you use?"

"A battering ram, sir," Sertor replied. "But that's to break through the doors of the gates."

"Suppose we used several to break their shield wall?"

"Crushing their forward lines, would ruin the African Corps' day," Pollio offered.

"And reduce the number of infantrymen we need to meet their mass," Sertor added.

Cornelius paced in front of his desk before stopping.

"See what you can get rigged, Sertor," Cornelius instructed. "If we can reduce the bridge to a shoving match, Captain Sibidiena and his infantry should be able to hold the gates. And I can use the Legionaries to defend against the flanking attacks."

"Why do you think they'll come at us from three directions, sir?" Pollio asked.

"Because somewhere in South Casilinum, the Corps' planning and strategies staff is having the same discussion as us. And they'll reach the same conclusion. Unless they break through on the original thrust, the bridge becomes a bog. A swamp where tactics and infantrymen die."

***

It rained for two days. Then the weather cleared and for two more, the sun rose against a clear blue sky. And the surge of water from the rain receded.

"Not sure I like the looks of that," Optio Sertor remarked.

"The sky?" Pollio inquired. "Or the militia?"

"Neither. I'm looking at the river."

Both Legion NCOs stood on the walkway gazing at the militiamen on the far side of the bridge. At the mention of the Volturno, they shifted their eyes. Freshly deposited leaves and branches littered the riverbank. The high-water mark from the recent rains showed the river had dropped considerably.

"If I was over there and wanted to get here, I'd take the lower level as a sign to bring my Century across," Pollio offered. "Are the Praeneste infantrymen ready?"

"They didn't like drilling in the rain," Sertor replied. "And they aren't Athenian Hoplites. But they improved."

"That's not an answer, Optio," Cornelius commented as he came up a ladder. "We have to decide how we'll disperse our Legionaries. Understand, Hannibal teaches his planners to think ahead before a battle. We will do the same."

"But sir, we don't know what the Corps will do," Sertor pointed out. "How can we make smart decisions before we know anything?"

"We know there are three points of attack. We know the African Corps will take the fastest way across to do the most damage. And we know holding the bridge is the same as holding the center of an assault line."

"Tribune, if the center is the most important location, our Legionaries should be assigned to hold it," Pollio advised.

"I would agree," Cornelius admitted. "But think of my second point. The Corps will want to get to the north bank as fast as possible."

"You're thinking they'll use the militia to assault the bridge," Sertor declared. "And use the Corps to flank us?"

"That's why you'll be here, Optio," Cornelius informed Sertor. "If Captain Sibidiena and his command staff runs, you'll rally the Praeneste infantrymen."

"What makes you think they'll follow me?"

"Because you drilled them in the rain for two days," Cornelius replied. "And who doesn't love a Legion NCO after marching around with him in the mud and rain for a couple of days?"

Cornelius stepped on the ladder and climbed down.

"What was the Tribune talking about?" a Legionary in the right guard tower asked. "I hate drilling in the rain."

"But you do it," Pollio challenged. "Why?"

"Well, because you tell us to, Optio," the Legionary replied.

The Legion NCOs smiled at each other.

"Maybe Tribune Scipio does know what he's doing," Sertor suggested.

"He knows men, and he knows Punic tactics," Pollio said. "But is his plan sound?"

"We'll know by midday," Sertor proposed. He lifted an arm and pointed upriver. "Because the African Corps has declared themselves."

On the south bank at the bend in the river, heavy infantrymen pushed boats into the water, climbed in, and shoved them away from shore.

"Stay well, Optio," Sertor exclaimed as he exchanged salutes with Pollio.

Pollio, Sertor, and the Legionaries on duty in the guard towers climbed down. Once on the road, Pollio jogged away with the Legion heavy infantrymen. Sertor, as the lone representative of the Republic, stood silently, staring at the closed gates.

"What's going on?" Captain Sibidiena inquired as he ambled up behind the Optio. "The Centuries are marching away and you're here."

Sertor raised both arms and used his hands to indicate the guard towers.

"We need men on the platforms and three hundred of your Praenestes staged here," the Legion NCO directed. "Send the rest of your Company downriver to Optio Pollio."

"To Sergeant Pollio. Where is the young Tribune?"

"Planning an ambush, I imagine, Captain," Sertor responded. "We, you and I, have the privilege of defending the bridge."

Sibidiena worked his jaw which made his beard ripple around his mouth. Finally, he patted down the facial hair and nodded.

"And defend it, we will."

***

From the south shore of Casilinum, a thousand feet upriver, the flotilla drifted and rowed a couple of thousand feet downstream. There was no attempt at stealth by the African Corps. The infantrymen even shouted and waved as they floated under the bridge.

"Pretty sure of themselves," a Praeneste Lieutenant observed.

"We have movement at the end of the bridge," an infantryman alerted him.

The officer stopped ogling the boats and switched to watching as militia gathered on the far side of the bridge.

"How can we hold here when the Corps is coming in behind us?" the infantryman pleaded.

"Because we aren't fighting the African Corps," Sertor told him. "We drew the militia. And we've beaten them before."

"And we'll beat them again, right Optio?" the infantryman asked. Then he looked to his officer for reassurance. "Won't we, sir?"

"We will," the Lieutenant agreed after swallowing hard.

But then the officer went back to scrutinizing the boats carrying the big shields, long spears, and strong bodies of the infantrymen from Hannibal's African Corps.

If there was any question about the coordination between the militia and the Corps, the answer came when a detachment of cavalry arrived on the opposite bank. As the boats reached the flat portion of the riverbank, infantrymen jumped to shore and set up a screen of shields to protect those coming off the boats behind them. On the other side of the river, horsemen rushed back to Casilinum.

Even as Legion javelins arched into the sky and fell towards the landing force, the militia paraded onto the bridge. Five abreast, they marched in a loose formation, fifteen men deep.

***

"That's a comfort," Sertor declared after making a show of counting the attackers. "There's only seventy-five of them."

"Only seventy-five," the Praeneste Lieutenant repeated. "That's a lot and their headed right for the gates."

"It's a bridge, sir," the young infantryman told him. "There's not a lot of room to maneuver."

Sertor turned and looked down at the roadway.

"Where are my warriors?" he shouted. A roar came back from the Praeneste infantry. "Pick them up, we need to clear the bridge of trash."

Below the walkway, men trained and equipped for the mission, walked to the stockade wall, and snatched long poles from holding racks. Shortly after the Optio issued the warning, five infantrymen faced the gates and locked their shields together. Behind them, ten more shuffled into position. All fifteen looked up, expecting the order to march to come at any moment.

The ladder creaked as Sibidiena climbed to the walkway.

"This is ridiculous. We need to go out in force and fight them on the bridge," the Captain complained.

A flight of arrows zipped over the top of the wall. While Sibidiena ducked down, Sertor slipped his arm through the straps of his Legion shield.

"That's feeding men into the jaws of a bear," the NCO responded. He glanced around the shield and judged the progress of the militia. "You might eventually kill the beast, but you'll waste a lot of lives doing it."

"And twenty against seventy-five isn't a suicide attack?" the Captain demanded.

"No, sir. I'll bet none of them even gets a scratch," Sertor promised. He spun while shifting the shield to protect his back. Then he addressed the infantrymen staged at the gate. "Hard and fast. And just as we practiced, hit your mark, and get out."

"Yes, Optio," the twenty responded.

Sertor slowly brought his right fist up. It hovered for a moment, before he slammed it into his chest. After the salute, the Legion NCO ordered, "Open the gates."

***

The militia expected javelins. When facing Legionaries, there were always iron tipped missiles. They had even drawn straws to see who would be condemned to the forward ranks while crossing the bridge. The two ranks of five at the front had picked the shortest straws.

One hundred and twenty-five feet across the bridge and the nerves in their guts fired. Anticipation alone caused the fear, because even the best Legionary couldn't throw a javelin halfway across the bridge. Death from the sky would start at sixty feet from the stockade wall.

But then, while still beyond throwing distance, the gates flew open. Something resembling the image off an old Greek vase appeared. From the portal marched a facade of shields. The moving screen alone posed little threat. The militia could stab between the shields with their eight-foot spears once they got close enough.

With the defenders in sight, the militia collapsed their ranks and closed up their files. Confidence filled their hearts for they faced Praeneste infantrymen and not red cloaked, javelin throwing Legionaries.

"The bridge is as good as ours," one boasted.

Then from the façade of shields, a row of four long poles popped out of the screen at shoulder height. Immediately following the top row, a second row of extremely long poles appeared at waist level.

The militia jabbed at the air and made noises to unsettle the moving wall of shields. But the twenty Praeneste marched forward unaffected by the battle cries and manic shouting.

***

"You trained my men to perform as a phalanx," Sibidiena exclaimed. "And you've given them long poles like the ones used by the army of the Macedonian King Alexander."

"I thought about rigging battering rams at the gates but that would allow the militia to get to close. Excuse me for a moment, Captain," Optio Sertor excused himself. Turning, he shouted to the infantrymen on the street. "Standby. In a moment, we'll go and finish the job. And remember, a wet militiaman is as good as a dead one."

"Standing by, Optio," they called back in the Legion response.

"The phalanx isn't all you've taught my men," Sibidiena noted.

"The fight is out there, Captain," Sertor said.

He pointed at the bridge where the packed shields and long poles of the infantrymen closed the distance with the front ranks of the militia.

The spears were steel tipped killing implements. Opposing them, the long shafts were sharpened poles. Before the spears reached the shield wall, the long poles began to undulate.

Forward and backward as if eight punching fists, the tips impacted militiamen before the spears could come into play. And to the shock of the attackers, the shafts didn't just knock them back, the poles pushed them to the sides.

The militiaman on the right side found himself suddenly shoved farther to the right. In an attempt to catch his balance, he stumbled to the rail, wobbled for a moment, then he fell over the barrier. His screams as he tumbled towards the river were echoed by a falling militiaman from the left side. Soon they were joined by other men who never had a chance to get close enough to attack the shield wall.

Of the first five ranks of militia, half were drowning in the river, pulled under the current by the weight of their armor. The rest backed away from the phalanx and the sharpened shafts, fearing they would be next to fall from the bridge. Their movement to the rear disrupted the rest of the militiamen on the bridge.

Sertor leaned far over the back side of the walkway.

"Men of Praeneste. The enemy formation is in shambles and our brave comrades are in peril," Sertor screamed at the waiting infantrymen. "What are you going to do about it?"

"Save our brothers and clear the bridge," they shouted back at him.

"Don't tell me," the Legion NCO responded. "Tell it to the militia. Forward!"

As he had coached, the infantrymen ran onto the bridge in two lines. Quickly, they reached and passed the men in the cocoon of shields. Once beyond the tips of the long shafts, the Praeneste infantry formed rows and assaulted the confused militia.

"Congratulation Optio Sertor, soon you'll have taken the bridge. Now what?"

"This fight is not over, Captain Sibidiena. Now we have to hold it."

Act 7

Chapter 19 – On the Edge of Disaster

Captain Sibidiena's forces filled the bridge from the north side to the southern end. Even at a distance of twenty-three hundred feet down the Volturno River, Optio Pollio could have identified sections occupied by the infantrymen. He might have, if he took a moment to squint through the trees in that direction. He didn't have the luxury.

"Optio Pollio, rotate our left side," Cornelius ordered. "And pull the wounded back."

Pollio repeated the commands while running behind his third rank. As Legionaries rotated off the assault line, they pulled wounded comrades back with them. A few stumbled from exhaustion and Pollio stopped to help drag the injured to the rear.

"Tighten up those shields," he bellowed. "Corporal, shove men into the gaps. Tighten up your Century."

Beyond the Legionaries, he moved to the detachment of infantrymen from Praeneste. Their fighting style had them grouped behind their assault line. It wasn't efficient by Legion standards but correcting them during a combat operation served no purpose.

Stretching to his full height, the Legion NCO peered between the heads of the Praenestes, gazing down onto the massed horde of infantry coming up from the river. Unsettled and mad at the outcome of the confrontation so far, he jogged back to the center of the assault line.

"Tribune Scipio, we've got more than we can handle," Pollio advised. "You should consider backing us up and moving into town."

"We might delay them by fighting street to street," Cornelius replied, "but it's a losing strategy. We'd end up trapped on the bridge. No, Optio. We're better off holding them here at the edge of the river."

Pollio wanted to point out that they were neither at the edge of the river nor had they stopped the landing force. At best, their action delayed the combined forces of the African Corps and infantry from Capua. Before the NCO could decide if he wanted to push the issue, a runner came from Casilinum.

"Sir, Captain Sibidiena reports that he has taken the bridge," the messenger stated. "And further, he wants to inform you that he will hold it against the militia, no matter the odds."

"What does that tell you, Optio?" Cornelius asked the NCO.

"No matter the odds, sir? That tells me we're not getting reinforcements from the Captain," Pollio answered.

"You are correct. We've got to collapse our formation and reestablish our three ranks," Cornelius suggested. "Once we get that accomplished, I'm going to check on Captain Ceionia. Pass the order."

The Tesserarii from the two Centuries were acting as their Centurions. But just filling the slot of a combat officer didn't make the Corporals proficient at the job. They were good at keeping the Century's records, tracking the Legionaries pay, and managing the funeral funds for the eighty-man units. But interpreting hand signals and translating them to field commands for a Century required more experience and training.

"Yes, sir," Pollio acknowledged before sprinting to his right. Once he reached the acting officer in that position, he explained. "Corporal, when I give the sign, move them towards the center. We're collapsing and strengthening our position."

"Optio, I've been in the Legion long enough to have dug my share of latrines," the Tesserarius remarked.

"Okay, get to the point," Pollio urged, although he sensed what was coming.

"And this, Optio, is a cesspool, if I've ever seen one," the acting combat officer declared.

"I can't argue," Pollio agreed.

He continued towards the irregular infantrymen holding the right flank.

***

Cornelius knew his detachment hovered on the edge of disaster. The landing force exceeded his expectations. In addition to the infantrymen from the African Corps, soldiers from the city of Capua had disembarked from the small boats. Although hard to judge during a battle, Tribune Scipio believed the combined force outnumbered his Legionaries and Paraeneses fighters.

However, something else was nagging at the back of his mind. Something worse than the embarrassment of retreating back to the bridge. It circled around the message from Captain Sibidiena, but he couldn't clarify the thought.

An injured Legionary stumbled out of the combat line. Throwing down his shield, he stabbed his gladius into the dirt and took a piece of cloth from a pouch. After wrapping the wound, he knotted the ends of the bandage and picked up his shield.

"African Corps my great, hairy cōleī," he cursed as he plucked the gladius from the soil. "They ain't merda. They just have the numbers."

The Legionary shouldered his way back into the combat line. While he returned to the fight, Cornelius silently repeated the words, "They just have the numbers."

His thought solidified and panic blinded him for a moment. He had passed five hundred infantrymen of the African Corps on the road from Nola. But no more than two hundred of them faced his Legionaries on the riverbank. If Hannibal's African infantry hadn't assaulted the bridge, and weren't in the landing force, where were they?

A vision of ancient granite steps buried in weeds, and three hundred battle hardened infantrymen marching up the steps from the river flashed through his mind.

"Ceionia's light infantry doesn't stand a chance," Cornelius concluded.

***

Just as he admitted the awful truth, a messenger from the east arrived at Cornelius' location. A moment later, Optio Pollio joined them.

"Tribune Scipio. Captain Ceionia asked that you send Legionaries to the steps," the messenger stated. "They've rigged lines across the river and are transporting heavy infantrymen on barges. And sir, there are a lot of them."

Pollio tensed at the news. In the midst of the battle, with men crying out in pain and rage, the Legion NCO waited calmly for instructions from his Tribune.

Cornelius scanned the assault line. Weaving like a drunken Legionary fresh off a long march, the even rows they practiced in training were anything but straight. He couldn't see any way to separate the Legionaries from the Africans and the soldiers from Capua.

"Can we disengage a half Century without getting overrun?" Cornelius inquired.

"A half Century, Tribune?" Pollio questioned. "They can't do much, if that many men are crossing over the river."

"It's all you can spare. I need them as a rally point to help me pull the Perugians out," Cornelius answered. "While I'm there, you'll conduct a controlled retreat. If the Goddess Fortūna is with us, we'll meet at the bridge."

"We'll trust in her luck, sir," Pollio acknowledged. "And make a bond to sacrifice to the Goddess when we meet again."

Pollio saluted then sprinted to the left. After speaking to the acting combat officer, he demonstrated to Cornelius how to separate men during combat. The Optio didn't attempt to pull the half Century off the combat line. Instead, he peeled the third line of Legionaries off the formation.

In moments, Cornelius had forty exhausted Legionaries gathered around him.

"Legionaries, you aren't a full Century," he announced. "And you've been fighting all morning. I appreciate your sacrifice. But to the east of us, an allied force of light infantrymen are fighting the rest of the African Corps. They need our help to break contact. Thus, I ask you. Can you find the strength, and the heart, to fight one more battle?"

Although young, Cornelius understood fighting men. Offering one more battle sounded good, but it was a lie. And not only did Tribune Scipio know it, so did the Legionaries.

With disdain for the lie and a willingness to help the light infantry of their allies, the heavy infantrymen of the Legion shouted their assurances, "Rah."

***

Foregoing his right to mount a horse and ride, Cornelius jogged at the head of his half Century. They skirted the edge of North Casilinum and soon reached the extreme of the bend in the river. No fighting or signs of battle were visible. Nothing until they reached the far side of the bend and broke from a tree line.

Clusters of light infantryman from Perugian clawed at the edges of a forming mass of men with big shields and long spears. Only where the African Corps had yet to form up, did the Perugians dare to get close. Unfortunately, it was a lesson hard learned. The results of many ill-timed attacks lay dead or dying in the grass and on the slope.

"Captain Ceionia, pull back," Cornelius shouted. "We'll cover your retreat."

"You're late, Tribune," the Captain scoffed.

"The blame is mine," Cornelius confessed. "I'm here now and we need to go."

But the sight of ranks of Legionaries gave the African Corps an objective. In a wedge, they ran at the forty Legionaries, covering the distance in several heartbeats.

"Draw and brace," Cornelius ordered.

Twenty shields wide and stacked two deep, the Legionaries bent their knees and locked their shields in place. As if a wave breaking on a rocky shoreline, the African infantrymen crashed into the wall of Legion shields.

Long ruts, the width of hobnailed boots, showed where the lines moved. Truly a testament to the power of the collision, the boot prints in the earth also spoke well of the

Legionaries' training. Despite the torn grass and displaced soil, the wall of Legion shields held.

***

In addition to giving the African Corps a focus, the lines of red shields and flashing gladii offered a safe harbor for the surviving Perugian light infantrymen. To the detriment of the Corps, the Perugians ran down the sides of the formation wounding Africans as they raced for the shelter of the Legionaries.

Captain Ceionia rounded the flank, entered the Roman formation from the rear, then stumbled as he approached Cornelius.

"I didn't think you would come, Tribune," the officer of light infantry uttered.

"Of all the things a man needs to keep," Cornelius avowed while standing Ceionia upright, "are his oaths to the Gods and his word to his allies."

While the officers talked, the four Legion squad leaders organized the combat line into a fighting square. With Legionaries forward, the light infantrymen became the second row backing up the Legion infantrymen. Once they had a box with solid sides, one of the Decani jogged to Cornelius.

"Sir, we need to step back," he informed the officer, "before we get breached."

"Order the movement," Cornelius instructed the squad leader.

At that moment, Averruncus, the God who Averts Calamity, seemed to turn his back on Tribune Scipio.

***

Although they missed the trek over the Alps, the African Corps had arrived from the Punic coast and participated in

190

most of Hannibal's recent battles. By holding their line against the Legions at Cannae, they were a deciding factor at the battle. Disciplined and experienced, the leadership of the Corps was just as professional as the infantry.

One of their Lieutenants backed away from the fighting. Calmly, he examined the tight formation of Legion shields and the lances of the light infantrymen in the second rank.

"It's like digging dung beetles out of a pile of addax droppings," the officer complained.

"Do you need something, sir," a file leader inquired.

The Corps Lieutenant scanned the solid walls of Legion shields.

"Yes," he directed. "Knock the corner off their formation so our warriors can get inside that pile of dung."

There was only one way to chop a log or remove a corner from a fighting square. It involved a sharp wedge, manipulated not directly at the target, but at an angle. An ax blade chopped above where the woodsman wanted to make the final cut. And a file of African infantrymen, in a tight wedge formation, needed to run diagonally at the corner of the square and not directly at the shields.

***

"Order the movement," Cornelius instructed the squad leader.

Before the Decanus could pass on the order, three Legionaries and four Perugians vanished. As quickly as stalks of grain dropped from view during the harvest, one moment the corner of the fighting square was closed and guarded. The next, an opening revealed a line of African infantrymen running by.

"We held them on the slope for as long as we could," Ceionia explained. "It was later that I sent the messenger…"

But the Captain's report was cut short when Cornelius shouted, "Breach. Right corner."

In response to his own announcement, Cornelius snatched a shield from the hands of a wounded Legionary, drew his spatha, and dashed towards the hole.

As with all sons of Roman noblemen, Cornelius had trained with the scutum and the sword since boyhood. But while his drills were exhausting and drew a little blood, none had been life or death struggles. On several occasions, he had drawn his blade in anger, but the fierceness of his spirit and righteousness of his cause forced his opponents to back down. The infantrymen of the African Corps didn't know or care about the Tribunes ferocity or his honor.

Two African shields bashed into the borrowed Legion shield. Rocked back, Cornelius flashed to his instructors. Following their practice, he bent his knees and stepped forward, while slipping off one shield so only the pressure from the one on his left was against him. In mid step, he blindly slashed downward and to the side with his blade. It connected with an African spear, driving the shaft and steel tip into the dirt. But the long weapon of the man on his right wouldn't remain down for long.

"One advantage of the gladius is the short blade," a master of the sword boasted. "There's nothing better for stabbing across a shield wall, chopping when an opportunity presents itself, or cycling back for a killing thrust."

A truth was always valid even if Cornelius' cavalry spatha was a hands width longer than a gladius. From the downward slash on the shaft, he arched the blade up, bringing it over and down behind the infantryman's shield. For a heartbeat, the blade hung up, caught in the top of the

African's chest armor. But as the injured man fell away, Cornelius' spatha came free.

He braced preparing for the attack from the other African. But the pressure against his shield lifted as Legionaries shifted sideways, sealing the breach.

"Tribune. I've seen officers brag about their prowess with a gladius while berating a Century for weak sword drills," a squad leader exclaimed. His face, although covered in sweat and spotted with blood from the fighting, glowed with enthusiasm. "But you sir. You are blessed of Bellona, the ancient Goddess of War. You know how to fight. And sir, I would be proud to follow you to Hades if you ordered it."

"Right now, Decanus," Cornelius admitted. "I'd be happy just to make it to the bridge."

"Yes, sir," the squad leader acknowledged. Bellowing so everyone in the fighting square could hear, he instructed. "Tribune Scipio wants us at the bridge. What say you?"

The collective Rah sounded more like a growl as the infantrymen took one step away from the slope. Another followed, then another. Gladii and lances dueled with spears to the front. But soon the clashes moved to three sides. And finally, as the African Corps surrounded the half Century and the Perugian survivors, the fighting took place on all sides. And their progress towards the bridge stopped.

Cornelius stormed around the inside of the square. Still carrying the shield and bloody sword, he reinforced sections when Legionaries fell and stood in the battle line at potential breaches. But while his presence bolstered the Legionaries and light infantrymen, the officer's courage alone could not make up the difference in numbers. For a moment, Cornelius stepped back and looked longingly over his shoulder in the direction of Casilinum.

"An illusion brought on by exhaustion," he mumbled at the sight of a mounted Tribune.

The staff officer motioned towards the fighting square. Then men shouted warning orders from outside the circle of Africans.

"Second Maniple, Gracchus Legion East, uncover your shields, and stand by."

From hundreds of voices, Cornelius heard the words that meant the salvation of his command.

"Standing by, Centurion."

Chapter 20 – By an Aedile of Rome

No sensible commander wanted to fight on two fronts or would willingly allow his troops to be surrounded. The Captain of the African Corps examined his positions and quickly realized that a third of his detachment stood between the fighting square and the newly arrived Legion assault line.

"Pass the word to pull us out and order a defensive screen at the barge landing," the Captain instructed his aides. Then, while walking towards the top of the riverbank, he complained. "It's a shame those reinforcements showed up. Given a few more attacks, we would have captured that young, foolish Tribune."

Just as water runs downhill after a rainstorm, African infantrymen flowed away from the fighting square and jogged for their Captain.

"Set a shield wall along the top of the hill, Lieutenant," the commander directed. "Your units will be the last ones off the north bank."

"Sir, I apologize for not breaking the fighting square," the Lieutenant admitted.

"No need to apologize. It's why yours is the last unit out. We'll let that serve as your penance."

Discipline was the heart of the African Corps. And just as no commander wasted good infantrymen in a losing fight, nor could he ignore failure. With the Lieutenant duly chastised for his inability to create a breach, the Captain hiked down the granite steps to the first barge.

***

The half Maniple stepped off. Four hundred and eighty heavy infantrymen in a triple assault line, guided by six combat officers, and controlled by a mounted Tribune, stomped towards the Africans. They moved fast, but not quickly enough to catch the fleeing infantrymen of the Corps.

"This is my left side, Second Maniple, Gracchus Legion East," the mounted Tribune greeted Cornelius. "Name's Thaddeus. Who are you?"

"Sir, I'm Cornelius Scipio. Your timing is impeccable."

"Battle Commander Ovid wasn't sure about your request at first," Thaddeus explained. "But when he got word Capua had deserted the Republic and declared for Hannibal, he realized the importance of controlling the bridge and North Casilinum."

"We have the bridge," Cornelius informed him. "But there was a third assault from across the river to the west. I was there before I got trapped here."

"You're very young, Cornelius," Thaddeus observed. "You'll learn that unless you have cavalry, you can't split your infantry."

"Today that lesson has been etched in my heart by the blood of good men," Cornelius admitted. "If you've a horse I can borrow, I need to go check on my other Century."

"I sent my right side ahead to the bridge," Thaddeus assured Cornelius. "They're under the command of my best Centurion. He's young like you and brash like you. But I have a few older combat officers to check his recklessness."

"Unlike me?"

"I would never publicly say anything like that, Tribune Scipio," Thaddeus remarked. Then he called to a Centurion. "Send a runner to our wagon train. Have him bring up a mount for the Tribune."

A shout came from the top of the slope. Legionaries hopped around in frustration. Experienced Centurions held them from descending to the river's edge.

"The Africans are clustered at the landing spot. If your Legionaries wanted to attack, they would have to wade out in the river," Cornelius noted. "Some might slip and drown, and anyone wounded would certainly go under and be swept downstream."

"And so, my experienced combat officers stopped the Legionaries for their own good," Thaddeus pointed out.

"Since you can't use cavalry."

"It's a little more complicated than that."

"Is it?" Cornelius inquired. "Because Tribune, it's a steep slope and a river. There's nothing complicated about it. It's simple geography."

When the runner returned with a horse, Cornelius mounted. After Thaddeus issued orders to his Centuries to guard the crossing, the two staff officers trotted away from the battle. They rode in the direction of North Casilinum, the bridge, and the survivors of Optio Pollio's command.

***

Five fresh Centuries controlled the streets leading into the town. A Centurion saluted as Thaddeus approached a Legion guard position. Then the combat officer waved him to a stop.

"We've got a problem, sir," the officer informed him.

"How many did we lose during the fighting?" Thaddeus asked.

"None, sir. We hit the Africans from behind and broke their lines. They ran like a pack of stray dogs," the Centurion assured him. "No sir, casualties aren't the issue. The Senior Centurion from Benevento rode in as we were removing the bodies."

Thaddeus didn't say anything. He kicked the horse and galloped towards the bridge. Not understanding the situation, but being curious, Cornelius put his heels into the mount's flanks and raced after the Tribune.

They shot by patrols of Legionaries, calmly walking the streets. For all the urgency of the Tribune for the Second Maniple, the Legionaries appeared relaxed.

As they came within sight of the gate wall at the bridge, the first sign of trouble appeared. An armed and armored Century filled the street. And not just in a haphazard manner, the eighty Legionaries were in an assault formation. Facing them were ten cavalrymen and a Senior Centurion.

"Thaddeus, get your people out of my way," the senior combat officer ordered.

"That's Tribune Thaddeus to you, Centurion," Thaddeus growled as he dismounted.

"Fine. Tribune Thaddeus. Produce the murderer," the Senior Centurion responded. "Or move these misfits out of my way and I'll get him myself."

"These men are Legionaries of Rome," Thaddeus insisted. "They've been trained, bloodied, pardoned, and accepted into the Legion of the Republic. Do not slander them or I'll have you up on charges of inciting a riot."

"Have it your way. I'll respect the Legionaries. But the Centurion hasn't been pardoned. And he's been convicted and sentenced to the wood by the Magistrate of Benevento. Just hand him over and I'll be on my way."

Thaddeus strolled to the wall of shields, leaned over the edge of one, and inquired, "How are you Optio Decimia?"

"Sir, we hit the African Corps hard and they broke contact," Sidia replied. "He had us come in on their flank. That really messed them up."

"It usually does," Thaddeus agreed. "Where is he?"

"He's in the office doing the after-action reports. We don't want him taken, sir."

Cornelius dropped to the ground and marched to the Tribune.

"I don't mean to tell you how to command a Maniple," he said softly. "But if you're harboring a murder in your ranks, he needs to be turned over to the sentencing authority."

"Every man in our Legion, until a few weeks ago, was a slave or a criminal," Thaddeus disclosed. "Now they are Legionaries of Rome."

"Except one," the Senior Centurion asserted.

"He's a special case," Thaddeus protested.

Behind the rogue Century, Optio Sertor had quietly shoved his Legionaries and units of Praeneste infantry into

198

position. When they were in assault lines, the NCO smashed his fist into the palm of the other hand. A signal telling Cornelius that he only needed to give the word and the Optio would punish the rebellious Century.

"He's nothing special," the Senior Centurion affirmed. "In two days, he's going to watch his last sunset from rooftop height."

"If you need help," Cornelius offered.

Before Thaddeus responded, the door to the command office opened and a ghost walked through the door. Cornelius rocked back from the impact of the shock.

Jace Kasia, with a Centurion's helmet under his arm, stepped into the street. Seeing his Century aligned in a combat formation and other infantrymen behind them, he raised his free hand.

"Legionaries of the Twenty-fifth Century," Jace declared, "it's been an honor fighting with you. But the fight is over. Stand by."

"Standing by, Centurion."

"Sheath your blades and break your formation."

As Sidia checked that the Century complied with the order, a curious murmur ran though the Legionaries and the officers. Not understanding, they watched as a Tribune splattered with blood marched to Jace, gripped Centurion Kasia's shoulders, then stepped back.

***

"I thought you were dead," Cornelius exclaimed. "Killed up north at Silva Litana."

"Not that it matters as I'll soon be crucified at Benevento," Jace replied. "But I heard you were killed at Cannae along with your Legion."

The two men gripped wrists. They held on for long moments as if the other would vanish when they let go.

"This is not a reunion of long-lost acquaintances or a social club," the Centurion from Benevento stated while urging his horse forward. Then to his cavalrymen, he ordered. "Take the criminal Kasia into custody."

The ten horses only took one step when Cornelius lifted an arm, pointed a finger at the sky, then made a circling motion with the hand.

"Optio Sertor. If the riders come another step closer, I want a shield wall around them," he directed. "Keep them penned in for their own protection. Understand?"

"Yes, sir," the NCO replied. "Century stand by."

"Standing by, Optio."

The Senior Centurion slipped from the saddle, dropped to the ground, and bellowed, "Are all of you insane? That man is condemned to death for murder."

"Only because of a technicality in his pardon," Thaddeus stressed.

"Gentlemen. Let's go into the office and discuss this," Cornelius offered.

"I've got a Tribune of Second Maniple who doesn't follow orders. A prisoner in command of a Century of infantrymen," The Senior Centurion listed. "And a boy Tribune who thinks he's a full-grown officer."

Cornelius reached up and used his palm to rub at the blood splatted on his face. Then he held the hand up and studied the red smear. Smiling, he peered across the street at his NCO.

"Optio Sertor. Put the cavalrymen in the dirt," he ordered. "And keep them there until I say otherwise."

In a rush, a hundred infantrymen dashed from side streets, leaped on the cavalrymen and in moments, the Legion riders were sitting or lying in the street. All protested and a few attempted to stand. They were rudely knocked down by Legionaries using the big infantry shields.

"Not until the Tribune says otherwise," Sertor informed the embarrassed cavalrymen.

"I have never," the Senior Centurion began to complain.

But Cornelius shoved his bloody hand in the man's face.

"This boy Tribune commands a thousand heavy and light infantrymen. And we've just fought a battle on three fronts and held the bridge against all odds," Cornelius informed the senior officer. "When I said let's go into the office and discuss this, it wasn't a suggestion."

Grabbing Jace's arm, Cornelius walked him back into the headquarters building. Moments later, Thaddeus strolled in with a smile on his face. They had all taken seats when the Senior Centurion stomped in, sulking like a child.

***

"Centurion Kasia earned his position in the battle of Benevento by saving the right side of Gracchus Legion East," Thaddeus explained. "The Proconsul himself wrote up the Centurion's paperwork, his pardon for crimes committed against Rome or citizens of the Republic, and a letter of commendation for a medal."

"That should have settled the matter right there," Cornelius remarked.

"It would have except the Proconsul had been given command of Legions composed of slaves and criminals. The nonstandard Legions were expected to break in combat," Thaddeus told him. "When Consul Fabius left for Rome, he gave the authority to command the Legions to Gracchus, along with the ability to pardon or free any infantryman he desired. But not the power to make a Legion officer of a wanted Hirpini tribesman. Especially after the tribe sided with Hannibal."

"And that's why I'm taking Kasia back to Benevento," the Senior Centurion boomed. "It's been several weeks and no one in authority has responded. And I don't expect them to because, in the eyes of the law, he is guilty. I'm sick of waiting for a magistrate from Rome to sign the pardon for a Hirpini. Let justice be served, I say."

"This does present an interesting dilemma," Cornelius admitted.

"The problem here, boy Tribune, is the trouble you're in for interfering with the duty of a Senior Centurion. And for abusing my detail. What command are you with?"

Thaddeus dipped his head as a way to show he couldn't help the young Tribune. Even Jace dropped his eyes. He felt bad about getting the Tribune entangled in the messy situation.

"If I come quietly, Senior Centurion, will you overlook the intrusion by Tribune Scipio?" Jace asked.

"I'll consider it. After we get back to Benevento."

Jace stood, and together with the Senior Centurion, they took a couple of steps towards the doorway. Thaddeus ground his teeth. And he locked his hands together to keep from drawing his gladius and doing something that would get him crucified.

When the arresting authority and the condemned man were halfway to the exit, Cornelius rose from his chair.

"Centurion?" he called out.

Both the senior combat officer and Jace glanced back.

"What is it now?" the Senior Centurion demanded.

"I wasn't addressing you," Cornelius whispered as if he was in deep thought. Then, in a clear voice, he stated. "I was addressing Centurion Lucius Jace Romiliia. You can't know this, Jace, but before you died, the Senate voted to recognize you as a descendant of Lucius Romiliia. And they decreed that your family be reinstated into the Patrician class."

"If you think I'm going to take your desperate lie as a reason to free this murdering tribesman, you are sadly mistaken."

"I thought nothing of the sort," Cornelius confessed. He dipped his hand into a pack beside the desk and extracted a small scroll. "But you will honor this."

As the Senior Centurion unrolled the scroll, Cornelius set a bottle of ink and a pen on the top of his desk. Then after brushing a piece of parchment flat, he wrote a few lines. When he finished, he handed the note to the senior officer and took the scroll back.

Without another word, the Senior Centurion of Benevento saluted, about-faced, and marched for the door. Cornelius rushed to the exit and leaned out.

"Optio Sertor. The matter is settled," he told the NCO. "Allow the cavalrymen to go about their day."

"Yes, Tribune."

As Cornelius ducked back into the room, Thaddeus confronted him.

"What just happened?" the Tribune questioned. "He left but you never answered his question. What is your command, Scipio?"

Cornelius took the scroll from the desk and passed it to Thaddeus.

Jace shrugged and inquired, "Am I not being returned to Benevento for execution?"

"No, you aren't going to be crucified Centurion Kasia, or should I call you, Centurion Romiliia Kasia," Thaddeus replied. "Because an assistant Aedile of Rome has signed off on your pardon."

"Just what is your command, Cornelius?" Jace asked.

"My command? I'm assigned to the Senate and answer to the people of Rome," Cornelius informed him. "My bosses are the two Consuls and the Director of the Temples of Rome. And you and I need to leave Casilinum before first light."

"Why me?" Jace inquired. "I'd like to stay with my Century."

"By law, an Aedile must be twenty-five years old to sign a legal document."

"You and I are the same age," Jace divulged. "And I'm not..."

Thaddeus dropped the scroll on the desk. Then he turned Jace to face him.

"Go say your goodbyes to your Legionaries and pack," he suggested. "Tribune Scipio and I need to discuss the transfer of command for the garrison of North Casilinum and the bridge detachment."

Chapter 21 – One's Own Ignorance

"Proconsul Claudius Marcellus, using a strategy built on foresight and nerve, waited for his Legions to be fully engaged against the Punic forces. Then, in a masterful tactic, he ordered the baggage train to storm through the gates of Nola," Cornelius described to the Senators of Rome. He took a few breaths to let the legislators puzzle out the meaning of the action. Most couldn't guess at where the report was going, causing them to grow impatient for the answer. Once Cornelius knew they were paying attention, he concluded his account of the battle. "When Hannibal Barca saw the clouds of dust from the 'reinforcements', his army retreated in a mad rush to get away from Marcellus' mules and his teamsters."

Laughter greeted his portrayal as well as cheers for Claudius Marcellus. Cornelius stood rigid, allowing the accolades to be directed at the absent Proconsul and not at the bearer of the story. But in his mind, young Scipio counted supporters of Marcellus who appreciated the report and the act of deference. At a date in the future, he would call on those Senators for a vote to gain him the command of a Legion.

For all the Plebeian support, he noticed many Patricians who didn't appreciate a nobleman's son, singing the praises of a new man.

"A fine report, Tribune Scipio," Valerius Flaccus complimented him. "If there is nothing else. I'll ask you to leave the Senate floor."

"Consul, I have one more piece of business," Cornelius revealed. He paused until the Consul gave him approval. "Last year, the Senate recognized Lucius Romiliia as the head of a Patrician family. Shortly afterward, we believed him dead. However, he survived the falling trees that murdered two Legions up north and now he has returned to Rome. And not just as a nobleman, but as a hero of the Republic. For his actions at Benevento, where he saved his Legion, I ask that every courtesy be extended to Centurion Lucius Romiliia Kasia."

Cornelius pointed to the gallery. In a new set of ceremonial armor, Jace braced, raised his arm in salute, and gazed over the Senate.

"I move that the Senate embrace Centurion Romiliia and reward his act of bravery," Senator Alerio Sisera declared.

One of Claudius Marcellus' associates stood, nodded to Cornelius, and announced, "I second the motion to extend all courtesy to Centurion Romiliia, a friend of Tribune Scipio."

Cornelius shivered a little at the mention of him in conjunction with honoring Jace. The reference probably cost him a future vote.

Hands shout up, everyone wanting to support a hero of Rome. Rather than call for a vote, Valerius Flaccus counted the enthusiasm.

"The motion carries," the Consul stated. "All services and departments will make special exemptions for Centurion Romiliia."

Cornelius saluted the Consul, left faced, and marched up the aisle.

***

As Valerius Flaccus brought up other matters, Cornelius reached Jace.

"How did I look?" the archer inquired. "Because I feel like a celebrant of Até."

"There's no hint of the Goddess of Fraud in you," Cornelius assured him. "You are a picture of…"

Before he could finish, Hektor Nicanor stepped between the two Legion officers.

"My, but you have changed," Senator Sisera's aide remarked. The Greek looked from one to the other. "Both of you."

206

"Have you come to admire the future of Roman nobility?" Jace teased.

"The Senator sent me to ask a former Legion officer which country he would like to be exiled to," Hektor answered.

"I won't go back to Crete," Jace said. "It's a hilly isle and feels confined after you're travel across it a few times."

"I'll remember that when it's your turn to temp the wrath of the Senate of Rome," Hektor told Jace. Looking at Cornelius, the Greek advised. "Be at the Senator's village before dark. And bring Centurion Kasia. Lady Gabriella will want to see him."

Hektor vanished into the crowd, leaving Jace and Cornelius looking at an empty spot on the tile floor.

"Apparently, Nicanor doesn't like the Romiliia name," Jace commented. Then after a moment, he asked. "You started to say what I looked like. What was it?"

Cornelius continued to stare at the empty spot.

"You would make a perfect model for a sculpture of a Centurion," Scipio said without inflection. "We should go."

"Absolutely, let's go. I'm hungry."

"We'll eat later. Right now, we're going to see an Aedile of Rome to get your documents signed properly."

"Wait. I almost forgot, it's you who honored Até, the Goddess of Fraud."

"Keep talking Kasia and I'll ship you back to Benevento in a cage."

"Is that an example of the courtesy extended by the Senate of Rome?" Jace questioned.

"No. That's the response of a worried Tribune."

The two marched towards the building's exit. Their hobnailed boots clicking a rhythm on the travertine floor as they left the Senate.

***

Aedile Sandalius had to search the piles of parchment on his desk before he located the correct one. If Cornelius hadn't insisted, the document from Proconsul Gracchus would have remained missing until next year when the new Aedile was elected. After signing, he demanded Jace, and Cornelius, stay for conversation and refreshments.

Later than Cornelius wanted, the two mounted and rode across the Capital to Villa Sisera.

The block of travertine at the entrance remained where it was the first time they visited. And in the bright afternoon sunlight, the chiseled message, *Memento mori*, almost appeared to be a natural part of the stone.

"Remember you to will die," Jace read as they stepped up to the door. "Senator Sisera holds the Goddess of Death close to his heart."

"If the scars on his body are any indication," Cornelius stated, "he's danced often in Nenia's presence."

The door opened and a household guard examined the two Legion officers.

"Tribune, Centurion, come in," he invited. "Colonel Sisera isn't back from the Senate yet."

"We can wait," Cornelius assured him.

They marched into the great room and stood looking across the space at a garden. Facing away from the hallway, they didn't notice Lady Gabrielle before she breezed into the room.

"Tribune Scipio, how nice of you to visit," Gabrielle DeMarco Sisera greeted them. As Cornelius and Jace turned to face the lady of the house, her eyes popped wide open, and her mouth formed a surprised 'O'. "Lucius. We heard that you were dead."

"I've come close recently but haven't been killed yet. It is nice, ma'am, to know someone cares."

"You sound like your father. He was a charmer as well," with dignity barely controlling her enthusiasm, Gabrielle rushed to Jace and hugged him. "Come, we'll have vino and talk."

She took Jace's arm and guided him and Cornelius into a side room. Servants brought wine and cheese and placed the snacks on tables besides sofas. Once their glasses were filled, the three reclined.

"Do you have any idea why the Senator wanted to see me here?" Cornelius asked.

"Specifically, I don't. But years ago, Alerio built warships to patrol the east coast to protect our trading vessels from pirates," she replied. "Republic fleets do the patrolling nowadays. But Alerio keeps in contact with people about the politics of Illyria and Greece."

"Yes, ma'am. But what does that have to do with me?"

"Two days ago, the Senator received a letter from Greece. Something in it disturbed him," Gabrielle informed Cornelius. "Then we received word that you had returned to Rome, and he brightened up. I don't know if the two are connected. But, it's probable."

From the doorway, Alerio Sisera declared, "It's more than probable, wife of mine. It's practical in several ways."

Gabrielle slid off the sofa and went to the Senator. As she kissed him, he attempted to take the glass of wine from her hand.

"Hektor, please pour my husband a glass of watered vino," she directed. Then whirling to face Cornelius and Jace, she told them. "You will be staying for dinner."

"Yes ma'am," they replied.

As she left, Alerio Sisera settled onto his wife's couch and accepted a glass of weak vino from his aide.

"What's practical?" Cornelius inquired.

"The Greek philosopher Socrates professed his ignorance of many subjects," Alerio Sisera described between sips. "Yet of this, he was sure; Human wisdom begins with the recognition of one's own ignorance."

"This is a trap, isn't it Senator?" Jace questioned. "Because in archery training, you don't learn until you do wrong, and your instructor points out your flaws."

Cornelius poured another glass of wine, settled back, and raised the vessel to the Senator.

"I expect the ignorance is directed at me," he suggested.

"Not in the way you might think," Sisera corrected. "You have a depth of supporters in the Senate. But Tribune Scipio, you seem ignorant of the reverse. All the Senators who want you gone."

"Gone, Senator?" Jace questioned.

"Like a puff of smoke," Alerio confirmed.

"I realize I have my detractors," Cornelius professed. "But my family has always had enemies."

"The ones I'm referring to are generated by your actions and not those of your father or uncle. Take for example the young noblemen you threatened at sword point."

"They were talking about deserting the Republic," Cornelius protested.

"Your heart was in the right place, but it resulted in a handful of new enemies. And just as the long memory of the

210

Senate began to forget your insurrection," the Senator told him. Cornelius sat up and opened his mouth to protest. But the Senator held up a hand to stop him, "you arrive in Rome declaring the virtues of a Plebeian Proconsul."

"Claudius Marcellus bested Hannibal on the field of battle. He made the Punic General break contact and run," Cornelius blurted out as he jumped to his feet. "He is the first Roman General to succeed. I will not apologize for carrying the word of his victory to the Senate."

"Nor would I ask you to," the Senator assured him. "But had I known about the report, I could have softened the impact on you by questioning you to draw out the information. As it stands now, you need to leave Rome before a group of Patrician Senators vote to exile you. And that's where practical comes in. I require your assistance."

"To go to Greece?" Cornelius scoffed. "I need to be where a Legion is facing Hannibal. Not sailing in the other direction."

"Human wisdom begins with the recognition of one's own ignorance," Alerio Sisera repeated.

For a few long moments nobody said anything. Then Jace cleared his throat.

"Need I remind you, Senator Sisera, I was raised on Crete," he emphasized. "Greek is my native tongue. And the customs are not foreign to me. But I am a coinless and homeless Roman nobleman. What does the job pay?"

"The reward is the gratitude of a grateful Republic," Sisera responded.

"No offense Senator but I can't eat that."

"True. But you can live on the salary of a Senior Centurion of the fleet or cavalry, whichever you prefer."

211

Cornelius dropped onto the sofa and slapped his own forehead.

"One's own ignorance," he whined. "This isn't a mission from the Senate. It's personal for you. And you are prepared to reward us with titles and positions."

This time it was Sisera who raised his glass to Cornelius.

"What does your newly discovered wisdom want, Tribune Scipio?" the Senator questioned.

"I want a Legion."

"That is politically impossible. Even if I loaned you the coins, the Senate would strip you of the Centuries before you had them trained."

"Seeing as I'm wiser than before, what do you suggest?"

"Complete the mission and next year I'll get you and your cousin elected as Aediles of Rome."

"Unfortunately, I'm but twenty years old, Senator."

"That's why I added your cousin. He'll sign everything you initial to keep the documents legal. After a year as an Aedile, you'll know rich and important men who will back you in any venture you desire."

"Including his building of a Legion?" Jace inquired.

"If the Tribune wants to be a Prorogatio of Provincial Legions, there'll be few who will stop him."

"Except the Senators with long memories," Jace proposed as Lady Gabriella appeared in the doorway.

"We'll both go," Cornelius announced.

"Go where?" Gabriella demanded.

"To dinner, wife of mine," the Senator told her. "The boys will need a good meal before leaving."

"Jace just got to Rome, and Cornelius has barely been home," Gabriella protested. "Where on earth are they going?"

"To Delphi to see the Oracle," Senator Sisera replied, "among other places. Now everyone, I am hungry, let us go and eat."

Act 8

Chapter 22 - Twine, Rail, and Constellation

As both a scholar and a Senator, Quintus Pictor was accustomed to getting his way. Understandably, he became irate when Cornelius and Jace arrived at the pier and disrupted his plans.

"I have, already, selected the representatives who will accompany me to Delphi," he complained. Then pointing to a Senior Tribune, an Optio, and four infantrymen, he stated. "And we have sufficient security. Why am I being burdened with two more Legion officers?"

"Pirates, sir," Cornelius replied. "I am a tactician and Centurion Kasia is a master archer."

"An archer at sea," Pictor scowled. "I see no value in the skill during a sea battle."

Cornelius ran his eyes down the length of the liburna. At one hundred and nine feet in length and sixteen in width, the ship was smaller than a trireme. Although the single banker accommodated thirty-six oarsmen, making her fast and agile, the upswept overhanging prow offered no ram to damage an enemy warship. The thought of a sea battle in the light vessel was laughable.

"Sir, you are charged with consulting the Oracle about how the Republic can defeat Hannibal Barca," Cornelius offered to Pictor. "We're simply an extra level of security to keep you safe."

"Senior Tribune Terrigenus, your thoughts?" Pictor asked his military aide.

"They are young. Probably have never seen the sight of blood," the officer projected. "But Kirra is a rough town, and two more men can't hurt."

"As long as they don't get in my way," Pictor declared.

The Senator hurried to where two other men stood surveying the birds flying over the Ionian Sea. One had on the toga of a priest while the other wore a multicolored robe.

"Which temple is the priest from?" Cornelius inquired.

"The Temple of Jupiter. He's Master Pictor's spiritual adviser," Terrigenus answered. Then he chuckled and added. "Don't even bother asking about the one in the bright robe. Ennius claims the spirit of Homer has been reborn in him."

"Can he tell us about the siege of Troy during the Trojan War?" Cornelius inquired.

"I really can't tell you," the Senior Tribune admitted. "He slips between Latin, Greek, and an old tongue I don't recognize. He's almost unintelligible."

Behind the senior officer, the NCO directed the four Legionaries to discard their armor and stow their shields.

"Do you want us in armor or in travel clothing?" Jace asked.

"It's a day and a half sailing over open water to reach the Island of Lefkada," the officer told him. "You might as well be comfortable. But keep your weapons nearby."

Cornelius and Jace located empty spots on the deck. After stripping off their armor and pulling on woolen trousers and shirts, they sat and peered down the length of the transport.

"We're going to cross the Ionian Sea in this?" Jace asked as he felt the hemp fibers on a piece of rope.

The poet in the bright robe moved towards the new arrivals. Distracted by the rigging and ships equipment, Jace and Cornelius didn't notice the man.

"We'll leave at moonrise," a rower informed them, "navigate by the stars, and make landfall tomorrow afternoon. If it pleases Neptune."

"And if it doesn't?" Jace inquired.

"Then no one will ever know we existed," the sailor answered.

The poet spoke, but to the rowers and Cornelius, it sounded as if he talked with a mouth full of pebbles. Only a few Latin and Greek words were clear. The rest blurred into incoherent syllables.

"Very profound," Jace replied to the poet.

"You understood him?" Cornelius asked.

"Sure, he's mixing Latin, Greek, and Oscan, the old language of the Samnite people," Jace explained. "He said everyone on this boat may drown and be forgotten. As for him, let no one weep for Ennius, or celebrate his funeral with mourning; for Ennius still lives, as his name will be passed to and fro through the mouths of men."

"He's pretty confident about his fame," Cornelius commented. "But I've never heard of him."

Ennius bowed, spoke in his unique manner, then turned and went back to Pictor and the priest.

"I think, possibly, the poet agrees with you," Jace speculated.

"You don't sound sure."

"I'm not. But what do you think?" Jace stated. "Ennius said, *the victor is not victorious if the vanquished does not consider himself so.*"

"If I don't consider him famous, then he admits he's not?"

"Well stated, don't you think?"

Before Cornelius could reply, the master of the ship shouted, "Get some sleep. We'll be sailing the dark and I need fresh eyes for the voyage."

Oarsmen pulled blankets from under their rowing benches and hopped to the pier. All thirty-six plus the navigator, the rear oarsman, and the ship's master stretched out and fell asleep. It happened so fast, Pictor, the priest, and the poet broke from their conference, glanced around, and ogled the bodies on the dock.

"Everything is fine, Master Pictor," Terrigenus promised the Senator.

Reassured that the crew hadn't died or taken ill, the three representatives continued to caucus.

***

"Stroke, stroke, stroke," the Captain called the cadence. "Keep it together. Stroke, stroke."

Under oar power, the liburna slipped from the dock at Crotone. Slowly, the vessel left the pier and the glow from the torches. As the black expanse swallowed the ship, the merriment from Legionaries and civilians on the streets of the port city faded until the splashing of thirty-six oars filled the night.

"Navigator, get your twine and rail," the master of the ship directed. "If we're to find land tomorrow, we'll need a good start tonight."

In the starlight, the navigator lifted the end of a piece of twine and put it between his teeth. Then he elevated a length of wood until the slat was held against the stars. With one end of the twine in his mouth and the other tied to the end of the slat, he formed an arrow with the apparatus.

"Starboard, a little," he mumbled.

"Come starboard," the ship's master instructed.

Aft of the Captain and the navigator, the helmsmen adjusted the rear oar and the prow of the ship drifted to the right. In response, the stick and stars lined up, and the taut twine pointed down the length of the ship.

"That's our heading," the navigator declared.

The Captain licked his forefinger and held it up.

"Wind from the northwest," he observed. "We'll ride a little north to offset the wind."

"Angle towards the Herdsmen?" the helmsmen offered.

"The Boötes constellation is fine," the master agreed. "But don't get us too far north."

Jace felt the movement as the liburna drifted left. Even if he didn't feel the change in heading, the stars overhead shifted letting him know they were on a new course.

"Check again," the master told his navigator.

The rail was lifted to the sky and the twine put back into the man's mouth. In moments, he held up his free hand and extended three fingers. Dropping one, he lowered the device.

"We're two fingers north of the direct course."

"Good enough," the master announced. "Sailors, unroll the main sail and set the headsail."

Selected rowers pulled in their oars before leaving their benches. Jace and Cornelius watched the shadowy figures move about the deck.

"Maybe I'll become a ship's master," Jace remarked.

"Not me," Cornelius said. "I'll stick with the Legions and solid ground."

As they talked, the big sail rolled free, and the sailors tied lines from the material to the gunwales. At the bow, the smaller headsail filled with wind, blocking the stars above the horizon.

"Let-her-run," the Captain called out. The rowers pushed down on their oars, lifting the blades from the water. Once the craft shifted from oars to wind power, he proclaimed. "Twine, rail, and constellation."

The navigator responded by placing the twine between his teeth and raising the rail to the heavens.

"Port a nudge," the navigator mumbled through clenched teeth.

"Give me a hands width port side on the oar," the Captain told the helmsman. Then to the waiting rowers, he ordered. "Way enough! Toss oars."

The rowers put pressure on the handles and lifted their oars with their outboard arms. For a moment, all thirty-six oars pointed at the stars. Then in sections, the oars were stowed along the inside of the gunwales.

Without the splash of oars, and the calls of stroke, stroke to keep everyone on pace, the ship quieted down.

"See, sailing is peaceful," Jace said. "Listen to the flapping of the sail cloth and the water along the hull. Nice, isn't it?"

"Twine, rail, and constellation," the master directed. "Sailors, check your tie lines."

As the navigator lifted the device to the stars, and sailors moved around the tight space, Jace asked, "How long will that go on?"

"Until sunrise," a rower answered. "You get accustomed to it."

"After how long?" Jace inquired.

"It took me two or three crossings of the Ionian," the rower told him.

Jace leaned into Cornelius.

"I may have to find a different form of employment."

"How about my Master of Horse," Cornelius joked.

"I can see you as a General," Jace said. "But me as your deputy? I'm an archer, not a Legion commander."

"You're a Centurion," Cornelius reminded him.

"That's right, I am. Without my Century, I forget."

Jace had just closed his eyes when the Captain instructed, "Twine, rail, and constellation. Sailors, check your tie lines."

"Definitely not a sailor," Jace sighed while trying to find a comfortable position between rowing benches.

***

Just before dawn a squall dampened the sails. The cloth sagged from the moisture but not enough to require the ship to go to oars. It did soak the men and equipment, while filling the hull with water. Working parties began to bail out the bilge. Beneath the headsail, one rower pulled buckets of water from under the forward deck and passed the containers to a second. At the railing, a third tossed the water over the side. In the aft, another team bailed out the water that was making the liburna sluggish.

"Allow me to point out that a horse doesn't require this many men to maintain it," Cornelius quipped. "And you know you don't have to do that."

In the weak rays of a new day, the Tribune leaned on the rail, watching Jace.

"I'm from Crete," the archer responded as he took a full bucket and dumped it over the side. "We prefer to run hills rather than ride horses around them. And I was sleeping here when the first bucket was passed over. I figured it was good exercise."

The master of the ship stepped in front of Jace.

"You don't have to do that," he told the archer. "No one realized it was a passenger at the rail."

"Captain, what was I to do, sit around while others work? That's not in my nature."

"You're an odd noblemen."

"You have no idea," Jace assured him.

He leaned around the Captain and took the handle of the next pail of dirty water.

"Change up," the Captain called out.

Fore and aft, fresh trios of rowers replaced the first shift. Jace stepped away, making room for the next oarsman at the gunwale. He stretched and smiled at Cornelius.

"You're correct, Tribune Scipio. I can't be a sailor because with or without a horse, there's no room to run on a ship."

As the sun appeared over the horizon, the sail dried and filled to capacity. Now in daylight, the liburna smoothly sailed towards the island of Lefkada.

***

For the rest of the day, the wind continued to propel them eastward. When the teal of the Ionian Sea became tinted with a spots of brilliant turquoise, the crew began pulling on the rails or pushing against each other.

"What's going on?" Cornelius inquired.

An oarsmen, bent over and braced against the side of the ship, looked under his arm at the Tribune.

"We're getting near land," he replied. "That means we're in the waters of coastal pirates. We're warming up in case we have to row away from them."

"Is there's a chance of them boarding us?" Jace asked.

"The costal scum? No way. We'll leave them sitting with a limp sail as if they were in the middle of a calm," the rower bragged. "But if we come across an Illyrian, that's a different matter."

"Are they faster?" Cornelius questioned.

"More determined," the oarsmen offered as he stretched his arms and back. "Once they spot your ship, it's not a matter of if, but when they catch you."

"Toss Oars!" the Captain shouted, which ended the conversation. In what could have been a confusing mess, the rowers, pulled their oars out in turn and held them upright. Once all thirty-six were weaving in the air, the ship's master commanded, "Blades down. Stroke, stroke."

The blades moved while the sails bellowed with air. And for a short spell, the ship raced over the swells, slamming into wave after wave.

"Neither man nor ship is meant to go at this rate," the Captain warned. "Sailors, roll the sails before we shake her apart."

In a rush to slow the ship, the designated sailors brought in their oars before attending to the main sail and the headsail. And just as the turquoise sea faded to teal, the liburna settled into the smooth rhythm of the oars. Not much later, the navigator announced, "Land sighted off the starboard side."

"Helm, give us a little starboard oar," the Captain instructed.

A few hundred strokes later, hand appeared in front of the ship.

And, as the sun lowered to the horizon, appearing under the upswept beam that hovered over the navigator, the Captain declared, "A good crossing. Thanks to you all and the blessings of Neptune."

"The blessings of Neptune," the rowers repeated as they stroked for dry land.

The God of the Sea had indeed blessed the voyage so far.

Chapter 23 – Deterring the Determined

The Roman delegation to Delphi learned that the crew had a system after crossing the sea. An exhausted captain, navigator, and helmsman stood briefly and delivered prayers to Neptune. When they finished, crewmen threw offerings of grain into the surf to honor the God. Then, while the three men who went sleepless rested, fires were built, and pots slung over the flames.

A few crewmen tossed nets into the sea to gather the fish that Neptune sent to eat the sacrificial grain. While pulling in the catch, the rowers repeated, "The blessings of Neptune. The blessings of Neptune."

Later, the Captain, navigator, and helmsman awakened to eat fish and grain before climbing back under their blankets. They barely spoke to Quintus Pictor and his company or the crew.

"I guess we aren't going anywhere tonight," Terrigenus noted. "Optio Perperna, set a guard for the night."

"Put me on the rotation," Jace told the NCO.

"Sir, we can handle the guard," Perperna assured him.

"Maybe so. But I'm a combat officer not a staff officer," Jace explained as he marched to face the NCO. "You will put me on the rotation. All the duty shouldn't fall on just four Legionaries."

The Optio glanced in the direction of Senior Tribune Terrigenus for guidance.

Before the staff officer could interject himself, Cornelius advised, "Senior Tribune Terrigenus, I would not get involved. Centurion Kasia doesn't wear the medal. But when he saved his Legion at Benevento, he stood in a volley of lances and charging horsemen to mark where he wanted the defensive line to reform. You can imagine, sir, he has strong feelings about how to manage Optios, Centurions, and Tribunes."

"By all means, Centurion Kasia, you do as you please."

"I intended to, Senior Tribune," Jace responded. He hooked the arm of the NCO and began walking the Optio up a hill. As they climbed higher and had a better view of the sea, Centurion Kasia told him. "We'll want two positions. One up here to watch for arriving ships and another on the far side of the camp..."

"That'll put us in a position to watch the trail leading to the crew, and Senator Pictor," the NCO said finishing the sentence. Then he nodded and declared. "I hadn't thought of two posts for the night, sir."

"I'm a Centurion of the Legion. It's my job to help," Jace told him. "I approve of your choice for two positions. Now walk us down and show me where you want the other guard post."

They hiked downhill, crossed the camp, and stopped at the beginning of a trail. Where the path crossed an open field, the NCO pointed to the ground.

"We can put the second guard position here."

Jace looked down the trail, turned and peered at the top of the far hill.

"Good line of sight. Now we flip a coin."

"A coin, sir?"

"Sure. To see which of us has to sleep down here with the bugs. And who gets to watch the sunset over the sea."

Moments later, Jace walked into camp and said good night to Cornelius. After collecting his gear and long pack, he gathered two Legionaries, and they hiked to the top of the hill.

Not far away, Perperna marched into camp with his head high and his chest puffed up.

"Did the Centurion give you any trouble?" the Senior Tribune questioned. He assumed, based on the NCOs posture, that there had been issues. "I can set him straight if needed."

"No problem, sir. He's a combat officer for sure," the NCO observed, "and he understands the need to have a line of sight between guard posts."

"Why, Optio Perperna, I'm surprised at your knowledge of field craft. All this time, I thought you were only a bodyguard and an NCO of the honor guard."

"I don't often get a chance to display my expertise while guarding doors to conference rooms, sir," Perperna bragged.

From where he sat eating a bowl of roasted fish and grain, Cornelius overheard the discussion. Between bites, he whispered, "Perhaps, Senator Pictor, you don't have as much security as you might think."

***

With just a hint of the coming dawn in the sky, the Captain ordered his passengers on board and the crew to cluster on three sides of the hull. Before he issued the launch order, the ship's master walked to the raised foredeck and peered over the side.

"I don't want to leave you in the surf," he notified the man not in his crew.

"Captain, I'm a better than average climber," Jace assured him. "And I have no intention of being left on the beach."

"Crew brace," the captain announced as he walked to the center of his ship. "Launch!"

Thirty-seven backs bent to the task and the liburna transport slid off the sand and gravel and into the gentle waves. When the bow section entered deeper water, rowers at the front scrambled up the sides and dropped onto their rowing positions. As more of the length transitioned from land to sea, oarsmen climbed and took their places on the bench.

"Stroke, stroke," the Captain called. "Pick up the cadence. Stroke, stroke."

With more and more rowers adding their oars to the strokes, the ship swiftly left the shallows. Then, fearing what might be a problem, the ship's master glanced at the shoreline to see if he left anyone stranded.

"A refreshing dip in the sea is a great way to start the day," Jace stated while squeezing around the Captain. "Excuse, me sir."

In his years of transporting cargo and passengers, the ship's master had seen all types of soldiers. The list included tribal warriors, mercenaries, more than his fair share of uptight staff officers, and Legionaries, both recruits and veterans. But he had rarely encountered a Centurion willing to stand guard overnight and voluntarily help push the ship into the sea.

"You are excused," the Captain said as Centurion Kasia made his way to Cornelius.

Jace sat beside his long pack.

"I'm not impressed by the skills of Senior Tribune Terrigenus' hand-picked security detail," he confided to Cornelius.

"We'll need to keep an eye on Senator Pictor, if things get out of hand."

"Agreed," Jace added.

The Legion officers watched as the island drifted by the rails of the ship.

***

Once beyond the tip of Lefkada, the transport tracked southeast, threading between islands. Near midday the crew and passengers lounged in the warmth of the sun. It appeared as if they were suspended in a living fresco. A blue dome capped the sky, the sails puffed out from the breeze, and sunlight reflected off white rock faces of a few islands. Setting a floor for those elements, the turquoise sea completed the mural.

Then the peace shattered.

"Illyrian raider," a lookout shouted, "off the starboard side."

In an orderly manner, the rowers took to their benches and lifted their oars from their resting places.

"Let fall," the Captain instructed. "Sailors, roll the sails."

As the crew prepared to race the raider, Optio Perperna begged his Legionaries.

"Get your gear on," he whined. "Hurry up. We may be in for a fight."

"But Optio, I can't swim in the armor," one complained.

"Just get ready. But stay down and out of sight."

In the aft section, Senior Tribune Terrigenus held his arms out as if he was a mother hen shielding Pictor, the priest, and the poet from a hawk.

"If it comes to a fight, we're sunk," Jace projected.

"Our leader is occupied guarding his political future," Cornelius remarked. "And our infantry appears to be lacking something."

"Training, discipline, and experience in an assault line," Jace offered. He rested a hand on his long pack. "If the Illyrians are as determined as the rowers say, we'll need to deter them."

"If you have an idea, Centurion Kasia, I'm listening."

"Strap on your chest plates, hook up your armored skirt, clip on your red cloak, and slip on your staff officer's helmet," Jace instructed as he slid his war bow from the case. "Then, Tribune Scipio, stand up and shout challenges until the Illyrian leader steps to the rail to answer you."

"And what will you be doing while I'm making a fool of myself?"

"Deterring the determined by wounding as many of their leaders as we can identify," Jase answered.

The archer carefully bent the bow across his knee. Gently at first, but as the wood, bone, and sinew coating warmed, he flexed it further and with more energy.

"How close do you need them?" Cornelius questioned. He lifted up on his arms and peered over the right side of the transport. Then he dropped back to the deck with a sour stomach and a facial expression to match.

228

"I can hit a target at seven lengths of this boat," Jace told him. He pulled and sorted several arrows from his quiver before explaining. "But that's a problem in this case."

"How so, Centurion Kasia?"

"Your voice won't carry that far, Tribune Scipio."

***

The oarsmen on the transport were as good as any civilian crew. But not as accomplished or as powerful as the one hundred twenty oarsmen on the two-banker.

"Tribune Scipio. What are you doing?" Terrigenus cried out. "Get down. We need to hide the value of our mission."

Beads of sweat dotted the foreheads of the rowers as they bent and pulled in rhythm. And for the last hundred or so strokes, they had prevented the raiders from catching up. But with each passing moment, the Illyrians gained on the transport.

"Captain, please lower your stroke rate," Cornelius told him.

"You'll do nothing of the kind," Senior Tribune Terrigenus barked. "You need to increase your rate."

Ignoring the senior officer, Cornelius indicated the rowers around him.

"How much longer can your crew maintain this?" he inquired.

"Not much longer," the Captain admitted.

"Then slow your stroke rate and rest your crew, while I talk to the Illyrians."

"Are you mad?" Terrigenus demanded.

He started to rush Cornelius, but Quintus Pictor clung to his cloak. Torn between enforcing his authority and remaining near his patron, the Senior Tribune stepped back and resumed his useless hovering.

"When I tell you," Cornelius instructed the Captain, "rotate us away from the raider and head north. Then when I signal again, turn around and resume the southern track."

"Do you know what you're doing, young fellow?" the Captain questioned.

"I'm a strategist," Cornelius assured him. While the Captain looked to his navigator and helmsman for the meaning of strategist or an answer, Tribune Scipio lifted his helmet with the bright yellow horsehair comb and slipped it over his head. Then he shouted. "Illyrian raider. I will have a word with your leader."

At four hundred feet, his voice barely reached the foredeck of the two-banker.

"Illyrian raider. I will have a word with your leader."

In a few strokes, the distance close to three hundred feet.

"Illyrian raider. I will have a word with your leader."

A slim man with scars on his arms and face stepped up on the deck of the raider and replied.

"Who wants to know?"

"I am Tribune Cornelius Scipio of the Roman Legion. And I am prepared to accept your surrender."

Closer than two hundred and fifty feet, Cornelius' voice was clear to the rowers on both the transport and the raider. Given the boldness of one officer standing on a liburna facing down a crew of Illyrian pirates, oarsmen on both ships laughed. One because they were confident, and the other laughed out of nervousness.

In a display of his mastery of the raiders, a heavy-set Illyrian shoved the slim man aside.

"You wanted Commander Artas?" he bellowed. "Well, much to your displeasure red cape, as you'll soon discover, I am here."

The pirate leader slapped his chest with a large hand to emphasize his presence.

"With that much confidence, I believe you," Cornelius mumbled. Then without facing the master of the ship, he ordered. "Turn us now, Captain."

***

With all the drama between the Senior Tribune and the Tribune, and Cornelius's declaration that he would speak with the Illyrians, no one noticed the hooded archer creep to the Legionaries.

"When we turn, get to the aft and form a shield wall facing the raiders," he coached. "And remember the ship will rotate. You'll need to adjust. Keep your shields tight and good luck."

"I don't understand, Centurion Kasia," Optio Perperna admitted. "Where's your armor?"

"I'm the tip of the spear," Jace told him. "Keep your shields tight and protect the Captain, and the helmsman. Without them, we're as good as dead."

Bent low, Jace moved quickly to a spot just below the steering platform. Four arrows were gripped between his fingers and the body of the bow and a fifth ended up notched and resting on the bowstring. Then, following years of training, he listened to the exchange.

'You don't need to have your eyes on a target,' Zarek Mikolas taught him. 'Direction can come from voices, breathing, or a footstep that snaps a twig. But you need to remember, your first arrow may be too high or too low. Before the second arrow reaches the target, you should have a view of the battlefield. If you don't, run.'

"I can't run on a ship," Jace said to the memory of his teacher. Then he lifted his eyes to the raised aft of the

231

liburna. Like the forward section, the beam curved up higher than the deck. And in the rear, the beam was more pronounced. It curled over the helmsman's position. "I can't run on a ship, Master Mikolas. But I can climb."

The echo of the pirate leader slapping his chest reached Jace. A moment later, Cornelius ordered, "Turn us now, Captain."

Master Archer Jace Kasia leaped onto the steering platform, raced to the rear, placed a foot on the rail, and pushed off. Twisting in the air, he flung the other leg up and out. As if mounting a tall horse, his leg slipped over the raised beam. Before falling off the other side and into the sea, he locked his legs, stabilized his position, and elevated his bow.

As the prow of the transport turned, Illyrian Commander Artas questioned, "Just where do you think you're going, Tribune Scipio?"

Zip-Thwack!

Chapter 24 – Anything but No

As happens with snap shots, the first arrow was off, in this case low. But Artas bent to tend to the shaft in his thigh and Jace adjusted. The second one clipped the Commander's clavicle bone before driving the arrowhead deep into his chest and through his heart. Seemingly exhausted but with a shaft sticking up beside his ear, Artas sat on the deck before falling onto his back.

The sudden demise of a strong leader always leaves a power vacuum. Jace took a moment to scan for anyone acting vigorous and proclaiming themselves the new leader.

Zip-Thwack!

A thin man with knife scars fell to the deck. His bid for the leadership position ended before he could assert any real authority.

Chaos broke out on the deck of the Illyrian raider. Several rowers left their stations and swung their big arms around trying to amass a following. Others stopped rowing to argue for or against their ascension.

'If an enemy is distracted, let them,' Zarek Mikolas had preached. *'Use those precious moments in a battle wisely.'*

Below Jace, the Captain shouted, "Port side hold water. Starboard, power twenty."

With eighteen oar blades stationary on the left, and eighteen more on the right digging into the sea in quick time, the liburna whipped around. Tracking north, the transport rowed alongside the southbound Illyrian raider.

Clamping his legs tighter to keep his balance as the beam swayed, Jace examined the deck of the Illyrian two-banker. The ships moved in opposite directions, and Jace picked targets for the last two arrows.

Zip-Thwack!

One of the two Illyrian helmsmen went from gripping a rear oar to grabbing an arrow shaft. He toppled to the deck. An Illyrian sailor noted the loss. Snatching a shield from a rack, he jumped between the archer and the last helmsman.

Considering the elevation of the archer, the natural route for the next arrow was a downward slant. The sailor held the shield up at shoulder height, protecting the helmsmen. To his amazement, the helmsman collapsed. An arrow had slid below the shield, cut the skin, severed the tendons, and shattered the bones of the helmsman's ankle.

As a gap opened between the two ships, Jace pulled a handful of new arrows from his quiver. Carefully, he sorted out another five with matching shafts and fletching.

***

From the foredeck, Cornelius Scipio signaled for another turn. One hundred feet away on the steering platform, the Captain glanced at the archer perched over his head. Then he perused the four infantrymen holding a shield wall, protecting him and his helmsman.

"I still don't understand what a strategist is. But I recognize sacrifice," he said. By standing up on the foredeck, Tribune Scipio would draw arrows that might otherwise target the transport's oarsmen. Trusting in the brave Tribune's plan, the Captain ordered. "Helm, bring us about. But keep us away from the raider."

"That'll be hard," the helmsman pointed out, "we'll be pulling alongside of them."

"Just do it," the Captain snapped.

Jace twisted around and peered down the length of the transport. The flashy armor and helmet of the Tribune made Scipio a target. His motion generated a salute from Cornelius.

"Not to worry Tribune Scipio," Jace uttered as he dipped the war bow in return, "I've got you covered."

The transport curved a gentle U-turn in the water and returned to its southerly route.

At the same instant, the Illyrian raider began a turn to port, intending to give chase. Someone noticed the change in course of the liburna and countermanded the order. An argument broke out among those claiming the command. During the power struggle, the inexperienced helmsmen allowed the raider to continue deeper into the left-hand turn.

234

While watching the raider get farther out of position, Jace reached into his quiver, and finger counted five more arrows. Those uninspected shafts, he pulled partially out of the case and allowed them to lean against the opening.

'Wound one and you take two out of the fight,' Zarek Mikolas instructed.

The five arrows in his hand were a matched set, useful for precision targeting. Once he eliminated their bowmen, the other arrows would serve to wound oarsmen and disrupt their rowing.

"Is that the best you can do?" Cornelius shouted as the transport caught up with the two-banker. "I am right here. Come and get me."

From the aft of the raider, men peered around the raised keel. Although not as high as the one on the transport, the beam supported the two rear oars, and the space was widened by the presence of twin helmsmen. Fists shook in Cornelius' direction and six Illyrians with bows in hand appeared on the deck.

One Illyrian bent over an oarsman and released an arrow in Cornelius' direction.

"This Herd barely knows they're archers," Jace sneered.

Zip-Thwack!

From hovering over the rower while lining up his shot, the bowman dropped between two oarsmen, disrupting their strokes.

"Sometime three, Master Mikolas," Jace whispered to the ghost of his teacher.

Then he swept right until his war bow and the next arrow targeted the face on another bowman.

Zip-Thwack!

235

Apparently, a leader emerged because the raider's prow swung to the right. But the ship required a lot of strokes and the aid of both rear oars to come around. Before it reached a southerly heading, the war bow sighted on another bowman.

Zip-Thwack!

Jace had dropped three, frustrating the remaining bowmen. The trio wanted the archer but realized they couldn't hit him on the raised tail of the transport. But the Legion officer in the fancy armor was different. He stood on the foredeck glaring at the Illyrians as the smaller ship drew closer.

The three lined up, notched arrows, and drew their bowstrings.

Zip-Thwack!

Zip-Thwack!

Of the three, the bowman on the left jerked away as an arrow took him out of the line. Then, the one on the right spun around and crashed to the deck. From three to a single bowman, the change was too much. The lone bowman's hands shook. His arrow traveled half the distance to the transport before diving under the surface of the sea.

Zip-Thwack!

The bowman never had a chance to chastise himself for the weak shot.

***

Cornelius posed on the foredeck. His arms spread as if he was a conquering hero, inviting the Illyrians to kneel before him. Angry, the raiders focused on the Tribune. Spears flew into the air but fell short of the transport. One Illyrian sailor picked up a discarded bow.

Zip-Thwack!

He would not regret the decision. A person must be alive to have an emotion about anything, least of all regret.

The transport slid by the raider and Jace Kasia released arrow after arrow. On the top tier, every other midship-rower collapsed on their oars. The oarsmen around them stopped rowing to tend the wounds of their crewmate. Despite the efforts of the helmsmen, with the power from the right side reduced, the raider's ship angled to the left.

Jace slung a leg over the beam and dropped. Before he crashed into the deck, he caught the top of the keel with his right hand. After hanging for a moment, he dropped to the steering deck.

"Nice job of navigating," he greeted the Captain. "I'm out of arrows. Sir, you might want to unfold the sails and row for your life."

After advising the ship's master, Jace strolled back to his long pack.

"Where did you learn archery?" an oarsman asked.

"I was raised on Crete," Jace replied as he tightened the straps for the chest and back pieces of his armor.

"Great Oizys," the rower prayed to the Goddess of anxiety, "you're a Cretan Archer."

"I was," Jace commented as he fastened the armored skirt around his waist. "Until I ran out of arrows. Now I'm a Legion Centurion."

From the steering platform, the Captain called, "sailors, lower and tie your sails. Everyone else, maintain your stroke rate"

With his helmet under his arm, Jace dodged men running out tie lines. At the foredeck, he saluted

"A fine job of shooting, Centurion Kasia."

"Thank you, sir," Jace said while returning the salute. "And to you Tribune Scipio. An excellent job of distraction."

"What do you suppose our chances are?" Cornelius inquired.

They both faced back, looking at the Illyrian raider as the ship corrected course, redistributed rowers, and prepared to come after the transport.

"They started the attack with around one hundred and twenty-five men and a clean deck," Jace answered. "Now they're under a hundred men and their deck is soaked with blood. So, what are our chances you ask? None, Tribune, absolutely, none."

"Then the question is fight, or swim?"

"Tribune, I didn't put on the armor to take a bath."

When a group of sailors approached to unroll the headsail, Cornelius and Jace relinquished the foredeck. They picked their way around personal possessions and made their way to Pictor and the Senior Tribune.

***

"We could have paid off the pirates," Pictor moaned. "But you've stirred them up and destroyed any hope of negotiations."

Jace stepped back and forcefully locked his jaw to keep from responding. As the archer pulled away from the confrontation, Cornelius nodded wisely.

"I see your point, Senator," he sighed. "The actions of Centurion Kasia have consequences. But so does making your kidnapper rich before your family pays the ransom."

"Well, I'm glad you see it my way. Wait. Are you saying the Illyrians would have taken me captive even had I offered them coins?"

"Yes, sir. You and I because our families can afford to pay silver for our release," Cornelius described. "Everyone else on this ship would be sold into slavery."

"You left me out?" the Senior Tribune challenged. "Do you take me for a poor man?"

"I take you for a man with political ambition," Cornelius snapped. "And I can smell desperation pouring off you like sweat off a fieldhand. So, yes."

Terrigenus bristled but the accusations wilted something inside of him and he deflated.

"Sir, what are we going to do?" the NCO asked.

"Optio Perperna, we are going to fight."

"How?" the Optio asked. "They have hundreds of warriors."

Cornelius placed an arm on the NCO's shoulder and turned the man to face Jace.

"Centurion Kasia is in charge of the defense."

"They have a new leader," Jace explained. "If we can identify him and take him out of the fight, the rest will back off."

"That's your plan?" Pictor blurted out. "Find one man in a mass of blood thirsty soldiers?"

"They're hardly soldiers," Jace stated. He winked at the NCO. "Most are rowers with long knives and no armor. We'll have to murder a lot. But eventually we'll reach the new Commander. Rah?"

The call-response used by marching Legions should have been part of the Roman garrison nomenclature. Yet, Optio Perperna stared back at Jace with a puzzled expression on his face.

"Two-Faced Janus, must I be both a politician and a staff officer," Cornelius prayed to the God who looks at the Past and Future. "Legionaries, lift shields and brace."

The four infantrymen on the steering platform stood erect with their shields tucked tight against their bodies. Cornelius hopped onto the platform and strolled around them.

"When Centurion Kasia says Rah, you repeat it with enthusiasm," Cornelius instructed. "Rah?"

Four weak, unsure responses came from the four Legionaries.

"Did the Tribune stutter? Was he unclear?" Jace shouted as he leaped to the platform. "Perperna. Get up here and show your detachment the proper comeback."

The NCO stepped up and rushed to stand beside his four infantrymen while Cornelius jumped off the platform. Jace drew his gladius. Using the flat of the blade, he slammed it into the first shield.

"Rah?"

Perperna replied, "Rah."

Jace peered around the NCO's shield and asked the next Legionary, "What about you?"

"Rah, sir?"

Stepping to him, Jace hammered his gladius into the face of that man's shield, "Rah?"

This time, the first two infantrymen, and the NCO responded loudly, "Rah."

"This must be the slow end of the formation," Jace remarked. He smacked the third shield, "Rah?"

In response, all five of the infantrymen responded in full voice, "Rah, Centurion."

On the deck, the priest touched Cornelius' arm.

240

"Two questions, if you'll allow them," he requested.

"I would hope, I always have an answer for a Priest of Jupiter."

"Why the drill on the word, Rah?" the cleric asked.

"These Legionaries are accustomed to ceremonial duty," Cornelius told him. "In combat, we need them to focus on the voice of the combat officer. And Centurion Kasia needs to know they heard his orders. We drill the response so no matter how desperate the fighting, the Legionaries respond automatically."

"I see," the priest acknowledged. "And what does Rah mean?"

Above them, Jace screamed, "No one is allowed on this ship without the express permission of Tribune Scipio. Rah?"

"Rah, Centurion."

"And I don't see any Illyrians carrying a pass from the Tribune. Rah?"

"Rah, Centurion."

Each call and response grew more intense as the infantryman gained confidence in the combat officer.

"The pirates will get off the Tribune's ship or they will die on our gladii. Rah?"

"Or they will die on our blades. Rah, Centurion."

Cornelius leaned forward and drilled his stare into the eyes of the cleric.

"Rah means anything I want it to," he told the priest. "Absolutely, anything except, no."

Cornelius vaulted to the steering platform and marched to the ship's master.

"What does my crew need to do, Tribune?" the Captain inquired before Cornelius said a word.

241

"I thought you'd require an explanation," he admitted.

"You and that Centurion of yours might be totally insane," the Captain proposed. "But you fended off a ship of Illyrian pirates and reduced their numbers while protecting me and my oarsmen. I figured there's more to your strategy. What do you need?"

"I need four of the meanest oarsmen on your crew. And another eight of your tallest and strongest."

"Now I must ask. Why?"

"We're going to build a shield wall and dare the raiders to break it or die trying."

Act 9

Chapter 25 – Politicians in Armor

The five infantry shields anchored the center of the defensive formation. Rowers filled in on the sides to stretch the wall across the width of the ship. The eight meanest oarsmen bracketed Pictor, the priest, the poet, and the Senior Tribune.

"This is going to get ugly fast," Jace whispered to Cornelius.

"I'm open to suggestions?"

"Don't get killed," Jace replied. "That's all I've got."

Centurion Kasia and Tribune Scipio separated. Each went to an end and spoke to the nervous crewmen. As the officers with combat experience encouraged the defenders, the Illyrian raider closed the distance between the two ships.

"Pull them back, Captain," Cornelius called over his shoulder.

The ship's master nodded before shouting to the rowers still manning their oars, "Way enough! Stow them and fall back."

Without power, the transport began to drift. But, crowding thirty-six oarsmen, four infantrymen, plus their NCO and officers onto the steering platform created a mass of muscle. Between the blades, boat hooks, and oars, the Illyrians would have a tough fight to take the ship.

"Tribune Scipio, stand down," the Captain advised.

Cornelius glanced back. He could not abide surrendering and was prepared to take command of the vessel. Expecting a scene with the ship's master, he half turned. Then he noticed the Captain's outstretched arm. Following the direction, he saw two quinqueremes coming from the south.

At that distance, they were unidentifiable. They could have been Corinth, Athenian, or Roman. It mattered little because for sure, the big warships were not Illyrian.

"Centurion Kasia, not today," Cornelius called to the other side of the formation.

Jace lifted his head from where he was reassuring a frightened oarsmen. "That's a relief, Tribune. May I inquire why no one is going to die today?"

"You know how moments ago the Illyrian raider was the biggest, baddest wolf in this part of the sea?" Cornelius asked.

"Moments ago, sir?"

"Yes. But not anymore. They have competition."

"We like competition. Rah?"

To both Jace and Cornelius' surprise, the Legionaries and the oarsmen bellowed, "Rah, Centurion."

Jace marched across the deck and admitted to Cornelius, "I was wrong. With this crew, we would have taken the Illyrian raider as a prize."

***

Once the warships appeared, the Illyrians turned north and rowed away. While the second warship chased the raiders, the first one checked down its oars and glided to a stop.

"Attention transport," the First Principale hailed from the Roman Navy vessel. He stood with a boot on the outrigger box of the top-tier rowing station, leaning over,

244

and gazing downward. The seven-foot difference between the five-banker and the single-banker gave the Naval officer a height advantage. "Are you in need of assistance?"

"I am Senator Quintus Pictor. And I am on a mission to Delphi for the Senate of Rome," Pictor informed him. "Your presence is all the assistance I require. Move along."

The dismissal was fine with the ship's first officer. He started to back away.

"First Principale. One question," Cornelius requested.

The officer bent over and made a come-on-with-it hand sign.

"How is it you happened to be in these waters?" Cornelius inquired.

"We're patrolling the coastline," the officer told him. "Praetor of the Fleet Laevinus assigned us the task of locating the Macedonian fleet."

"Has there been trouble with the Macedonians?"

"Their King Phillip signed a treaty with Hannibal Barca," the Principale reported. "But we caught his representatives on their way back to Macedonia. Phillip plans to attack our east coast from ports in Illyria."

"Does he have bases in Illyria?" Cornelius asked.

"No. And he won't, because we're patrolling the coastline. Any more questions?"

"No. Thank you."

"Gods save me from infantry staff officers," the First Principale grunted before stepping out of view. Then his voice drifted down to the transport. "Second Principale. Stand by rowers to fall in."

"Do we have your permission to get underway, Tribune Scipio?" Senior Tribune Terrigenus sneered. "Or do you have more questions?"

"Sir, intelligence is hard to come by out here," Cornelius offered.

"So, I've noticed," Senator Pictor scoffed. "Captain, onward to Delphi, if you please."

"Yes, sir," the master of the ship agreed.

***

Once under sail, Jace strolled to the foredeck.

"The warrior's role is always under appreciated by noncombatants," he remarked while stepping up beside Cornelius.

"I don't think that's correct. There are plenty of cases where Legionaries are celebrated."

"Yes, sir. By other Legionaries and their officers. Men who depend on our blades and shields to stay alive on a battlefield," Jace stated. "But as you've seen, step on the self-image of an important man, and your bravery is reduced to interference."

Cornelius gripped the rail and inhaled deeply. Then as he exhaled the sea air, he questioned, "Did you sense anything while we were in combat? I mean, really, was there anything else we could have done?"

"Next time, I'll bring more arrows."

"I'm not talking about supplies."

"I know what you're asking, Tribune Scipio," Jace assured him. "We created tactics for a battle with no planning and little communications."

"You understood what needed to be done and acted," Cornelius said. "Normally, it's me at the center and everyone around me speculating on what the boy Tribune is going to do next."

"You did more than save a ship," Jace reminded him. "No matter how the Senator or the Senior Tribune sees it, today, you saved the mission to Delphi. And maybe the Republic."

"They did look upset," Cornelius admitted, "after the fight was over."

"The warrior's role," Jace repeated, "is always under appreciated by noncombatants."

The two Legion officers watched birds fly overhead and listened as water swooshed by the bow of the ship. From the deck, they scanned for pirates and raiders as the transport sailed south.

With the warm sun on his face, Jace recalled a lesson from Zarek Mikolas. Jace was a little boy and upset at a vender who owed Neysa money but refused to pay her.

"We should go into town and beat the coins out of him," Jace declared.

"*Although unappreciated, Cretan Archers are always ready to defend an ungrateful client. At least, until we collect our coins.*"

"Meaning what, Master Mikolas?"

"*Meaning we don't touch the vendor until he pays Neysa,*" Mikolas explained. "*But once he pays, well, we'll see if we can persuade him to be more honest in the future.*"

With that memory in mind, Jace Kasia glanced over his shoulder and down the length of the transport. Briefly, he examined Senior Tribune Terrigenus before turning to face forward.

"What are you thinking about?" Cornelius inquired.

"A vender who doesn't understand the debt he owes a friend of mine."

"What are you going to do about it?"

"Not a thing," Jace replied. "Absolutely nothing, until the mission is over."

***

A deep V-shaped inlet marked the northern tip of Oxia Island. With a final stroke as the light faded, the transport drifted to shore.

"Get us dry," the Captain ordered.

After the close call with the Illyrians, the crew had the enthusiasm of survivors. Leaping over the sides while laughing, they splashed through the shallows and happily beached the transport.

"Optio Perperna, your thoughts on the guard position?" Jace asked the NCO.

Perperna scanned the darkening hillside.

"One post above the ship can oversee the curve of the beach and out to sea."

"I agree. Get it set and I'll be up to stand my watch."

Terrigenus shuffled to Jace and crowded into the Centurion.

"I don't think my Legionaries or my Optio require the help of an archer," the Senior Tribune asserted while physically pushing Jace with his chest.

The senior staff officer didn't notice the hand move, or the fingers grip the war hatchet. Fortunately, Cornelius did.

"Centurion Kasia, a word if you please?"

"But sir, the Senior Tribune and I are having a discussion."

"Now, Kasia," Cornelius insisted.

Jace released the weapon and placed the hand on the left side of Terrigenus' chest.

"Do you know what this is?" he asked.

"No. What?"

"This, Senior Tribune, is the shortest distance to your heart," Jace informed him. Then he walked away while saying. "Coming, Tribune Scipio."

When he arrived, Cornelius guided Jace to the rear of the transport.

"You know the Legion doesn't hold archers in the highest esteem," Cornelius pointed out. "Stabbing a senior staff officer over his prejudice is a bit extreme."

"Hacking is more appropriate. I was going to dig his heart out in the messiest way possible. Not with a knife but with my hatchet," Jace explained. Then he eyed the stars and reflected. "Isn't it odd that garrison Legionaries and their officers only adopt the customs of fighting Legions that please them?"

"Marching and garrison forces once intermixed during the off season. They shared officers and NCOs," Cornelius described. "But since Hannibal's invasion, the idea of seasonal Legions has given way to year-round units. A gulf is developing between assault Legionaries and those who sleep in a barracks every night."

"And between combat officers and politicians in armor," Jace remarked.

"As much as I want to argue against it, I'm afraid you're right," Cornelius admitted. "The Senate has added to the number of Praetors because they ran out of Proconsuls to fill all the command positions. That allows for career staff officers who will never see combat. Creating, as you said, politicians in armor."

"So, one less, shouldn't be a problem?" Jace mentioned while nodding in Terrigenus' direction.

"I hope you're joking."

"Only half, Tribune Scipio," Jace revealed.

***

The transport shoved off at daybreak and by mid-morning, they sailed between points of land.

"Are those islands?" Jace asked a rower.

"No, sir," he replied using the honorific. "Those are points of land on the coast. We've entered the Gulf of Patras."

"It still looks like we're at sea," Jace observed.

"Just because you can see land doesn't mean you can't be eaten by a sea monster," the oarsmen told him. "Or simply go under one last time."

"Not comforting thoughts," Jace said.

The rower slapped the deck with an open palm. The wood rang from the force of the strike.

"It's why we have almost three and a half feet of hull under us."

"Again, not a comforting thought."

"Try being out here without a ship."

"I'm not happy being this far from land at all," Jace confessed. "After this trip, it'll be a while before I'm comfortable going for a swim."

The wind pushed the transport until the afternoon. While they had seen few ships or merchants on the voyage across the sea, once in the gulf, they passed a steady stream of ships and boats.

When the transport drew close to land, the Captain instructed, "Roll the sails. We'll row into the harbor."

"Is Patras a large city?" Jace asked while the rowers lifted oars from beside the rail.

"After Athens and Corinth, it's the third largest in Greece," one replied.

"And home to the Achaean League," another oarsman added.

"And they have spices from Egypt and the east. The food is great."

Jace moved to Cornelius and smiled.

"What's funny?"

"Patras is headquarters to the Achaean League."

"If we can locate Aratus of Sicyon and deliver Senator Sisera's message," Cornelius proposed, "this part of our mission will be over."

"This part?" Jace inquired. "I thought this was our mission."

"I have come to a realization, Centurion Kasia. For as much as Senator Pictor and Senior Tribune Terrigenus don't want us, they need us more."

"To coin one of your phrases, I'd like to argue against it," Jace admitted. "But you're right. They do need us."

***

After nights spent on empty beaches and days of seascape, the harbor town of Patras promised to be a delight. Streets crisscrossed the ancient city and a few avenues deadened at cafes on the shoreline. But the river bisecting the metropolis defined two different visions of civilization.

"That's the Glafkou River," a rower said between strokes. "We'll beach on the left with the rest of the commercial traffic."

"What's on the right?" Cornelius asked.

"The government, the army, and folks better than us," another stated. "That's why we'll stay on the left side with our kind."

Cornelius studied the landscape of Patras. It appeared as if a giant had flattened the mountains near the gulf into the shape of cupped hands. Then he placed separate sets of buildings and paved streets on opposing palms, before dividing them with a river.

"Jace, wake up."

The archer lifted his arm and peered at Cornelius from under his elbow.

"Have we reached land yet?" the archer asked.

"I didn't know you hated sailing this much."

"I don't. It's an easy way to travel," Jace explained. "But when you grow up on an island, you begin to dislike the panorama of the sea. On the north coast you have a view of the ocean. Travel eighteen miles to the south and there you go again, another view of the ocean. It's like growing up on a huge boat."

"You should have a look at Patras," Cornelius suggested. "We'll have to navigate the town."

Jace pushed to a sitting position before standing.

"The left side is warehouses, and businesses with a lot of cafes. Seems like a fun place," he described. "On the right of the river are villas and defendable buildings. I'd say they're prepared to repel invaders. Is that a problem for a pair of Legion officers?"

"It depends on where the headquarters for the Achaean League are located," Cornelius submitted.

The transport angled for an open stretch of sand. As it neared shore, the Captain ordered it turned and then backed towards the beach.

"Over the side," he instructed his rowers. "And get us dry."

Once the ship was motionless, Cornelius made his way to Terrigenus.

"Centurion Kasia and I need to go into town," he told the Senior Tribune. "We should be back before dawn. If we're not, wait for us."

"Of course, Tribune Scipio. We are at your beck and call, Tribune Scipio. Whatever you desire, Tribune Scipio,"

Terrigenus emphasized the sarcasm before advising. "We'll shove off when the ship's master orders it. Not a moment before or after. If you want to pub crawl through Patras, that's none of my business. Nor are you, my responsibility."

When Cornelius returned to his gear, Jace asked, "What did the Senior Tribune have to say?"

"He wished us luck."

"That bad?"

"Yes."

Chapter 26 – The Gods of Fear and Terror

They decided to go in civilian clothing, taking only a Legion dagger in Cornelius' case and the war hatchet for Jace. After dressing, Cornelius hung the strap for a courier's pouch over a shoulder. They dropped from the ship to solid ground.

"I'd prefer to have my bow," Jace complained as they shuffled through the sand.

"As a talisman?" Cornelius inquired. "Because if I remember correctly, you're out of arrows."

"I can always buy arrows," Jace told him.

As they approached an outdoor café, clapping greeting them.

"It's the General and the Master of the Seahorse," several oarsmen announced. "Come, defenders of our ship. We owe you drinks."

"Tell you what," Jace offered, "you drink them for us. We've got an appointment in town."

"*Opa. Yamas,*" the oarsmen shouted before draining their glasses.

"That?" Cornelius asked.

"Opa is an expression of enthusiasm," Jace reported. "And Yamas is short for 'Stin Yeia Mas', meaning to our health. Get accustomed to hearing it."

"Why?"

"Well Tribune Scipio, sailors have little to do when ashore," Jace explained. "Like Legionaries on liberty, they tell stories. And it seems, you are the story of the year. I imagine you'll be famous for taunting a warship full of Illyrians by the time we leave Delphi."

"And you for sitting on the tail beam putting arrows in those pirates," Cornelius injected. "Come on, Master of the Seahorse, we have a message to deliver."

They took three steps before breaking into a Legion jog. The steady pace carried them away from the beach.

***

Three blocks into the city, they looked around for a leatherworker's shop. Of all the trades, a man who worked leather would make harnesses for teamsters, saddles for wealthy riders and cavalrymen, and handles for buckets. In short, a leatherworker knew all the gossip and where everybody resided.

At one shop, they entered and walked to a man carving leather at a workbench.

"Where can we find the headquarters of the Achaean League?" Jace inquired. "Specifically, we want to know if Aratus of Sicyon is in Patras."

The craftsmen drew a sharp, hook-nosed knife along the edge of a piece of leather. In the wake of the blade, a leather strap curled up until it fell to the floor, pulled down by its own weight.

"You're looking for Aratus of Sicyon?" the leatherworker asked. "Why not look in Sicyon?"

254

"He's the head of the Achaean League and the League is based in Patras," Cornelius stated while easing in front of Jace. "Tell me. Is Aratus of Sicyon in the city or not?"

Reaching around the Tribune, Jace dropped two bronze coins on the workbench.

"They are simple questions," he commented while sliding the coins to the craftsman.

"Where is the League headquartered?" Cornelius summarized. "And is Aratus in Patras?"

"Go up the Glafkou for three miles," the leatherworker directed. He snatched the coins from the workbench. "Cross the river and continue south. Follow the big road into the foothills. The League is in an estate in the village of Achaia Clauss. Aratus should be there. He was in town yesterday."

"There, that wasn't so hard, was it?" Jace remarked.

He and Cornelius left the shop.

Once the visitors had gone, the craftsman called his assistant from the backroom.

"Those Latians are up to no good," he declared.

"How can you tell, Master?"

"They were impatient for information anyone could have provided. And they were too free with their coins," the leatherworker told his helper. "Go find an officer of the guard. Tell him two Latian assassins are heading for Achaia Clauss to murder Aratus of Sicyon."

***

Although the day grew late, Cornelius and Jace continued along the left bank of the Glafkou.

"We could have stopped for a meal with the oarsmen," Jace whined.

"Centurion Kasia, we're charged with delivering this package to Aratus of Sicyon," Cornelius reminded him.

"Once we've completed the task for Senator Sisera, we'll find food. Maybe Aratus will feed us."

"I'm looking forward to tasting the spices the rowers were bragging about."

"Truthfully, so am I," Cornelius admitted.

They counted steps and judged when they had traveled three miles. A few paces beyond, Cornelius spotted a trail leading down to a fording spot.

"This works. It's not too deep," he offered while wading out into the current. Jace walked a little behind the Tribune. Cornelius observed the behavior. "You're falling behind, Centurion Kasia. Please don't tell me you can't swim."

Jace kept a hand near the strap to the courier's pouch.

"I swim just fine, Tribune," he replied. Silently, Jace added. 'I just want to be sure you can.'

At waist deep, the two Legion officers plunged into the river. With sure strong strokes, they crossed to the other side and splashed out of the Glafkou.

"How far did the leatherworker say?" Cornelius asked.

"He didn't. Only that we follow…"

A bush on the bank moved and a military officer stepped from behind the greenery.

"Follow the road to Achaia Clauss," he completed Jace's sentence. "But first lift your hands away from your weapons."

Jace might have argued with the officer if ten spearmen hadn't rushed over the embankment.

"We're here to see Aratus of Sicyon," Cornelius informed the officer.

"And King Phillip of Macedon stationed me here to keep people like you away from Aratus," the officer replied.

"People like us?" Cornelius questioned.

256

"Assassins," the officer responded.

"We're not assassins," Cornelius protested. "We're representatives from the Roman Republic, here to deliver a message to the General of the Achaean League."

"Even worse. Spies," the officer remarked. Then to the spearmen, he instructed. "Bind their hands. And if either man gives you a reason, kill him. I can always question the other."

Cornelius put his hands behind his back. But then he noticed Jace holding his arms to the front and offering his wrists to a spearmen. Cornelius quickly followed the example of the archer.

***

A large estate house and a barn were the highlights of Achaia Clauss. Outside a stone wall, huts created the actual village. But the surrounding countryside revealed why the place existed. Grapevines covered the rolling hills, and the aroma of fermenting wine filled the air.

Given the location, Jace was not surprised when they passed through a gateway and were directed down into a wine cellar. The shock for him came from the rows of huge wooden barrels and the high stone ceiling supported by beams.

"Hang them from hooks," the officer ordered.

After slinging ropes over iron hooks, the ends were tied to the bindings. Spearmen pulled the ropes until Jace, and Cornelius were hoisted and stretched. With their arms overhead and their heels off the stone floor, the ropes were tied to iron rings.

"That'll hold them until I'm ready," the officer declared. "Leave two men on guard. The rest of you go eat."

"Thank you, Captain," one of the spearmen said.

"Say Captain," Jace requested, "any chance of getting fed. I missed supper."

"I plan to question the other one first," the officer replied. "But I'll get to you. Don't you worry."

"You could skip a meal now and then," Jace said as the Captain walked up the steps. The comment stopped the Macedonian. "You know because you're getting soft around the middle."

Although he was muscular from exercising, the Captain self-consciously touched his waist.

"You don't want to get fat again," Jace warned.

With a huff of dismissal, the Captain rushed up the steps and vanished into the night. The last of the spearmen to leave closed the cellar doors. Left behind, the two guards rested their spears against the wall and sat at a tasting table. They barely looked at the two prisoners hanging in front of the huge wine barrels.

"Why did you feel the need to antagonize the Captain?" Cornelius demanded. "It'll make it harder to reason with him."

"He considers us assassins and spies," Jace pointed out. "Would you reason with us if the situation was reversed?"

After thinking for a moment, Cornelius confessed, "Probably not."

***

Much later, two guards came and relieved the original pair. Deep in the night, two more guards arrived accompanied by the Captain. With a flip of his hand, he dismissed the extra guards.

"It's a beautiful facility, don't you think," the Macedonian said as if he was giving a tour and not preparing to question prisoners. "One benefit of the cellar is it's quiet."

"Are you also hard of hearing?" Jace questioned.

The Macedonian unstrapped his sword belt and placed the scabbard on the table beside Jace and Cornelius' weapons. Then he brushed a hand over the hilt of the dagger on his hip as if contemplating using it in the interrogation. Instead of following through on the implied threat, he reached for the courier's pouch.

"What have we here?" he quipped. After unstrapping the pouch, the Captain lifted out a folded piece of oiled leather. Carefully, as if the waterproof wrapping held a blade or was poisoned, he peeled back the edges. "Just as I suspected. There is no message. Only a dagger and a hatchet for the evil act of assassination."

It would be hard to disagree with his supposition. The oiled skin contained a piece of string and a straight length of wood with a rough notch cut on one end.

"We never looked in the pouch," Cornelius explained. "We were simply asked to deliver it to Aratus of Sicyon."

"Yes, but who sent you? Are there others on the way?" the Captain asked. "And how much is the life of a Greek General going for these days?"

"We are not assassins," Cornelius protested.

The Macedonian strolled to a bank of shelves. Along with mugs for tasting, there were taps, plugs, and tools. He selected a mallet and walked to Cornelius while tapping his hand with the wooden hammer.

Halfway to the Tribune, Jace inquired. "Tell me, Captain, wasn't that old King Alexander a Macedonian? I hear your people are proud of the lush."

The Captain stopped and pivoted towards Jace.

"You will speak respectfully when talking about the great King Alexander."

"Maybe you can clear something up for me," Jace suggested.

Cornelius stared at Jace in confusion. It was as if Jace wanted to be abused. Then, it occurred to Cornelius that Jace was saving his Tribune from the punishment.

"I have read extensively about the King," the Captain bragged.

"So, what's the deal," Jace sneered. "Alexander's father had a horse that no one could ride."

"Yes, the stallions name was Bucephalus."

"Yea, whatever. So, no one could stay on the beast until a groom pointed out to an intoxicated Alexander that the horse was afraid of its own shadow," Jace recounted almost as if he was a nasty drunk. "Then with the courage of a belly full of wine, the coward Alexander had the horse's eyes covered. I heard he fell off the first time he tried to mount the blinded horse."

The Captain leaped forward while swinging the mallet. It impacted Jace low in the stomach. Responding to the blow, Jace bent in two. Involuntarily, his legs jerked up and off the ground.

"Oomph," he bellowed as the air was driven from his body. His head hung for a heartbeat before he raised his face and inquired. "I thought you Macedonians were tough. Is that all you've got?"

Hunching his powerful shoulders, the Captain reared back and lifted his leg. Then stepping forward, he delivered a power swing at the chest of the insulting Latian.

***

When the Macedonian drew back, Jace twirled on the end of the rope. As if climbing a wall, he raced up the face of the wine barrel until his feet reached the overhead stones. Then, bug like, he walked across the ceiling before launching his body towards the room. Swinging at the end of the rope, Jace Kasia used his knees and momentum to drive the Captain into the wine barrel.

Dazed and confused by the result of the attempted hammer blow, the Macedonian staggered. Jace pulled himself up on the rope and captured the Captain's head between his knees. From the height of the man's shoulders, Jace reached up and detached the rope from the iron hook.

"Excuse me," Cornelius asked the two stunned guards, "do either of you have a bag of salt? This beef is really tasteless."

Rather than rushing forward, the spearmen hesitated. They looked in the direction of the other prisoner, trying to understand where he got beef.

The pause allowed Jace to pull the Captain's dagger and sling his still bound arms over the Macedonian's head. Then he sank to his knees using the Captain as a shield.

"The last thing I want to do," Jace announced to the spearmen, "is to kill your Captain before dying."

"How?" one guard questioned.

The tip of the dagger pointed at the exposed throat of their officer. Although Jace sawed at the ropes binding his wrists, it was understandable how he could kill the Captain. Or maybe the how wasn't that obvious.

"How what?"

"How did you get free?" the spearman inquired.

"On Crete we learned more than how to handle a bow and fight," he replied. The knife finally cut through, and the bindings separated and fell away. Jace held up his arms and declared. "We practiced escape and evasion, a lot."

"Phobos and Deimos protect us," the other spearman prayed to the Twin Gods of Fear and Terror.

Both were anxious at the thought. But only one said it, "You're a Cretan Archer."

"More than a Master Archer, I'm a Cretan File Leader," Jace described. "Sent to protect Cornelius Scipio on his mission to deliver that pouch to Aratus of Sicyon."

"But there's nothing important in the pouch," the Macedonian officer exclaimed. "You can't…"

Jace tapped the side of the Captain's head and instructed, "I don't mind blood on my hands if you don't mind bleeding. Or you can shut up until I finish."

The Macedonian nodded his understanding when the dagger tapped the bridge of his nose.

"As I was saying," Jace continued. "Our only goal is to hand the pouch over to the General. But I want to keep everyone safe before that. Put your spears on the floor and step away."

With their Captain in danger, they had no choice. The spearmen placed their weapons on the ground and moved away from them.

"Now, one of you go and bring back Aratus of Sicyon."

"Aren't you going to escape?" a spearman asked.

"If I wanted to escape, I would have killed the three of you," Jace bluffed. "Then Master Scipio and I would have walked out of here and gone to town for a hot meal. But seeing as you asked, you go inform Aratus that he has a visitor."

After the guard ran up the stairs and left the cellar, Jace sat the Captain and the other guard at the tasting table.

"Jace? Master Archer?" Cornelius called to him. "Would you mind cutting me down?"

"Yes, sir. I was preoccupied with saving your life."

"Duly noted, Kasia."

Chapter 27 – Repaying an Old Debt

As soon as the cellar doors opened, Jace moved into the shadows on one side of the stairs. Cornelius shifted to the dark corner on the other side. Both leveled spears at the opening. If spearmen came down, there would be a fight.

Briefly, night sounds spilled through the double doorway. Then, five armored Hoplites filled the opening. As they charged down the steps, any thought of fighting by the Legion officers fled.

"Cornelius Scipio?" one asked.

"That's me."

"Where is the archer?" another demanded.

"I'm over here," Jace replied.

Three shields spun and faced Jace. They locked together and one of the heavy infantry instructed, "put down your bow."

"No bow, no arrows. Only a spear," Jace assured the armored men. He bent and placed the shaft on the floor. The steel tip illuminated in the candlelight. Even with it in plain view, Jace announced. "I've put the spear down. I am unarmed."

"Step out of the shadows."

The Hoplite helmets obscured their faces, and the big shields defended their bodies. What wasn't hidden by the gear were their xiphe. The short sharp blades targeted Jace as he stepped into the candlelight.

"Cornelius Scipio come forward," another of the Greek infantryman instructed.

Cornelius simply dropped the spear. Bouncing from tip to butt end, the shaft rocked back and forth creating a ruckus in the wine cellar. All five Hoplites bent their knees and braced for an attack.

No attack came, only Cornelius from the shadows with a sheepish look on his face.

"Captain are you alright?" the fifth Hoplite asked.

Moving slowly, the Macedonian officer lifted his face and blinked while trying to focus his eyes.

"Kill those two," he slurred. "They have disrupted the good order of Patras."

"Sir. Are you injured?" the Hoplite inquired.

"The Latian made me drink too much wine," the Captain complained. "Too much. Kill them."

The Hoplite moved to the base of the stairs and proclaimed, "General Aratus. The area is clear."

A man in his mid-fifties and wearing a robe of office descended the steps.

"This had better be important to get me up in the middle of the…"

Aratus of Sicyon rushed to the table and gently picked up the wooden slat and the piece of string. He held them to the candle and admired the insignificant items.

"How is my friend, Alerio Sisera?" he inquired.

"Sir, the Senator is in good health," Cornelius responded.

"Come with me," Aratus said. As he reached the stairs, he acknowledged the Hoplites. "Thank you for stepping into the fire for me."

"It's our pleasure, General."

***

264

Later in his quarters, Aratus dropped into a chair. He held up the stick and the piece of string.

"On the worst night of my life, Alerio Sisera protected me. After the coup and during the carnage in my hometown of Sicyon, he spirited me away and took me to my Uncle's place at Argos," Aratus explained. "With these simple items, Legionary Sisera guided us through the mountains by reading the stars. He knew the stick and string would identify someone I could trust."

Cornelius assured him, "We are at your disposal."

"Let me explain why I'm doing what I am," Aratus described. "When King Philip the Fifth came to the Macedonian throne, he was a dynamic leader. We all wanted to be part of his vision. But he's grown power hungry and arrogant. He has become the type of ruler one does not want as a neighbor. Two weeks ago, he loaded his army on transports and sailed from Macedon."

"The Republic Navy has warships out patrolling for the Macedonian fleet," Cornelius informed the General.

"Then your fleet will be out of position to stop Philip from taking Illyrian cities," Aratus told Cornelius. "The Gods have provided his fleet with favorable weather. They will reach Illyria this week. After Philip captures a few Illyrian forts, we'll both have a nightmare neighbor on our border."

"Not if I can get word to the fleet," Cornelius proposed. "If you'll excuse us. We need to get to the beach."

"In addition to the soldiers stationed here, Philip has spies everywhere. For my own protection, I can't give you anything official," Aratus said as he stood. "You'll just have to take the word of a man repaying an old debt."

"Sir, if we could have you hand draw a map of the coast and mark the landing site of the Macedonian Fleet," Jace suggested. "That would add credibility to our report."

Aratus pulled out a piece of parchment, sketched in a coastline, added an inlet, and labeled the location, Orikum. Then he pressed a carved stone stamp of the Achaean League into a corner of the rough map.

"I'll tell Senator Sisera that you've repaid the old debt," Cornelius promised as he rolled the parchment.

Jace and Cornelius slipped out the rear door, sprinted across the yard, and climbed the stone wall.

***

Once in open country, they settled into a Legion jog. In the moonlight, they had no trouble locating the road as the lush landscape contrasted nicely with the hard surface.

"It'll be dawn soon," Jace remarked. "Do you think Pictor will divert the transport to warn the fleet?"

"He has no choice," Cornelius answer. "We can't allow a third front to get hot."

"A third front?"

"The fighting in the south of the Republic against Hannibal. My father's war in Iberia with the Punic army. And now the threat of Macedonians across the Adriatic Sea," Cornelius listed. "If King Philip can land soldiers on the east coast of the Republic and resupply them from Illyria, the Legions will be hard pressed to throw the Macedonians back into the sea."

Motivated by the seriousness of the situation, Cornelius and Jace sprinted to the Glafkou, splashed into the current, and quickly swam across. On the far side of the river, they turned west, and ran for the beach.

***

The moon hung over the horizon but didn't set. Instead, the rays of the rising sun washed out the moonglow, leaving only a pale, partial disk in the sky. When Cornelius noticed the colors of the buildings, and the aroma from cookfires, he slowed to a walk.

"I had the same thought," Jace agreed. He dropped from a run and fell in beside Cornelius.

"Which one? That the Senior Tribune didn't hold the transport for us?" Cornelius asserted. "Or that we're in possession of important information, in need of transportation, but short of coins."

They continued through the wakening town for another block before Jace concluded, "All of that."

At the end of the buildings, the two stopped beside the café where the rowers had offered to buy them drinks.

"No transport," Jace reported.

The day before boats, fishermen, merchant ships, coastal traders, and other vessels crowded the beach. Now, shortly after dawn, they had an unobstructed view of the bay.

"The water's pretty," Cornelius observed. Then he remembered Jace's dislike of a water view and apologized. "Sorry, I didn't think."

"You inconsiderate mentula," Jace swore.

Cornelius jerked back at the curse.

"I said I was sorry," he protested. "What more do…"

But Jace had dashed towards the surf. In a heartbeat, Cornelius understood, and he sprinted for the stack of gear carelessly dumped on the beach.

It might not have been their equipment. Except, the Senior Tribune had opened the bow case and mounted the war bow like a flag on top of the pile.

Cornelius reached Jace as the archer inspected the weapon.

"Did the Senior Tribune damage it?" he asked with trepidation.

In addition to harvesting the wood, Jace Kasia shaped and trimmed each piece of the bow with his own hands. As well, he hunted and brought down a mountain goat for the hoofs, the sinew, and the horn. With those items, he made glue, mixed the fiber coating, and cuts slats of horn to strengthen the bow. However, the war bow represented more than craftsmanship to the Cretan Archer. It represented Jace's identity. If Terrigenus damaged the bow, Cornelius feared he would soon be attending a murder tribunal.

"A war bow will keep you safe, fed, and employed," Jace chanted as he examined the limbs for cracks or breaks. "A war bow will keep you safe, fed, and employed."

"Did he damage the weapon?" Cornelius questioned again.

"No damage to the bow," Jace replied with deep furrows in his brow. "But you know I'm going to hurt Terrigenus. When this is over, he will pay for his insolence and for touching my bow."

"Just be sure there are witnesses and that he draws his blade first," Cornelius warned. Then he shoved the chest armor, the helmets, and bags aside, while searching through the gear. "I don't see my travel purse."

Jace slipped the war bow into the case and sealed the opening.

"Load up, Tribune Scipio," he encouraged. "We need to find an armorer and buy arrows."

"Buy arrows? Whatever for."

"This war bow," Jace answered while patting the cover. "It will keep us safe, fed, and employed."

"We have blades to keeps us safe. And coins for food. Are we in need of employment?" Cornelius inquired.

The two began packing their Legion and personal gear.

"I'll need arrows if the war bow is to fulfill its duty," Jace stated. "Because we do need to raise passage for a ship."

"One heading north and in the direction of the Republic warships."

"That's correct, Tribune Scipio."

***

A roar rocked the structure of the café. Almost fifty sailors, oarsmen, and ship's officers crowded the small outdoor patio. Others, forced off the stone floor, stood in the dirt.

"Nobody can do that," one shouted. He pushed his way to the front and slammed coins down on a table. "This will be the easiest bet I've ever won."

His declaration drew even more men to the table. They paused before placing coins in either a small stack or on the much larger pile.

"I hope you know what you're doing," Cornelius offered. "Because this could go bad. We don't have the coins to cover the bets."

"Keep taking them," Jace said with confidence. "It'll help when we get to the money round."

"Money round?" Cornelius questioned.

Before he could get an explanation for 'money round', a server tapped him on the shoulder.

"A regular customer just got here," the server told Cornelius. "Captain Norbert is a Noricum out of Trieste. If he's heading home, he maybe the ride you need."

"Thank you," Cornelius said while handing her a coin. "I'll go see him after the betting ends."

"That's crazy, you know that?" she commented. Her arm extended, pointing to Jace and the bow.

"I tend to agree with your premise."

"Tend to agree with my premise?" she mimicked. Lifting her nose in the air, the server chuckled as she went to wait on another table. "His Nobility tends to agree with my premise."

When Cornelius turned back to the table, Jace scowled at him.

"What part about blending in, did you not understand?" the archer whispered.

Cornelius leaned over the coins and the tabletop.

"I have studied and strived my entire life not to blend in," Cornelius Scipio informed Jace. "It's very difficult to put aside my position in society and my training to participate in this subterfuge."

"At least, you didn't call it a circus," Jace remarked.

"Only because at a circus, I'm not likely to be one of the performers. And have little chance of being beaten by a disgruntled audience."

"What did the cute waitress have to say?"

"There's a Noricum Captain here who may be heading north," Cornelius reported. "I'll talk to him after this. What did you call this?"

"An archery demonstration," Jace replied. He stood and called to the sailors, oarsmen, and ship's officers. "This is a Cretan war bow. There are many like it on the island. Or in the arsenal of Cretan mercenaries. But few can be found in the hands of non-islanders."

Jace walked a circle, holding the bow overhead and displaying it to the crowd.

"Just seeing one is unique. In the hands of a Latin, almost impossible," he described. "But this Cretan war bow has been blessed by Artemis, the Goddess of the Hunt."

"It's heavily constructed, I'll grant you that," a sailor challenged. "And probably requires a powerful draw. But blessed. How do you prove that?"

"The target, way out there, would be a challenge for the best archer," Jace suggested. "And I've claimed that I can hit the coin mounted on the board. A lot of you doubt my abilities. I can tell by the mound of coins bet against me."

A murmur of agreement ran through the crowd.

"But what would you say to a validation of the blessing?"

His question brought a circle of men forward. They tossed coins on the 'against' pile. Cornelius had to use an arm to scoop the overage back to keep the coins from falling off the table.

"Was that the money round?" he mouthed.

"No," Jace responded. With enthusiasm, the archer suggested to the crowd. "Let's up the difficulty. Boys?"

From the side of the café, three local boys appeared. Two carried old oars and the third toted a three-board section of hull. They marched to a spot halfway to the target. The boards were set in the sand and the oars placed behind it to keep it upright.

"The legend states that an arrow launched from a bow blessed by Artemis will always find its target," Jace boomed. "This is such a bow."

"Hold on Latian. Are you saying you can use a Cretan war bow and hit a target hidden behind those boards?" an oarsmen questioned.

"That is the bet," Jace confirmed. "Anybody else want to place coins on the outcome."

In response to his declaration, more sailors, rowers, and ship's officers pushed to the table and dropped coins on the small mountain. Cornelius needed both arms to confine the coins to a section of tabletop.

Reluctantly, he asked, "Is this the money round?"

"No," Jace stated. To the crowd, he announced. "I need an honest man to keep me honest."

A big man shoved through the crowd and approached Jace.

"I'm Norbert the Noricum," he boomed. "I'll keep you honest."

"You'll do," Jace acknowledged. "Show me where to stand so the barrier is between me and the target. And be sure I can't see over or through the boards."

Norbert used the side of his hand to line up the target and the boards. Then he stooped and studied the section of hull for holes.

"There is no way for him to see the target coin," Norbert exclaimed.

More bets dropped on the 'against' heap. But a few were added to the 'for' stack.

"Not the money round," Jace said before Cornelius asked.

Jace strolled to Norbert and took his place. Down range, the boards blocked the view of the target. The Cretan Archer selected an arrow from his quiver and examined the shaft.

"An arrow from a bow blessed by Artemis will always find its target," Jace said to the crowd. Stepping back with one foot, he turned sideways to the target, extended his left arm, and drew the bowstring across his chest. "Always."

He released the bowstring. The wabble of the shaft far exceeded a normal launch. In an absolute miss, the arrow flew to the right, not only way off target, but completely missing the section of hull.

A few laughed at the absurdity of the demonstration.

But then, as if the hand of the Goddess interceded, the shaft veered left, and missed the boards before burying the arrowhead in the coin.

Silence fell over the crowd.

"Blessings be to Artemis, the Goddess of the Hunt," Cornelius whispered.

Jace called out, "If the Goddess is truly in this bow. I should be able to do it again. Does anyone care to take that bet?"

Fully half the men stepped back, having already lost money. But the ones who stepped forward were the hardcore gamblers.

"The money round?" Cornelius inquired while scraping the winnings into his cape to make room for the new bets.

"Yes. This is the money round."

As the new pile grew, Cornelius' stomach tightened. The amount bet against Jace exceeded the coins placed on the first shot. Plus, these men were more intense, probably dangerously so.

Act 10

Chapter 28 – With This Intelligence

When Zarek Mikolas taught Jace the trick shot, he explained, '*An enemy behind an obstacle feels safe. But when your arrow comes around the barrier, it removes the illusion of security. However, bending the flight of an arrow reduces the impact of the arrowhead. So, after you flush him out, you'll need to take him down with a proper arrow shot. Another benefit, when away from Crete if you need coins, you can always fool the uninformed. And that's fine because the goal of every Cretans, after all, is to earn a profit.*'

Jace examined the arrows he and Cornelius had purchased while waiting for the pile of coins to grow. He weighed each arrow on the palm of his hand before flexing the shafts. To the crowd, he appeared nervous. The effect drew more coins to the pile against him. Several however, placed bets for the Goddess to bend the flight of the shaft, and guide the arrow to the target. Before that trend caught on, Jace went to Cornelius.

"Close the betting," the archer directed. "We're starting to give too much back."

"Thank the Gods. I can't believe we're doing this a second time," Cornelius conceded. "But tell me why you're closing the betting. Before you had me take bets almost until you shot."

"Some men enjoy the game more than the winning," Jace replied. "If we continue this, they will begin to place coins on both piles."

"The betting is about to close," Cornelius announced.

Jace Kasia walked to Norbert and indicated the hull boards and the target.

"Norbert the Noricum, if you will check the range for the people," Jace requested.

Norbert stared hard at the boards. Bending sideways, he studied the coin on the target. Then he returned to inspect the hull section. Seeing nothing out of the ordinary, he shouted, "the archer cannot see through the boards."

After stepping to the line, Jace dropped his right foot back. Then he extended his left arm and the war bow towards the boards. In good order, he notched the arrow level with the top of his thumb and held the loaded weapon across his chest. Until then, he operated as a Cretan Archer intending to hit a target directly.

The change came as he drew back the bowstring. First, he bent his left elbow, shortening the depth of the draw. Not only would the bowstring be short of a full pull, but he also slipped the notch of the arrow down the string. A partial draw and an arrow cantered below level, were two elements of bending the flight. The third being an arrow with a thin, flexible shaft.

In a normal shot, the power from the bowstring caused the shaft of the arrow to wrap around the body of the bow. Flexing as it flew, the undulating along the shaft continued from the bow to the target.

When Jace released the misaligned arrow, the thin shaft flexed only from the power of the bowstring. It didn't burn off energy bending around the body of the bow. Minus the violent warping as it left the string, the arrowhead traveled away from the boards and the target with an upward attitude. But as it floated through the air, the flexing increased, driving the arrowhead downward. Once it dipped, the arrow wobbled around to the left as if tuning a corner.

Or, as most of the sailors, oarsmen, and ship's officers witnessed, the hand of the Goddess reached out and directed the shaft. At the end of the odd flight, the arrowhead struck the coin on the target.

"Blessings be to Artemis, the Goddess of the Hunt," Jace and Cornelius prayed.

The sailors, oarsmen, and ship's officers stood silently after witnessing the miracle.

Then someone shouted, "You are a cheat and a liar."

Another bad loser cried, "He cheated us."

As in all cases with a mob, they didn't have a leader. There was no one to reason with, just the animal energy that took away thought and motive, leaving an emotionally charged crowd with no purpose.

Jace selected five arrows. Notching one, he slipped the others between the fingers of the left hand and the body of the bow.

"Cornelius on my left hip," he ordered.

In that instance, a small but significant change came over Tribune Scipio. He had always approached everything with intelligence and had thirsted for knowledge. And, once sure of his path, he was fearless as he'd displayed on several occasions. But habitually, he balked at following orders. The situation at the café, however, was beyond anything he'd ever encountered. A red cape full of coins, an angry crowd, and he had no idea how to handle it.

"Cornelius, get on my left hip," Jace insisted.

***

At that moment, a leader emerged. Not Jace Kasia. The Cretan Archer had proven his ability to command in a close fight. No, the birth concerned Cornelius Scipio. For he learned that to be a leader of men, one must first be willing to follow orders.

Moving swiftly, Cornelius hammered aside two spectators. Another reached for him. The Tribune paused briefly to run a knee into the man's gut. Then he was in the open and coming at Jace from the right. Remembering the instructions, he ducked under the notched arrow and ran to the archer's left side.

"What's the plan?" he asked.

"I was thinking a beef dinner with baked turnips," Jace replied. "But now."

"But now what?" Cornelius demanded.

"I am Jace Kasia, a Cretan Archer," Jace said to the front ranks of the mob. "More so, I am a file leader of an Archer Company. Understand this before you take another step. I will murder ten of you before you can reach me. And another five when you come in range of my war hatchet. Cornelius, please select the first ten men to die."

The Tribune bent the elbow of his left arm and lifted the hand over his head. Then as if throwing a curse, he straightened and pointed at a sailor.

"You are a dead man," he pronounced. Following the same actions, Cornelius dropped his arm, pointed, and stated. "You are a dead man."

It might have been the command voice or having a Cretan Archer shifting an arrowhead with each condemnation. But on the fourth 'you are a dead man', the crowd broke ranks and walked away.

"Thank you," Cornelius said. "Thank you for stepping into the fire for me."

Aratus of Sicyon's phrase to his Hoplites had the weight of a leader's appreciation. Now, Cornelius Scipio's sentiment held the same sincerity.

"We did it together, sir," Jace pushed back.

"No, Centurion Kasia. You held the command together when I was trapped and indecisive."

Jace froze from the adoration. He had been through a lot with the nobleman and had been thanked before. But he'd never felt this level of gratitude.

"Hopefully, sir, I will always be there when you need me."

The big Noricum strode to the two Legion officers.

"The waitress tells me you needed a ship," he uttered. "I have a ship. But she's not cheap."

Cornelius jostled his shoulder, and the cloak full of coins jingled.

"It just so happens, Captain Norbert. We have lots of coins."

Cornelius felt Jace's hand slip into a fold. A moment later, he extracted a handful of coins.

"A Cretan always makes a profit," Jace explained as he dumped the coins into a pouch. "It's part of our heritage."

"Is threatening men with an arrow through the heart also part of your heritage?" Norbert inquired.

"A heritage of threat?" Jace said in a thoughtful manner. "Not necessarily. Unless, of course, Tribune Cornelius Scipio orders it."

"In that case, I'll be extra kind to Cornelius Scipio," the Noricum proclaimed. "Come to my table. Let us drink, eat, and discuss your needs and my fee."

***

Two days out of Patras, the swift Noricum trading vessel rounded a point of land.

"Preveza was originally called Berenike. King Pyrrhus founded it seventy-five years ago. He named the new city after his mother-in-law, Berenice I of Egypt," Norbert explained. "If your warships came this way, they surely stopped here."

When the bow cleared the point of land, a city of stone and painted clay brick homes greeted them.

"Looks like a nice place to visit," Jace remarked.

"And an excellent place to catch a ship bound for Delphi," Cornelius added.

Jace and Norbert missed his meaning until they noticed the ships. Both Republic warships rested on the beach just south of the city.

"Captain Norbert you can beach here," Cornelius told him. "We'll depart. Thank you for the ride."

"We'll drop you in the surf and continue onward."

"But Preveza is right there, Captain," Cornelius pointed out. "I'm sure it's a good trading spot."

"That city is too cosmopolitan for a boatload of rustic Noricums like us," Norbert claimed. "We have some daylight left. We'll use it."

"If you don't mind me asking," Jace inquired. "What are you hauling?"

"Artwork from Sicyon," the Captain answered. "The city produces fine sculptures, paintings, and jewelry. They're worthless for trading along the coast. But to the right buyers, priceless."

"Then you're not a coastal trader?" Cornelius blurted out. "And we didn't pay you to skip ports of call. Because you weren't going to stop at any."

"You are a very smart young man, Tribune Scipio. And it's been a pleasure knowing you," Norbert informed Cornelius. "Good luck on your future endeavors. Rowers, hold water."

The four broad shouldered Noricum crewmen stopped rowing but left their oars in the sea. The drag of the blades slowed then stopped the transport.

Jace jumped into the shallow water. Cornelius tossed down their gear before turning to face the Norbert. He saluted the Captain then leaped over the side.

Behind them, Norbert shouted, "Back her down."

The trading ship pulled away as Jace and Cornelius splashed to the beach.

"Do we change and dress the part of Legion officers?" Jace inquired.

"Earlier, I wanted a bath, and a beef dinner with baked turnips," Cornelius replied. "But now."

"But now what, Tribune?"

"I want done with this intelligence business."

The two trudged through the sand. In the distance, Legionaries standing guard at the Roman warships took notice. They picked up spears and shields and watched the intruders.

"Do you know what I just noticed, Centurion Kasia?"

"I have no idea, Tribune Scipio."

"There are no command tents," Cornelius sighted as a squad of Legionaries jogged towards them.

"Does that mean the command staff for the warships are quartered in the city?"

"Yes. And we get to deal with inexperienced, ambitious, and aggressive Centurions out to prove themselves."

"We should have gone for the beef," Cornelius said as ten Legionaries leveled their spears and surrounded them.

"You are being detained by order of the Senate of Rome," the squad leader announced, "under the direction of Centurion Juvenal."

Jace stopped in front of Cornelius and inhaled sharply.

"Before you begin ordering around a Tribune of the Legion and an assistant Aedile of Rome, you might want to get Juvenal over here," Jace barked.

"Thank you, Centurion Kasia," Cornelius acknowledged the presentation. "Well, Decanus. Why are you still standing there?"

"I'm under orders to…"

"Centurion Kasia, please," Cornelius requested.

"Stop talking, squad leader. Tribune Scipio asked you a rhetorical question," Jace explained. "It was designed to give you a chance to run and get your Centurion."

From one of the warships, a Centurion strutted down the ramp and power walked towards the squad. The set of his shoulders showed he was everything Cornelius described in a young combat officer.

"Is that Juvenal?" Jace inquired.

"That is Centurion Juvenal," the Decanus confirmed.

"Tribune Scipio, you might want to take the lead on this," Jace suggested, "or allow me to take out my war bow."

Cornelius dropped his baggage and pulled out his breast piece. Juvenal arrived as Cornelius was fitting it on.

"Who are you and what are your names?" the Centurion spit out.

Neither Jace nor Cornelius replied. But Cornelius strapped on his spatha, then his red cloak. Finally, he took the cover off the Tribune's helmet with the yellow horsehair comb.

"I am not accustomed to speaking with junior officers," Cornelius growled as he walked up to Juvenal. The helmet, although tucked under his arm, conveyed the authority. "Where is your ship's Centurion?"

"Sir, Senior Centurion Italus is in Preveza."

"I gathered that. Go and get him," Cornelius instructed. "And if you must, tell him it's by order of the Senate of Rome and for the good of the Roman Fleet and the Legions of the East. As commanded by Tribune Cornelius Scipio."

Faced with a haughty staff officer, he couldn't manage, Centurion Juvenal saluted and marched away in the direction of the city.

"It's near mealtime," Cornelius mentioned to the Decanus. "Would your squad have any extra stew for a couple of Legion officers?"

"Yes, sir," the squad leader stammered.

"Then lead us to your bivouac. We're hungry."

***

The four horses kicked up sand as the ship's officers galloped from the city. At the aft of the warship, they dismounted.

"I will have his cūlus up on charges," the Senior Centurion declared as he marched up the ramp. "Where is the Tribune?"

"Sir, he and Centurion Kasia are with the infantry," the sentry reported.

"With the Legionaries," the ship's senior officer repeated. He spun and ran into his First Principale. "Get out of my way."

After squeezing by the First, the Second, and the Third Principale, the warship's commander was out of patience.

Upon reaching the bottom of the ramp, he shouted, "Tribune Scipio. Where in Hades are you?"

"I'm with the fighting men, Senior Centurion Italus," Cornelius replied.

He stood and the campfire backlit his shape.

Italus stomped to the fire and asked in cold fury, "what have you done to my command?"

"I've got word that the Macedonian Fleet will pass by here in the next five days," Cornelius told him. "They plan to land at Orikum. Then march up the Ajose River and assault the fort at Apollonia."

"How could you know that?"

Cornelius pressed Aratus' map into Italus' hand.

"You have a day to cross, a day to meet with Praetor Laevinus, and a day back with the fleet. That's cutting it mighty fine. If the Macedonians take Apollonia, the Legions will have a hard time digging them out. If they capture two Illyrian forts, we could lose the east coast of the Republic."

"Sir, we don't have to listen to an unknown Tribune who came out of nowhere," the warship's first officer proposed. "We should take him into custody."

"I can't be detained," Cornelius argued. "Centurion Kasia and I are on the expedition sent by the Senate to see the Oracle."

"Stand down, First Principale," Italus said. "Don't you want our ship to get credit for finding the Macedonian Fleet."

"Yes, sir but how can…"

"Tribune Scipio has a reputation for unorthodox behavior," Italus explained. "There are Senators who love him. And others who wouldn't mind seeing him up on the wood. But none will argue against his love for the Republic or his bravery. I'm taking Cornelius' message to Laevinus and claiming the credit for our ship."

Cornelius turned to the campfire and the Legionaries.

"Thank you for the stew," he said.

"Rah, Tribune," the infantrymen responded.

Then Cornelius, while addressing Italus, waved Jace to his feet.

"We'll take three of the horses, Senior Centurion. You won't be needing them."

"You can keep the deposit when you return them to the stable."

"Very generous of you," Cornelius said.

He and Jace collected their gear and walked to the four mounts.

While strapping their baggage to the third horse, Jace guessed, "I take it, we're not going to spend the night with the Navy?"

"They'll be launching before dawn. And I don't plan on rising that early."

"Back to Delphi after a late breakfast?" Jace assumed.

"If you don't mind giving up some of that Cretan profit from the archery demonstration," Cornelius ventured.

"I guess the elders on Crete would understand."

They mounted and rode for the city of Preveza.

Chapter 29 – Fat Priests

In the vastness of the sea and the protective coves and islands of the long coastline, it was possible for a fleet to hide. At least that's what it felt like to Cornelius. All the way back to the Gulf of Patras, he scanned the horizon searching for Macedonian ships of war.

"It's as if the sea swallowed them," Jace commented.

"If only that was true," Cornelius speculated. "But I don't hold out much hope for their demise. Hopefully, the Republic Fleet launched in time to intercept King Philip."

"You did what you could, Tribune. And now, we've come full circle."

Ahead, the beach of Patras expanded from a thin line above the waves to a widening stretch of sand and dirt.

"I suggest on this visit, we use the café only for finding a ride to Kirra and for dining," Cornelius directed.

"But we could pick up some extra coins," Jace protested.

"No more demonstrations, please."

"As you wish," Jace allowed.

From the steering platform, the Captain of the transport called to his six rowers, "Port side, hold water. Starboard, power fifteen. Bring us about."

With the oars on the left creating drag in the water, and those on the right stroking hard, the ship rotated until the prow faced away from shore.

"Back it down," the Captain ordered.

A moment later, the rear of the ship entered the shallows.

"Way enough. Stow your oars and get over the sides," he called. Then he issued the final landing directions. "Get us dry."

Moments later, the crew shoved the transport up and onto the beach.

285

Jace jumped down and caught their bundles. Cornelius joined him and they hiked to the café.

***

"Well, hello, my nobleman," the waitress greeted Cornelius. "I see you've brought you circus back to Patras."

"Not this time. We're here for food," Cornelius corrected. He extended a coin to her. "That's for your help in procuring transportation to the Port of Kirra."

She took the coin then buried her face in a hand to hide her amusement.

"Calling Kirra, a port, is a joke. And procuring transportation is the funniest thing I've heard all week. If you need a ride, say it," she chuckled. "But I'm disappointed. I figured you two were mercenaries for hire, off on some grand adventure. Instead, you're just a couple of worshipers on a pilgrimage to the Temple of Apollo."

"Is getting a ride to Kirra a problem?" Cornelius inquired.

"There are a number of boats to Kirra for pilgrims," the server answered. "It's a day's travel and expensive for most."

"For most?" Jace questioned.

"My brother has a boat and a crew of fishermen who you can hire," she explained. "And he'll give my nobleman a better price than most."

"It sounds like the best way to go," Jace said. "One more thing. Do you love your brother?"

"What a horrible thing to say. Of course, I love my brother. Why do you ask?"

"Just so we're clear. If he attempts to rob us, I will cut his throat and gut the fishermen. Is that clear?"

286

"Wine for you, gentlemen?" she inquired, decidedly changing the subject. "Today we have baked fish on a bed of radishes, carrots, and cabbage."

"For both of us," Cornelius told her. After she went to fill the order, he addressed Jace. "Does that mean we won't be meeting her brother?"

"I assume not," Jace concluded.

**

The waters of Corinth Bay grew choppy. On the rocking boat, the wealthy men clung to their gifts for the Oracle and their bodyguards clung to their clients.

"How many are swimmers, do you think?" Jace asked.

"From the looks of them, none," Cornelius answered. "But, even if they know how, it's hard to swim with a purse of silver around your neck."

"Then, it's a good thing we're poor," Jace offered.

A couple of the affluent petitioners scooted away from Jace and Cornelius. And their bodyguards shot warning glares at the pair.

The shuttle boat had loaded ten pilgrims with men at arms and shoved off from Patras at first light. The gulf had been smooth and the sailing good until mid-afternoon. Then, dark clouds moved in overhead and the calm surface became sawtooth waves.

"We may be heading for the Temple of Apollo," Jace observed. "But right now, my prayers are to Poseidon."

"You aren't a Greek anymore," Cornelius advised. "You're a Roman and Neptune is our God of the Sea."

"Yes, yes, I keep getting my heritage and my Gods confused," Jace exclaimed. "There must be something wrong with my mind. Do you believe The Pythia can help me?"

Thinking they were trapped with a madman, the wealthy moved farther away. Unfortunately, the shift put them near the rails, and they were soon soaked with saltwater.

"You know full well, the High Priestess gives prophecies," Cornelius scolded. "She's not a healer. Why did you do that?"

"Because I wanted more room," Jace replied while stretching out.

A side benefit of the rough and wet ride, the wind blew from the sea and across the Gulf of Patras. After passing through the narrows, the breeze drove the transport swiftly over the Gulf of Corinth.

***

"Kirra, the gateway to the Temple of Apollo," the Captain announced. "A favorable voyage. We accept offerings in the name of Poseidon so your crew can offer sacrifices to the God for our safe passage."

Jace turned his head and whispered, "See, around here it's Poseidon."

"You, my friend, take the Gods too lightly," Cornelius cautioned. "Do you never practice deference to the Gods and Goddesses?"

"Just to the deities who can kill me outright," Jace replied while sitting up. "Poseidon who can drown me, of course. The Goddess Mefita who can suffocate me with her poison fumes. And the bolt thrower, the God of Thunder, Zeus."

"Jupiter," Cornelius corrected.

"Him too. I'll honor them both if it keeps me from getting hit by lightning."

288

As if the Gods heard Jace, the heavens cracked open, and fingers of silver light raced across the sky. Moments later, the boat and passengers trembled from a mighty clap of thunder.

"Which one do you think made that demonstration?" Jace asked while pulling a coin from his purse.

"A display of power from the God Jupiter is not one of your archery demonstrations," Cornelius protested.

"Certainly not," Jace agreed. "You can't bet on an outcome from a God. You can only make an offering and say a prayer."

He flipped the coin to a crewman.

"The blessings of Poseidon on you, sir," the sailor responded.

***

Near the beach of Kirra, the transport swung sideways. Crewmen leaped off the deep side and pushed the hull against the sandy bottom. In spite of their efforts, a space of surf separated the boat from the beach.

"Aren't you going to land us?" a well-dressed man inquired.

"On Master, my apologies. We have a problem and need to get to the port of Itea," the Captain made the excuse as priests and porters moved down the beach, heading for the boatload of pilgrims.

"I wouldn't beach here either," Jace observed. "Come Tribune Scipio. Let's get ahead of the mob."

They grabbed their bundles, made their way to the rail, and jumped into the water.

"Why does a horde of simple priests and a handful of porters make you uneasy?" Cornelius inquired.

They reached dry land and shook water from their hobnailed boots.

"When I was with the Legions up north, before the Boii Tribe ruined our campaign, a tracker warned me about fat priests and starving citizens," Jace described.

Cornelius scanned the crowd as it descended on the load of worshipers. The description of well-fed holy men and gaunt workers matched the trackers warning.

"You're thinking greedy priests and desperate citizens," Cornelius proposed. "I agree. Let's go see if we can locate Senator Pictor and his entourage."

Cornelius and Jace hurried off the beach. They planned to search for someone in authority to ask, once they entered Kirra.

***

They roamed the streets, fending off beggars, rough men who offered to carry their bundles, drama girls looking for coins and company, and priests of all types. Growing frustrated, Cornelius stopped in an alcove between shops.

"This is a waste," he whined. "We should find shelter for the evening and start again in the morning."

"An excellent idea," Jace agreed. "The God Fames touched me a few streets ago."

"I saw you consume a large breakfast," Cornelius countered. "There is no way the God of Starvation has had a chance to counter that feast."

"Just when I honor a God, you complain," Jace groaned. Glancing up and down the street, he searched for the sign of an inn. "But you're correct we…"

Stopping, the archer indicated a direction and walked off. Cornelius, having no idea what Jace was after, followed. They were both tired and in need of a place to rest.

Two blocks away, he discovered what Jace had seen. A sign hung from a building. A bow and arrow and a leaping deer were displayed on the banner.

"I can eat," Cornelius said, assuming the place was a restaurant.

"Sorry to disappoint, Tribune Scipio, but this is a chapel dedicated to the Goddess Artemis."

"The Goddess of the hunt, the bow, and animals, like the Goddess Diana?"

They pushed through a door and entered into a candle lit chamber.

"How may the Goddess Artemis help a Cretan Archer?" a Priest inquired. "And his traveling companion?"

"You recognized the bow case?" Jace asked.

"No archer. Anyone could carry a bow case. It's the manner of assembly of your long pack. Only Cretan Archers pack so much while leaving access to their weapons."

Jace pulled out several coins and handed them to the Priest.

"That's very generous," Cornelius noted. "I hope the coins are more than a reward for flattery."

Jace held up a finger signaling wait. Then he tapped Cornelius' shoulder.

"What about him?" he asked the Priest.

"A brave commander, if I ever saw one," the Priest replied.

"Not flattery, Tribune Scipio, gossip," Jace reported. "The oarsmen and sailors from our transport have been spinning tales about our engagement with the Illyrian pirates."

291

"Tell me, Priest of Artemis, where can we find Quintus Pictor and the delegation from Rome?" Cornelius asked.

"There was a schedule change and they have been denied The Pythia until all of their party is in attendance," the Priest explained. "You'll find them camped at Chryso. A place where all those seeking guidance from the High Priestess of Apollo wait to be called to her chamber."

"How do we get to Chryso?" Jace asked.

"Head north out of Kirra. Follow the trail to the top. Where it levels out, go east. It's a little over five miles."

Cornelius handed the Priest a few more coins and they left the chapel.

"So, they finally arrived," an older Priest said as he walked from a shadowy corner of the chamber. "The Chief Priest of Apollo will be grateful for the information."

"The wealth of visitors allows them to pick and choose from supplicants. Why those two?"

"As you said, the Temple of Apollo has many petitioners. They can manipulate them in ways and for purposes a poor Chapel, like ours, cannot even imagine."

***

On the street heading north, Jace looked at Cornelius.

"Tell me, Tribune Scipio. Did it strike you as strange that the High Priestess denied Senator Pictor an audience," Jace questioned, "until all of his party was in attendance?"

"I didn't think anything of it," Cornelius admitted.

"But officially, we aren't part of his entourage," Jace remarked. "No one would have missed us after we finished with the fleet business, if we had returned to Rome."

"If you put it like that, Centurion Kasia, it is strange."

The trail began to climb. Soon the buildings of Kirra fell behind and the two Legion officers hiked into the long shadows at the end of the day. Adding to the fading light, the clouds opened, and it began to rain.

"Oizys," Jace mumbled from under the oiled skin.

"What did you say?" Cornelius called from under his waterproof wrap.

They walked a few more wet, slippery steps.

"I was praying to the Goddess of Misery," Jace said. "Thanking her for reminding me that I'm alive."

"Because only the dead are without suffering?" Cornelius offered.

"Rah, Tribune."

Cornelius whispered, "Thank you, Miseria."

The stockade gates came out of the blur from the sheets of rain.

"Didn't expect that," Jace remarked when he noticed them.

A sentry stepped out of a shed and asked, "Expect what?"

"A barrier," Cornelius replied.

The security didn't have the feel of military. He was more temple guard than infantry. Proving the comparison, the sentry walked in close and the three conversed under overlapping waterproof wraps.

"Names?" he inquired.

"Cornelius Scipio and Jace Kasia," Cornelius volunteered.

Jace shrugged at the question. The names couldn't have any meaning to the sentry.

"We've been waiting for you two," the guard said. He whistled and a second guard appeared out of the dark. "Scipio and Kasia. Take them to the Roman compound."

Jace leaned towards Cornelius in a conspiratorial manner.

"Not now," Cornelius whispered.

They followed the guard along a well-maintained stone path. After hiking up the muddy trail, the flat solid surface was pleasant. It branched several times, but the guard remained on the main pathway.

"That is your tent," the guard informed them. He pointed to an end tent set in a semicircle of dwellings. "There's wood in the brazier so you can dry your clothing. We'd light it but, in this weather, you're better off getting fire from the neighboring tent."

Jace studied the overhang that provided a dry sitting area in front of a mid-sized tent. Turning, he asked, "How did…"

But the guard had vanished in the rain.

***

With a fire going in the iron disk, cloaks draped over their shoulders to ward off the chill, Jace and Cornelius sat in a stupor. Their brains and bodies numb from traveling. They watched the flames in the brazier and listened to the rain fall.

"Kind of pleasant once you're out of the weather," Cornelius proposed.

"If we had wine, it would be perfect."

A moment later, Quintus Ennius dashed from his tent to the shelter of Jace and Cornelius' overhang. The young poet carried a wineskin in his hand.

"Did someone say vino?" he inquired.

294

"What happened to the triple language act?" Cornelius questioned as he took the wine.

"I use it to build my mystique as a poet and an educated man," Ennius told him. "It worked great until Kasia talked back as if I wasn't confusing at all."

"Oscan is the language of my people," Jace commented. "And I was raised as a Greek on the Island of Crete."

"Oscan, your people, and Greek?" Ennius listed in confusion. Grabbing at the one thing that might explain the different languages, he said. "I didn't know Rome had colonies on Crete?"

"The Republic doesn't and Jace's tale is a long one," Cornelius stated, stopping any rehash of the archer's history. "Tell us what happened here."

"We arrived five days ago, and Senator Pictor met with an important Temple Priest," Ennius the Poet described. "On the appointed day, he was preparing to go and see The Pythia. Before he left, another priest arrived and told him there was a problem and he had to wait until it was resolved."

"The holdup happened because all the members of Pictor's party weren't here?" Jace proposed.

"Yes. How did you know that?"

"I'm a Cretan Archer and the Goddess Artemis blesses each bowman with the ability to see…"

"Centurion Kasia, not tonight," Cornelius groaned. "Just sell him the arrow and we can move on."

"I have no blessed arrows with me," Jace admitted.

"But, members of Pictor's party, is exactly what the priest said," Ennius gushed. "You must tell me how you did that."

"I owe it all to the Goddess Artemis," Jace reported.

He locked eyes with Cornelius, challenging the Tribune to deny the hand of the Goddess in bringing them to the chapel and learning the reason for the delay. Cornelius said nothing. He simply handed the wineskin to Jace.

Settling into a pattern, they passed the vino around and enjoyed the patter of rain from the dry shelter.

***

Much later, three bodies appeared on the pathway. One went to Pictor's tent, one waited on the path, and the third headed towards Jace and Cornelius.

"What have we here?" Jace uttered. His hand slipped to the war hatchet.

Quintus Ennius noted the move and consoled him, "you've nothing to fear. We're less than a mile and a half from the Temple of Apollo. And in a guarded compound for pilgrims."

Cornelius dropped a heavy hand on the poet's shoulder.

"This isn't the grounds of a wealthy patron of poetry," he warned. "You're a long way from the safety of powerful friends and the Legionaries are on the other side of this cluster. If Jace Kasia reaches for a weapon, do not call attention to it. Just relax and be grateful."

The figure came from the dark as if floating. For all his control during the approach, the cleric stood close to the warmth of the fire.

"Tribune Scipio. Centurion Kasia. You are invited when the sun reaches its pinnacle, to enter the chamber of the High Priestess."

"What about Senator Pictor?" Cornelius asked.

"His appointment is directly after yours."

With the message delivered, the Priest of Apollo spun and glided away.

"Did I hear that right?" Jace stammered. "We're to have an audience with The Pythia."

"What should we ask the Oracle?" Cornelius muttered.

"That's easy," Quintus Ennius volunteered. "Ask her why she wanted to see you two."

Jace took a stream of vino and repeated, "We will ask her why she wanted to see us. That was easy."

***

In the morning, the sky cleared and Jace fell into the Legionaries' camp routine. He helped chop vegetables and added a few spices and a ration of salt to the pot. When the stew boiled, Jace ladled out portions and carried a bowl back to Cornelius. They had taken a bite when Pictor emerged from his tent.

"Why does the High Priestess of Apollo want to see you two?" Pictor demanded as he stomped towards them.

Pictor, the poet, the Priest of Jupiter, and Terrigenus must have had breakfast inside the Senator's tent. It was the first appearance by any of them. And based on his absence from the Legionary's cookfire, the meal was prepared by Optio Perperna.

"The NCO is multitalented," Jace remarked rather than answer Pictor's question. "Apparently, he can cook for important people. Get lost on a simple guard layout. Hide under the cloak of a senior officer when things get dangerous. And look good doing it all, I have no doubt."

"I asked you a question," Pictor reiterated. "I expect an answer not a chariot race commentary."

"That's a good one, Senator," Jace responded. "You see, sir, we have no idea. But I figured if you were coming over, I might as well give you my professional opinion of the NCO in your party."

"Tribune Scipio, have you nothing to say?" Pictor challenged.

"I have found, Senator, when in combat, I need my combat officers and NCOs to think for themselves," Cornelius replied between bites of stew. "When my detachment was surrounded by Hannibal's African Corps, my Optios were invaluable in forming the fighting square. They saved my life, I'm sure of it."

As Pictor stormed away, he growled, "Senior Tribune Terrigenus, get over there and discipline your Legion officers."

"And Senior Tribune," Cornelius reminded Terrigenus, "don't forget my travel funds when you come."

***

As if they couldn't see the sun near its peak, two priest came from outside the pilgrims' compound.

"We'll escort you to the Temple of Apollo," they said once.

Then as if statues, the pair waited on the stone pathway.

Senator Pictor came from his tent in a toga. Cornelius and Jace arrived on the path in tunics that were semi clean and still damp from washing.

"Don't you have something more appropriate?" Pictor scolded.

He scanned the limp travel tunics.

"Yes, sir. Back at my father's villa, I have a complete wardrobe," Cornelius told him. "But that's in Rome, Senator."

Before the conversation could progress into an argument, the priest indicated the path. One led the way and the other followed behind the trio of pilgrims.

"Tribune Scipio, is something wrong?" Jace inquired. "Lately, you've been short tempered with some people."

"But not with everyone?"

"No, sir, only with important people. Which is odd for you. Truthfully, you're usually a better politician than that."

"Jace, I realized that no matter what I do, some people won't support me," he answered, his eyes flashing with a moment of passion. "It takes forethought and tact to pretend to bow to people who hate you. And it gives them power. I've decided, if I'm ever going to get my Legions, I have to treat my friends well. And display scorn to my enemies. This is a fight I must win in order to face Hannibal across a battlefield."

Jace nodded and walked beside Cornelius. They were silent until the group rounded a bend. Then mighty columns towering into the sky came into view.

"The Temple of Apollo at Delphi," Jace whispered.

"Indeed, it is," the Priest behind them confirmed. "If you'll follow the path to the steps, we'll get you prepared for the High Priestess."

***

Preparation consisted of Cornelius making a healthy donation to the temple for both him and Jace. Afterward, a priest placed laurel wreaths on their heads. Next, they were beckoned by another priest from inside the temple. Cornelius and Jace took the stairs up to the sanctuary level.

"Nice view of the Bay of Corinth," Jace remarked after glancing behind them.

"This is serious, Kasia," Cornelius mumbled. "Behave accordingly."

"I am serious. We should run."

"I thought you weren't afraid of the Gods?"

"Not until I saw this temple. It feels wrong to me."

Halfway across the sanctuary floor, the priest stopped and indicated a dark opening.

Jace peered downward but couldn't see anything beyond the first step.

"I'll go first," he volunteered. "If I fall, run."

Cornelius put a hand on Jace's shoulder and walked them both to the opening.

***

At first, a light aroma of spices came from the opening and both Cornelius and Jace relaxed. How bad could it be if it smelled like a Saturnalia feast?

They descended and, as the stairs took them lower, the light aroma changed to a heavier flower fragrance. Lower still and the odor changed to musk scents as if furry animals were present. Then at the bottom, a haze surrounded them.

"Goddess Mefita is here," Jace warned. "I detect the sharp aroma of her realm. I pray she doesn't suffocate us with her vapor."

Through the veil of the mist, they saw a mature woman sitting on a three-legged stool. In one hand, she held laurel reeds and in the other a porcelain bowl of water. Her ability to balance impressed Cornelius as her stool bridged a fissure in the floor.

"Ask your question," she requested.

Her voice sounded younger than she appeared.

"Why are we here?" Cornelius asked.

Boiling up from below her, mist escaped the crack and shrouded the Priestess. As if looking through a thin fabric, they watched her inhale and roll her head back.

300

"Victory resides, my General and Master of Horse, not on these shores," the Oracle breathed in a heavy sigh, *"nor in your homeland, or on another."*

The mist swirled and for a moment, Cornelius and Jace lost sight of her in the fog.

When she spoke again, her voice came from far away, *"Victory resides as much in your memory and in your heart, as in your battle formation."*

In an assault on their senses, the vapors rushed up their noses. Both young men threw their heads back. Their attempt to avoid the acid stench failed.

"Victory resides," the High Priestess of Apollo whispered. A hiss was all she required as her lips brushed the ears of both Cornelius and Jace. *"Not in your deeds, but in your oaths."*

Her words still echoed in their minds when hands pressed against their backs. Cornelius and Jace were propelled from her chamber and up the steps. They emerged in the temple room, were hurried across the floor of the sanctuary, and then deposited on the steps of the Temple of Apollo.

"What did The Pythia want with you?" Quintus Pictor demanded. "Did the High Priestess say anything about Hannibal Barca or the Republic?"

"The Oracle mentioned victory in a far-off land," Jace informed the Senate's representative to Delphi.

"No, sir, nothing about the defeat of Hannibal," Cornelius informed him. "Maybe your audience will be more fruitful."

A pair of priests came from the temple, flanked Pictor, and escorted him up the steps and into the temple.

Jace peered down the line of wealthy petitioners waiting to see the Oracle. Then he refocused on Cornelius and asked,

"Is it true that King Alexander of Macedonia visited the Oracle to ask if he would be successful before starting on his conquests?"

"The story I heard was The Pythia told the King to come back later," Cornelius recounted. "Being young and having no patience, Alexander grabbed the High Priestess by the hair and began pulling her from the chamber. As she slid along the floor, the Priestess screamed, *You are invincible, my son.* The King stopped and dropped the Oracle on the floor. Then he announced as he left the temple, now I have my answer."

"We've seen The Pythia," Jace emphasized. "Did we get an answer as to why she wanted to see us?"

"I don't remember," Cornelius Scipio admitted. "But, at least, we didn't assault the High Priestess."

Jace Kasia rubbed his hands together. Then he cracked the knuckles on one and suggested, "Maybe we should have."

Inside the temple, the Chief Priest stood with a young cleric. They peered at the two Legion officers on the steps.

"Will it work?" the young cleric asked.

"Sometimes it does and other times the chosen are failures," the Priest explained. "But giving prophecies to future leaders is how the Temple of Apollo at Delphi has stayed relevant for thousands of years."

In the Oracle's chamber, the High Priestess answered Quintus Pictor's question, "*Practice supplications to the Gods and Goddesses and observe the proper rituals. Honor the Gods and victory in the war will belong to the people of Rome.*"

The End

A sample from book #4 in *A Legion Archer* series

A Legion Legacy

Chapter 00 – Help a Lowlife

Pugnus ambled down the sidewalk. Tradesmen driving oxen carts, pedestrians enjoying a pleasant summer afternoon, and shopkeepers sorting their merchandise turned away. He took no offense at them avoiding eye contact. Their reaction of fear kept the Legion veteran in business.

His stomach rumbled and he stopped to gaze up and down the street. As if a wealthy nobleman surveying his farm, Pugnus looked upon his property. Every shop and residence in a two-block area gave deference to their protector. He could expand beyond the blocks, but the former Legionary had no interest in taking on assistants. The Legions had shown him to be a bad leader and a worse follower. So, the street lord ran the business with himself as the sole employee.

"I am not a greedy man," he uttered. "Just a hungry one."

Spying a new load of fruit at his produce shop, Pugnus strolled to the entrance, sniffed the fresh aroma, and walked into the store.

"Centurion Pugnus. Good day, sir," the produce seller greeted him. "We have some lovely grapes, figs, and pomegranates. Plus, quinces, and plums but they aren't quite ripe yet."

Pugnus pointed to a cluster of figs and a bunch of grapes.

"Excellent choices," the proprietor gushed. He took a woven grass mat from a pile. After placing the figs and grapes in the center, he folded the mat around the fruit and handed the package to Pugnus.

"No charge, sir," the shopkeeper told him.

"That is no way to run a business," Pugnus instructed. "You must in every purchase charge the highest rate a customer can afford."

"Yes sir, I understand."

Reaching into the wrap, Pugnus pulled out several grapes and popped them into his mouth. As he chewed, grape juice ran down his chin.

"If memory serves me correctly, last week you were short on your payment," Pugnus asserted. He pulled a couple of figs from the package and shoved them into his mouth. "You know every enterprise pays dues to the Shop Keepers Collective. When one misses a payment, it puts undue burden on the other owners."

Pugnus kicked the side of a basket. Four pears shot from the container and dropped to the floor. Rushing over, the proprietor bent to pick them up.

"When one doesn't pay, others get ideas," Pugnus explained.

Lifting his right foot, he kicked the stooped man in the ribs. The shopkeeper rolled onto the basket, crushing the wicker weave, and smashing several pears.

"No charge. No charge," Pugnus snarled. "You owe me bronze from last week and more from this week. And you say you understand business. Here's something you will understand."

Pugnus grabbed the produce vendor by the back of the neck, jerked him to his feet, and smeared the remaining grapes and figs onto the man's face. Choking from the pulp up his nose, the proprietor attempted to pick it away. Punching with less power than he was capable of, Pugnus drove his fists into the shopkeeper's fingers and nose.

Something cracked. Either the man's nose or a finger. Neither bothered Pugnus.

"I'll be back tomorrow, and you better have the dues," he warned.

On the street, Pugnus brushed his fist on his shirt, leaving smashed fruit, juice, and blood on his chest. Ignoring the stain, he crossed the street to the meat market.

Although the butcher was up to date on his dues, he was friends with the produce seller. Pugnus aimed to stop any rebellion against the Shop Keepers Collective before it became a problem.

***

Cornelius stooped before strolling down the steps. He paused on the last riser to allow his eyes to grow accustomed to the dim interior. Stacked wine casks filled three walls of the brick lined wine cellar. The fourth wall was left open for the staircase and a few tables.

"Good afternoon, Aedile Scipio," the proprietor greeted him. "Did you notice the new doors and the ironwork at the entrance?"

"I did notice," Cornelius replied. "They enhance your property and compliment every business on the street."

"Thank you for giving me the extra days to get the work done. Are you in a rush or do you have time for a glass of vino?"

"A glass would be welcomed," Cornelius told the proprietor.

Lifting the hem of his toga, he went to the table farthest from the steps and sat.

"Here you are, Aedile."

The glass was heavy and filled to the brim with red wine. While he appreciated the man's generous portion, Cornelius feared a spill and a stain on his toga. To avoid attending afternoon meetings with a soiled garment, he bent in a most undignified manner, and slurped from the vessel.

In mid gulp, Cornelius noted a pair of dirty cavalry boots walk into his peripheral vision.

"I always suspected once you let go of that prideful exterior," the wearer said. "You would lose all control and end up living in a wine shop."

"I didn't know you had that much imagination," Cornelius confessed between sips. "But seeing as you've found me, have a seat."

Jace Kasia pulled out a chair, threw a leg over the back, and sat on the seat.

"Vino, my good man," he called to the shopkeeper.

"Aedile Scipio," the property inquired, "is this cavalryman bothering you?"

"For years," Cornelius conceded. "But Centurion of Cavalry Kasia has saved my life on occasion. I would think that earns him a glass of vino."

"Nice place," Jace remarked as a not so full glass landed on the tabletop. "But the ceiling isn't high enough to properly string up a pair of assassins."

"It's one of the reasons I like it," Cornelius explained. "And it's near the edge of my quadrant of the city. Few people can find me here. Which begs the question, how did you locate me?"

"Two stops. One at a leather workers to get a general direction of your route," Jace answered. "And another at the biggest and loudest pub in the area."

"Why there?"

"Because, it wasn't your type of establishment," Jace informed him. "But it was almost a public nuisance. Every customer there had an opinion about their Aedile. I sorted the opinions. Disregarding the stories of you with sheep and drama girls, I picked the ones that mentioned a small cellar with excellent vino."

"Sheep and drama girls?" At the notion, Cornelius spit out a mouthful of wine. "I think I'll shut them down for a week and request an offering to Bacchus before allowing them to reopen."

"I'm sure the God of Wine will appreciate a sacrifice," Jace remarked. "But you didn't call me all the way from Lucania to talk about your bad reputation."

"Lucania," Cornelius repeated. "How I envy you, being in the field against Hannibal."

"Hannibal is still on the west coast," Jace informed him. "Mostly, we chase the Libyan Cavalry around the countryside. What happened to your plan? I thought you gave up Legion duty to build your support."

"I have and I am," Cornelius confirmed.

"Why am I here, Tribune Scipio?" Jace asked. "Certainly not to sit in a wine cellar and drink. Not that I'm complaining."

"There are four Aediles, and each takes a quadrant of the city to manage," Cornelius explained. "My cousin Marcus Cethegus has a section of Rome under his care. But he also, because I'm underage, has to sign my contracts and notes of violations. That extra duty keeps him away from his sector."

"I'm not a magistrate type," Jace proposed. "But if you need an archer to fill a shopkeeper with arrows, I'm your man."

"Aedile Cethegus can do the façade inspections, manage the markets, and check the temples in his quadrant," Cornelius described. "What he can't do is linger in his district looking for lowlifes."

"Ah, tracking criminals, I can do that. Except, isn't that the job of the city guard?"

"The guard is very good at crowd control, arresting gang members, detaining the accused, and sometimes, capturing thieves," Cornelius replied. "What they can't do is get peaceful citizens to testify against violent men."

"You want me to coach shopkeepers on how to find their courage? You know as well as I do, bravery is not an amulet I can hang around a weak person's neck. No number of awards, or amount of talking, or encouragement will turn a sheep into a hero."

"You're close, Centurion Kasia," Cornelius said. Jace gave him a half smile and waited. "What the right man can do is break the spirit of a criminal."

"Help a lowlife see the error of his ways?" Jace summarized. "Now that is something I'm well qualified for. Do you have anyone in mind?"

"Actually, I do," Cornelius admitted. "He claims to be a veteran and goes by the title of Centurion. A big man, he uses his size to terrorize the shopkeepers. None of them will bring charges or testify against him."

Jace drained his glass. It clicked on the tabletop when he set it down.

"Another?" Cornelius asked.

"After a long ride, I wanted a beef dinner, boiled radishes, and a hot bath," Jace said as he stood. "But now."

"Now what?"

"I'm already dirty," Jace declared. "A little blood on my clothes won't make a difference. Where can I find this Centurion?"

***

Pugnus came out of the meat shop licking the knuckles of his right hand.

"That butcher's head is harder than the thigh bone of a bull," he whined. Examining the raw spots from where he'd hit the man several times, the thug decided to change his approach. "It was fun hitting people with my fists when I was younger. But not anymore. I better find a club and save the skin on my knuckles."

The sun had dipped to the height of the buildings, creating shadows in alleyways and alcoves off the sidewalk. Despite the lateness of the day, Pugnus headed for the cooper's shop.

"An oak barrel stave, cut down with a trimmed handle would make it easier to collect," he said to himself. "And add to the intimidation. Hades, I might bust up a few shops, just to show off my new toy."

Ten steps later, a voice called from behind him.

"Centurion? Are you the one they call Centurion?"

Pugnus twisted around. Other than a short stretch in the Legions, he'd been on the streets his entire life and didn't trust anyone coming up behind him.

"Who wants to know?" he replied to a man in a hooded jerkin. "Come on, out with it or be on your way."

Pugnus smacked his fist into the palm of his hand. The raw knuckles stung, and he grimaced.

309

"Yup, a piece of oak will definitely help," then he realized the stranger hadn't said anything. "Yes, I'm the Centurion. Who wants to know."

"I'm thinking about opening a store," the hooded man replied. To stress his seriousness, he wrapped his fingers around a heavy purse, and jingled the coins. "I was told I had to see you before renting the shop."

Greed clouded his reasoning and the street lord only had thoughts of the coins in the purse.

"There's a deposit to join the Shop Keepers Collective," Pugnus informed the would-be vendor.

The stranger peered from under the hood that hid his face. After looking up and down the street, he informed Pugnus, "I'm not comfortable displaying coins on a public sidewalk. Can we go into the alleyway to conduct our business?"

End of Sample

Order your copy of A Legion Legacy

A Note from J. Clifton Slater

Thank you for reading *Heritage of Threat*. If you're new to my historical adventure books, you may not realize Senator Alerio Sisera's story is told in the 19-book series *Clay Warrior Stories*. From a young swordsman and Legionary, Alerio rose during the 1st Punic War to command a Legion. But not after many hurdles were thrown in his path by enemies and friends. The first book in the series is titled *Clay Legionary*.

Let's get started with the notes from *Heritage of Threat*.

Carthalo and Ten Legion Officers

After the Battle of Cannae, Hannibal sent Carthalo, one of his commanders, to Rome with terms of surrender for the Republic. Refusing to admit defeat, the Senate ordered Carthalo away from Rome, giving him until sundown to vacate the area. Seeing as Carthalo never entered the city, I thought it would be fun to insert Cornelius into the story and give a reason why the Roman's refused to grant the commander entrance into Rome.

Also arriving in Rome with Commander Carthalo were ten Legion officers. They represented 8,000 captured Legionaries who were taken while guarding the Legion camp at Cannae. Each of the ten swore an oath to return to Hannibal if they failed to secure a ransom of 3 minae for each Legionary. (The Aeginetan *minae* weighed 623.7 g or 22.00 oz.) I estimated the total ransom would amount to 528,000 total ounces of silver. A sum high enough that just paying it would weaken the Republic financially and prevent Rome from fielding her Legions.

The Senators debated the pros and cons, according to historian Livy, of whether to pay the ransom or not. In the end, despite the loss of so many sons of Rome, the Senate refused to pay.

They did allow 9 of the 10 captured Legion officers to make their own decision about keeping their word and returning to Hannibal or remaining in the Republic. One attempted to game the system by returning to Hannibal's camp shortly after being released. In his opinion, he had left and returned thus satisfying his oath. The Senate had the man bound and returned to Hannibal as an undesirable. Oddly enough, after treating the trickster badly, the Senate later downgraded the citizen status of the other nine Legion officers because none honored their oath to return. Of the 8,000 captured Legionaries, we can only guess that Hannibal Barca executed some and sold the rest into slavery.

Oath by Cornelius Scipio

After the Battle of Cannae, four disheartened Tribunes began discussing leaving Italy and sailing off to join a foreign king's army. When Cornelius heard about the plan, he pulled his gladius and, at sword point, made them swear an oath not to desert the Republic. While historian Livy placed the exchange at the town of Canusium right after the escape of the ten thousand from Cannae, I moved it to the Senate of Rome to fit the story.

Marsican Brown Bear

Although depicted as a monster in the story, the Marsican is also known as the Apennine bear and is a gentle creature. However, an adult male weighs around 478 pounds and the female near 310 pounds so they fit the description of monsters. Unfortunately, these magnificent beasts are an endangered species. Mostly due to loss of habitat and poachers.

Aedile Scipio

To the best of my knowledge, Cornelius was never an assistant Aedile, and he did not put on a festival by himself. He did, however, run for the position and was opposed because he was under the legal age to sign contracts. But due to his strong public image, war record, and his political allies, a couple of years later, he won over the voters. He was elected as an Aedile of Rome along with his cousin. I imagine, Cornelius Scipio needed a relative as the second Aedile to have someone who would not argue with him about signing his documents.

I did my best to display the many tasks of the Aediles in the story. After the battle at Cannae, their responsibilities included reminding citizens that the Roman Senate outlawed public crying, mourning, and any talk of defeat or surrender.

Proconsul Claudius Marcellus II

After the death of Lucius Paullus at Cannae, the Senate of Rome elected Postumius Albinus as the second Consul. But Albinus was killed by the Boii tribe before assuming the Consulship.

Quickly, the Senate of Rome elected Claudius Marcellus to fill the slot alongside Tiberius Gracchus. For a day in 215 B.C., the Roman Republic had two Plebeians Consuls to run the war and the government.

Then, the Patrician class complained about having two Plebeians as Consuls. After another vote, they revoked Claudius Marcellus' Consulship and replaced him with Fabius Maximus the Third, a nobleman and the son of former Dictator Fabius.

We don't know how Claudius Marcellus took being rejected. But he did take a Proconsul's position, based on his limited day as a Consul. As a General, he won the Battle of Nola. The next year 214 B.C., he would be elected and serve out the year as a Consul of Rome.

Hannibal at the Siege of Nuceria 'Alfaterna'
(Modern day Nocera Inferiore, Italy)

The siege of the ancient city with towering walls of granite stone lasted for six months. Although both the Republic and Hannibal used the time to recruit and train fresh troops, the Legions were the biggest beneficiary of the lull in the action.

When the town council opened the gates of the city to release surplus population, Hannibal Barca turned them around. Then he drove other people, the prisoners he held, back into the town. According to Historian Livy, the ploy more than doubled the population of the city. The enormous number of people to feed in a besieged city proved too much and a short while later, Nuceria Alfaterna surrendered.

Hannibal allowed the population to leave with only the clothing on their backs. Then he released his army to plunder the city. After taking everything of value from the rich town, he demolished the walls and the buildings, destroying Nuceria Alfaterna as punishment for defying him.

The Battle of Benevento

There were passes through the Apennine Mountains other than the Via Appia. In his haste to reach Hannibal, and his arrogance founded on earlier victories over the Romans, Lieutenant General Hanno marched his reinforcements along the Via Appia towards Benevento.

Tiberius Gracchus force marched the Consul's two proper Legions and his slave Legions (only a few records mention criminal in those Legions) to block the route. Before the battle began, he promised his two non-standard Legions that in order to win their freedom and pardons, they needed to collect heads. At the start of the battle, Historian Livy reported that Legionaries broke ranks in order to harvest heads. Others strolled around displaying heads instead of fighting. Once it became clear that rewarding decapitation had caused disruption, Gracchus changed the order to simply winning the battle to earn the reward.

After a day of fighting, General Gracchus only lost 2,000 Legionaries. On the other side, 16,200 of the fresh troops destined for Hannibal Barca were killed during the fighting. Hanno and two thousand men escaped the Legions' final ring of death. And while Hannibal Barca marched to Nola with confidence, the expected reinforcements would never reach his army.

The Trick at the Battle for Nola

Nola lay just 18 miles southeast of Capua. With Capua declaring for Hannibal Barca, both the Punic General and the Roman Republic wanted possession of Nola, the gateway to the south.

Proconsul Claudius Marcellus arrived first and entered the city. Shortly after, Hannibal reached Nola and the two parties skirmished with no winner. Then word reached Claudius Marcellus that when he marched his Legions out to battle Hannibal, rebels would seize the gates and lock the Legions outside Nola. Caught between the defensive stonework and the Punic army, the Legions would be annihilated.

To negate the plan, Proconsul Marcellus sent Legionaries to the five gates of Nola to take command of the portals and he placed extra guards on the Legions supply trains. Then

Marcellus had the walls, gates, and guard towers abandoned and the western gate left open.

Seeing the opportunity, Hannibal Barca marched his army directly at the open entrance. Before Hannibal reached the opening, one Legion poured from the west gate and formed battle lines. And just as Hannibal shifted to mirror the Legion, the second Legion came through the two flanking gates. History tells us Valerius Flaccus and Caius Aurelius led the half Legions through the gates. But as often happens, ancient historians didn't tell us the ranks or positions of minor leaders.

With the battle joined, the Carthaginian mercenaries fought on three fronts. Although pressed, they battled the Legionaries until the fight became a stalemate. Hannibal Barca again proving to be a General who could rally men from different geographical areas.

But then, Claudius Marcellus performed a tactical trick worthy of Hannibal. From the western gate, a third Legion appeared. In the dust raised by the stomping of thousands of feet, this Legion seemed to be reinforced with cavalry.

Upon seeing the flags and dust kicked up by the third Legion, Hannibal's army broke ranks and ran. Claudius Marcellus prevented his Legionaries from pursuing out of fear that the retreat might be one of Hannibal's tactical stunts.

Plus, when the thick cloud of dust settled, the third Legion was revealed to be the animals and carts from the Legions' wagon trains and teamsters carrying banners and flags. Because of the trick at Nola, Claudius Marcellus became the first Roman General to defeat Hannibal Barca in face-to-face combat.

Geographical Location of Capua, Italy

Around 856 A.D., the city of Capua was rebuilt at its current location beside the Volturno River. In antiquity, Casilinum served as the town on the river where the Via Appia crossed the water course. The site of ancient Capua was 3 miles southeast from the Volturno. And while Capua has a long history at both locations, Casilinum has vanished.

Via Ponte Vecchio Romano Bridge

Construction of the Via Appia connecting Rome to ancient Capua was finished in 312 B.C. For the highway to pass over the Volturno River meant the original Via Ponte Vecchio Romano Bridge was constructed around 313 B.C., making it around 98 years old at the time of *Heritage of Threat*. Unfortunately, little beyond the approaches remains of the original structure. On the north side, medieval ramparts bookend the road at the bridge. And during WW2, the bridge was destroyed and rebuilt after the war. With no other description available, I used the current bridge and ancient bridge designs as a guide for this story.

In *Heritage of Threat*, Cornelius commands a mismatched garrison at the north end of the bridge. History does not show Cornelius Scipio at the bridge during the fighting. However, the troop strength and makeup of the Republic forces defending the north end of the Via Ponte Vecchio Romano Bridge comes to us through the writings of Historian Livy, in Book 23, Chapter 17.

Quintus Ennius

Ennius (239 B.C. – 169 B.C.) was a Roman poet from southern Italy who claimed he possessed the spirit of Homer, the author of the Iliad and the Odyssey. Beyond Latin, Ennius spoke Greek and Oscan. No records show him accompanying Quintus Fabius Pictor to Delphi. But I thought a poet might have been included in the party to help decipher the Oracle's esoteric answers. Famously, The Pythia, the temple priestess channeling Apollo, replied in rhyming, verbal puzzles. When Jace meets the poet, I paraphrased the note Quintus Ennius wrote just before he died. *"Let no one weep for me or celebrate my funeral with mourning; for I still live, as I pass to and fro through the mouths of men."* Ennius would have been a young man of 24 when the Senate sent Quintus Fabius Pictor to consult with the Oracle about how to beat Hannibal Barca.

Oscan language

Oscan was spoken by a number of tribes, including the Samnites, the Aurunci, and the Sidicini in Southern Italy. In *A Legion Archer* books, Oscan was portrayed as a language known only to old chiefs, priests, and a few scholars. In reality, Oscan survived among bilingual people along with ancient Greek until around 100 B.C. Eventually, Latin overshadowed both languages as Rome colonized the Italian peninsula.

Although today it has no known native speakers, Latin was so influential in history that it's considered a dead language. Oscan, on the other hand, is an extinct language, only known to us through artifacts.

Philip V of Macedonia

The Macedonian King blustered and threatened battle with the Roman Republic. He went so far as making a treaty with Hannibal. Unfortunately for Philip, the treaty document fell into the hands of the Navy when his courier was intercepted.

In an attempt to grow his territory, he sailed to Illyrian and attacked cities. But the Navy of the Republic learned of his passage from their patrol boats along the Greek coast.

After crossing the Adriatic Sea, Praetor of the Fleet Laevinus trapped the King and his army as they lay siege to Apollonia. Beaten in the field, Philip V escaped over the mountains and returned to Macedonia. As much as I wanted to include Jace and Cornelius in the fighting, their story in Heritage of Threat was moving in a different direction. Thus, there is only a hint of the history in this book.

Aratus of Sicyon

At age 7, Aratus narrowly escaped death after his father was executed in a coup. I related this story in *Clay Warrior Stories* book #7 *Fatal Obligation*. Only because he was spirited away in the middle of the night by the wife of the man who murdered his father, did Aratus survive. Years later, Aratus returned and captured the city of Sicyon.

17 times, he was elected as the head of a confederation of Greek cities known as the Achaean League.

The meeting between Cornelius and Aratus never took place. And we don't have any records showing Aratus warned the Republic about the invasion of Illyria by Philip the 5th. However, Aratus of Sicyon was an adviser to the Macedonian King and a year after the failed invasion of Illyria, an otherwise healthy Aratus died at age 58.

Temple of Apollo at Delphi

Quintus Pictor returned to Rome and built an altar to Apollo where he regularly sacrificed to the God for victory. But the God wasn't popular with the Romans nor was his worship seen as an advantage in the war against Hannibal.

History does not record Cornelius Scipio accompanying Pictor's expedition to Delphi or any instance of him meeting the Oracle. But for the story, I felt it was important to contrast the usual obscure prophecies by The Pythia to the one she delivered to Pictor.

And here's a final thought on the Oracle of Delphi. She only granted prophecies once a month and travel at the time was imprecise. Most visitors to the temple would arrive at Delphi days or weeks early. And while priests interviewed the people seeking an audience to see if they were worthy, the Temple of Apollo could have had spies. Gossip from the servants and men-at-arms would give information that would help The Pythia in delivering meaningful prophecies.

And that's the end of the history. Here's hoping you enjoyed the notes for *Heritage of Threat*.

***

I appreciate emails and reading your comments. If you enjoyed *Heritage of Threat*, consider leaving a written review on Amazon. Every review helps other readers find the stories.

If you have comments e-mail me.

E-mail: GalacticCouncilRealm@gmail.com

To get the latest information about my books, visit my website. There you can sign up for my monthly author updates and read blogs about ancient history.

Website: www.JCliftonSlater.com

Facebook: Galactic Council Realm and Clay Warrior Stories

I am J. Clifton Slater and I write military adventure both future and ancient.

Other books by J. Clifton Slater

Historical Adventure of the 2nd Punic War

A Legion Archer series

#1 Journey from Exile

#2 Pity the Rebellious

#3 Heritage of Threat

#4 A Legion Archer

Historical Adventure of the 1st Punic War

Clay Warrior Stories series

#1 Clay Legionary

#2 Spilled Blood

#3 Bloody Water

#4 Reluctant Siege

#5 Brutal Diplomacy

#6 Fortune Reigns

#7 Fatal Obligation

#8 Infinite Courage

#9 Deceptive Valor

#10 Neptune's Fury

#11 Unjust Sacrifice

#12 Muted Implications

#13 Death Caller

#14 Rome's Tribune

Printed in Great Britain
by Amazon

39097741R00185